"You're divorced... because of your brother?"

Sarah stared at him as she asked the question.

"Yeah." Luke's answer was soft. Then he added, "But for the record, it's not as tabloid as it sounds. She was engaged to Matt first. He went missing on a classified army assignment and they told us he was dead. We got married, Erin and Jen were born. Then after five years he came back."

"Five years!"

"He was a POW the whole time. Kristin hadn't ever stopped loving him, and...and it was tearing her apart, being with me when he was around. That's the whole story."

"You're very honorable to set her free."

"A regular white knight."

"Do your daughters live with you?"

Luke ran out of brittle comments. "Not full-time. We've been sharing custody since I moved out a year ago. But now that they're married..." Luke couldn't bear to think about the changes in his life.

How could one translate anguish into words?

Dear Reader,

I remember being awakened at midnight, when I was six or seven years old, so my brother and I could climb into the back of our big station wagon and fall asleep again while my father drove straight through the night, heading east.

Sometime the next afternoon, we would park on the deck of a ferryboat that took us to the isolated Outer Banks of North Carolina. We camped just behind the dunes in a canvas tent and cooked on a gas Coleman stove. Showers were optional—we spent most of the day in the ocean. Cape Hatteras Island became a dear friend we looked forward to visiting each summer. I still find my greatest sense of peace and freedom when I can sit and watch the sea.

So I've written a book set at the beach. Police officer Luke Brennan and photographer Sarah Randolph have lost the people they care about, the people who cared for them. The joining of these two solitary souls requires courage, determination and, of course, deep and abiding love. I hope you enjoy your time with Luke and Sarah as much as I have. They are very special people.

As are all the Superromance readers. Please feel free to write me at: P.O. Box 17195, Fayetteville, NC 28314. Thanks for reading!

All the best,

Lynnette Kent

P.S. The second BRENNAN BROTHERS book will be available in September. Luke's brother, Matt, lives with three females, and he doesn't understand any of them! Look for *Matt's Family* to share his dilemma…and to celebrate his joy.

LUKE'S DAUGHTERS
Lynnette Kent

HARLEQUIN®

TORONTO • NEW YORK • LONDON
AMSTERDAM • PARIS • SYDNEY • HAMBURG
STOCKHOLM • ATHENS • TOKYO • MILAN • MADRID
PRAGUE • WARSAW • BUDAPEST • AUCKLAND

ISBN 0-373-70901-3

LUKE'S DAUGHTERS

Copyright © 2000 by Cheryl Bacon.

Visit us at www.romance.net

Printed in U.S.A.

For my mom,
who showed me the wonders of the beach,
the glory of the mountains,
and all I know of love.

CHAPTER ONE

SARAH HEARD his voice first.

Not the words, not even the sense of what he was saying, just a warm, smooth rumble counterpointed against the never-ending crash of the waves. The timbre of that voice resonated inside her, making her push back her hat and open her eyes.

She couldn't have designed such a picture in a thousand years. The owner of the voice wore a starched white shirt, a black bow tie and vest, and the satin-seamed trousers of formal dress, rolled halfway up his calves. He'd left his sleeves buttoned; they shivered crisply over his arms in the afternoon wind blowing off the ocean.

Just as her eyes focused clearly, he tugged the band out of his shoulder-length hair, letting it blow free with that same wind. Putting up a hand, he pulled the straight, black strands out of his face and laughed as he glanced down at his companions.

Creatures from a fairy tale they were, two princesses in rose-and-green flowered gowns, with puffed sleeves, high necks and long, full skirts. Sunlight glinted on their blond heads, one a bit darker than the other, both braided neatly from crown to nape. As they looked up at the man, Sarah could see flowers woven into those braids...baby's breath and pink sweetheart roses.

Automatically, she reached for her camera.

She captured the gentleness with which the man held

each little girl's hand to help her down the sandy bank, the care the children took to hold up their skirts as they crossed the shallow inlet separating them from Sarah. The setting sun and the contrast of such formal clothes against a backdrop of sea and sky and sand provided near perfect composition.

As the trio came close, Sarah relaxed into her chair and let the camera rest in her lap—their awareness of what she was doing would spoil the effect. She stared back the way they'd come, across the rocks and the deep green grass that separated the public beach from the exclusive Sandspur Country Club. Light flashed behind the club's tinted windows, silhouetting the impression of a crowd.

Now she understood—they'd been to a grown-up party of some kind. The man must have taken pity on two bored little girls and brought them out across the manicured grass to look at the ocean.

But looking obviously hadn't been enough, not for the girls and not for him. With just a little pleading on their part, he'd agreed to an adventure no anxious mother would ever allow—a walk on the beach in all that finery. Sarah could just discern the white-and-black splotches of their socks and shoes, abandoned at the brink of the lawn.

When her camera lens found them again at the edge of the ocean, the girls were bent over a fisherman's bucket, inspecting his bait and his catch. But their companion stood straight and tall, staring north along the shoreline. His hair blew back, leaving his profile stark against the sky. Sarah snapped the picture, thanking all the saints that she'd brought the zoom lens—and thinking that, for a party guest, he didn't look much like he was celebrating.

After a few minutes, he turned and spoke to the girls.

The children pranced and danced across the beach, heading back toward the club. But the man lagged behind, head down, hands in his pockets, dragging his bare feet in the sand as if reluctant to return.

Reluctant or not, he *was* leaving. Sarah jammed the camera into her bag, dredged up a couple of business cards and a pen, then struggled out of the low sand chair to her feet. By the time she clambered up the opposite bank of the inlet, the girls had nearly reached the rocks. But the man had just come level with Sarah.

"Excuse me," she called.

He stopped and looked over, his dark, straight brows lifted in question.

Up close, he was bigger than she'd realized, taller. Not thick or brawny. Just…strong. "My name is Sarah Randolph." She extended a card. "I'm a photographer."

"That's…nice." He stared, expectantly.

Suddenly she felt intrusive. She gathered up the remnants of her professional nerve. "You must know—the three of you made an exceptional picture on the beach in your formal clothes."

"I didn't think about it," he said. The hint of a drawl flavored his voice, like a ribbon of caramel through milk chocolate.

"I did." Sarah gathered her thoughts. "And I took pictures."

His gray gaze darkened. "And you want me to pay you for them? Sorry." He lengthened his stride to catch up with the girls. "Not interested."

"No!" She jogged after him, reaching for his arm to slow him down. His muscles felt like carved driftwood. "No, I don't want you to pay me."

He stopped and looked over his shoulder. "What do you want, then? I need to get them back inside."

Something in his face made her let go of him. Quickly. "Are they your daughters?"

His mouth tightened. "Yeah. They are."

She tried a smile. "You see, I might want to use the pictures in a…in a professional capacity. And for that, I need a release."

He started to shake his head. "I don't think—"

"No, really, all it says is that you agree to allow the photographs to be used for publication. I may never use them, they might not develop. But if they do, I'd be glad to give you copies, in exchange for the release. Please?"

For a long moment he watched the girls, now involved in investigating a jagged black rock. Finally, he sighed. "I'd have to see them first. Otherwise, I'm not agreeing to anything."

"Sure. No problem." Sarah held out the extra card and the pen. "Just write down your address and I'll bring them over as soon as I can. Probably in a day or so."

His face was stern as he took the card and wrote quickly across the blank side. "Nice to meet you, Ms. Randolph." He gave back the card.

Before she could answer, or even read his name, he strode across the sand to his daughters and swept them before him, over the rocks, up the bank, and back into the club.

COMING IN from the beach, Luke stopped on the threshold of the country club dining room. The girls ran toward the crowd inside. Given a choice, he wouldn't have followed. But then, nothing about today was his choice.

Or maybe everything was. Maybe that was his problem—he'd made the decision and he hated living with the consequences.

When Erin and Jennifer found their mother at the center of the swirl of people, she turned immediately to give them her full attention. No one could say Kristin wasn't a great mom—the girls came first, every time. He loved that about her.

And she made a beautiful bride, in an ivory dress with a lace top and a bell-shaped skirt, holding orchids in the curve of her arm. Under a lace veil, her rich blond hair shone like sunlight. Laughing at something Erin said, she tucked a stray curl behind Jen's ear, then glanced up at the new husband who stood by her side. The meeting of their eyes came straight out of an old-fashioned romance. The kiss they'd shared at the wedding deserved fireworks, like the end of a fairy tale.

Luke took a deep breath and pivoted away from the reception. He wasn't going to stay. He'd done his part, kept up appearances for the sake of the girls and his parents' friends. No one would miss him, anyway—

"Luke Brennan! What happened to your hair?"

He turned to face his mother, resisting the urge to neaten up. "The girls and I went outside for a walk. It's windy."

Elena Brennan raised aristocratic eyebrows. "You took them out on the beach? In those dresses?"

"We were careful. We left our shoes—"

"Honestly, I don't know how you ever came to be so irresponsible!" Her cultured Southern accent always deepened when she got upset. "The photographer is still taking pictures, for heaven's sake. Just once I'd like to see you think ahead…" She pivoted and stalked toward the girls with her long-legged grace, a contemporary Southern belle in blue silk, severely ticked off.

"Bad move, son." His father stepped up on Luke's other side. "Worse still to tell her what you'd done."

Luke jammed his fists in his pockets. "I didn't *do* anything. The girls were going crazy trying to act like porcelain dolls. I just let them have a little fun.''

"You know how important this wedding is to your mother.''

Luke dragged his thoughts back from freedom of the beach…and the sweet sympathy in a strange woman's golden eyes. "Yeah, I know.''

His mom hadn't gotten a chance to plan *his* wedding— the bride and groom had eloped in the middle of the night, coming back with the vows taken and a baby on the way. That was not how things happened in the prestigious Charleston social circles where Elena Calhoun Brennan had grown up.

"We didn't do anything wrong,'' Luke insisted. Now *or* then.

His dad's hand fell on his shoulder and drew him farther into the room. "Well, what's done is done. Tame that damn hair, put your coat on, then come get a glass of champagne so you can celebrate with the rest of us.'' Thirty years in the Army turned every request into an order.

Luke looked at the man beside him. They were the same height—six-two—but Colonel William Brennan's military bearing always made him seem taller.

Beyond his father, he caught sight of Kristin, finishing a slow waltz with her new husband. They ended with a kiss. He took a deep breath. "No, thanks.''

The Colonel's gray eyes went steel-cold. "Listen, son, I expect you to cooperate—''

Luke jerked out from under his dad's hand. "How much more cooperative can I get? I let him take them away. I stepped aside and gave him my whole life. I even played the part you wrote for me today.''

He lowered his voice, stepping close enough to guarantee his words would stay between them. "But if you think I'm happy about it, you're crazy. And if you think I'm going to come in there and toast this marriage—give them my blessing, for God's sake!—you're more than crazy. You're sadistic."

"Luke—" Strong fingers gripped his elbow as cheers from the other end of the room drew his attention. Dread tightened his throat, but Luke looked over.

Kristin stood balanced on one slender leg, her skirt lifted to reveal the other foot in its high-heeled slipper resting on a chair seat. Her groom, wearing Army dress blues, knelt in front of her. As she laughed, he slipped a lacy blue-and-white garter down her thigh and over her smooth calf. Applause broke out as he stood and flourished the scrap of fabric.

"All single men to the front, now!" He grinned widely. "This lady's mine and I'm not sharing, but if you catch her garter, you're guaranteed to find your own!"

As he looked around the room, the groom's gaze came to rest on Luke. Even from a distance, the antagonism in his face was clear to see. The crowd chuckled, murmured, and finally ebbed into silence.

Luke broke away from that stare and glanced at his father. "There is a limit to brotherly sacrifice." He turned on his heel, heading toward the club exit. "Your *other* son," he said over his shoulder, "just crossed the boundary line."

Then, as if chased by demons, he ran for his life.

ERIN COULD HARDLY stand still long enough to let her grandmother unbutton the back of her hot, scratchy dress. "Are you done yet, Grandmom?"

"I'll never be done if you don't stand still, young

lady.'' Grandmother Brennan was pretty strict. You didn't go to her house and put your feet in the chairs or eat with your elbows on the table—not if you were almost seven years old. Babies who were only four—like Jenny—could still get away with just about anything.

Such as whining when she didn't want to change clothes. ''I want *this* dress,'' she told Grandma Jennings. ''I want to see Mickey Mouse like this!''

''Well, you can't.'' Erin turned toward Jenny, and was pushed back in place by a firm pair of hands. ''We're goin' on a plane, Jenny. You can't wear that dress on a airplane.''

Jenny started to cry. ''I want Mommy!''

Erin felt the last button on her dress give way. ''Oh, boy.'' She pulled away, dragged the dress over her head and let it drop. ''That feels so good!'' She whirled in the middle of the room, her arms spread out like wings. ''I hate dresses!''

Grandmother Brennan picked up the stupid pink-and-green dress and put it on a hanger. ''Get your shorts on, Erin, dear. You'll be leaving soon.''

''Disney World!'' Erin ran to the chair with her clothes and stepped into her favorite blue shorts. The itchy flowers in her hair got caught in her T-shirt, so she pulled them out. That pulled out some of the braid, too, which was okay, because braids hurt. She tugged the rest of her hair free. ''Where are my shoes?''

''Right here.'' Her grandmother held up a pair of white sandals with pink flowers on top.

''Those aren't mine. I want my red sneakers that Daddy bought me.''

Grandmother Brennan brought over the yucky shoes. ''These will look better with your outfit, sweetheart.''

Erin crossed her arms. ''I...want...my...red...shoes.''

She wasn't gonna cry, like Jenny. But she wasn't going anywhere in those stupid white sandals.

The door of the room opened, and Mommy came in. Jenny jerked away from Grandma Jennings. But Erin reached their mother first. "Tell her I don't have to wear those shoes, Mommy. I want to wear my red ones!"

Jenny arrived. "I wanna wear my dress for Mickey Mouse!"

Mommy got down on her knees. She put one arm around Erin and one around Jenny. "Erin, sweetie, your red shoes are in the suitcase under the window."

Erin flew to the bag and found her shoes right on top of all her other clothes. She sat down and started to pull one on.

"Socks first," her mother said.

"Yes, ma'am," Erin groaned. She put on the socks, then the shoes, and tied the laces herself. Daddy had taught her to tie her own shoes over spring break from school.

With Mommy to help, getting dressed and ready to go was easy. Jenny put on the plain yellow dress she was supposed to wear and let Mommy brush her hair. In just a couple of minutes they were all done.

Mommy's new husband waited for them in the hallway. "All set for Disney World?" Jenny put her thumb in her mouth and hid her face in Mommy's neck. He looked at Erin. "What do you say? Ready to go?"

Erin looked back at him. He'd told her to call him Matt. Mommy said she thought Daddy Matt would be better, since he was a part of their family now. Because Mommy asked, Erin tried to remember. But he didn't feel like much of a daddy to her.

He was tall, and kinda big—bigger than Daddy, even if they were brothers. And he was more like Grandmother

Brennan than Daddy. Daddy played games. He laughed and joked and called her funny names.

Most of the time, Daddy Matt talked about rules.

Suddenly, Erin didn't know if she *was* ready for Disney World. "Mommy, where's Daddy?"

"He's right here, love." She looked surprised.

"No. I mean my *Daddy*. I need to tell him something."

Erin saw Mommy look at Daddy Matt. Then Daddy Matt came over and squatted beside her. "He had to go to…work, Erin." Daddy Matt had blue eyes. Even when he smiled, his eyes stayed serious. "He said to tell you to have a great time in Florida. He'll be thinking about you, and he'll see you when you get back. Okay?"

When you were almost seven, you could usually tell what you could get out of and what you couldn't. Erin knew she wasn't going to see her dad again before they left. She sighed and nodded. "Let's go."

Daddy Matt stood up and took her hand. Erin went with him, with Mommy on her other side. Outside the front door, all the people who had come to the wedding were waiting. They started cheering and throwing bird seed from the little packets Erin had helped tie. She and Mommy and Daddy Matt ran in between the lines of people to the van waiting by the curb. Erin helped Jenny into her car seat and buckled her own seat belt the way Daddy had taught her.

Then, laughing and waving, Mommy and Daddy Matt shut their doors. They pulled away from all the people, and the car got quiet. "Next stop," Daddy Matt declared, "is Disney World!"

Jenny yawned and closed her eyes. Erin looked out the window without answering, wondering why she didn't feel so excited anymore.

SARAH HELD her breath as the picture developed, like a ghost materializing out of the mist. She hadn't run a proof sheet this time. She wanted to see each print full-size right away.

There. More than twenty-four hours later, she was struck yet again by the sheer beauty of Luke Brennan's face, the grace of his stance. From a professional—and personal—perspective, he made a truly breathtaking picture.

And the little girls were every bit as lovely as she remembered, as photogenic as she'd hoped. The energy of those children endowed each shot with an intense impression of...of...*life*.

"Pretty," a voice commented behind her.

Sarah jumped, then swore. "You scared me!" She retrieved the tongs she'd dropped. "Why didn't you knock, Chuck? You could have ruined everything."

Her business partner—they'd inherited joint ownership of the photography shop where she developed her work—rolled his eyes. "The door was already open, so I figured it was safe. You've been in here for hours."

He stepped past her and stared at the pictures on the drying table, arms crossed over his stomach, the fingers of one hand tapping his elbow. "Not your usual style, but pretty. Are you planning a calendar?" She could hear the sneering tone in his voice.

Sarah put the tongs down before she used them as a weapon. Chuck belittled her work whenever he got the chance. Why get upset about it now? "No. Those are some shots I took yesterday, that's all." She drew a deep breath. "What time is it?"

"After seven. I've closed the shop. Are you ready to leave?"

She'd printed the pictures in eight-by-tens. Some of

them might look good even larger. "I think I'll stay and work some more. Go ahead and lock up. I've got a key."

"I know." He smiled thinly. "You're okay to stay here alone after dark? This part of town's pretty much deserted on Sunday night."

Sarah put confidence into her voice. "I'll be fine."

Chuck lifted a thin, pale eyebrow in doubt, but turned without a word and left the darkroom. Shortly afterward, while she was still mixing developer, she heard the back door shut and the roar of his Cadillac's engine. She couldn't deny the relief of finally being alone.

As she printed the larger versions of the beach pictures, though, she did ask herself exactly what she would do with them. The weekly news magazine she worked for, *Events,* didn't publish "pretty" photos. Her New York editor wanted grit—the grittier, the better. She'd given him just that for six years now, first in Africa, more recently in Eastern Europe and Afghanistan.

They'd been a damned good team, she and James Daley, even after she ended their brief engagement. Despite the pain caused by James's unfaithfulness, Sarah had stayed on the job. Anger and hurt feelings had, with time, given way to mutual respect; together they'd earned a notable reputation for delivering *the* story with his spare reporting and her uncompromising pictures.

Then, between one heartbeat and the next, James was gone. A witness to the shooting—she stood only a few steps behind him as he fell—Sarah remained at the scene and finished the story for James…for them both. She'd managed to work through the memory of his sightless eyes, the smell of blood and munitions in the air, the one ragged cry he'd given before dying.

Until that last morning, by a pit in a field outside Kabul, a vast cavern filled with the bodies of women and girls, when the shaking had gotten so bad she couldn't hold the camera steady, and there wasn't any way to make it stop. She'd seen herself falling into that grave. She could still hear the voices of the dead—James's among them—crying all around her, waiting for her...

On a deep, shuddering breath, Sarah jerked her mind back to the present. This was not a war-raped field in Central Asia. This was Myrtle Beach, South Carolina, USA, where the sun sank gently behind the dunes, shedding an amber light over little girls dancing on the beach in their best clothes.

Eyes closed, she focused on that peaceful scene, recalling each lovely detail. Gradually, her heartbeat slowed, the shakes went away.

See, she *was* getting better. Six months of therapy had restored her ability to cope, to function. She'd been tired when she got back to the States...well, okay, exhausted. Yet she'd had trouble sleeping. The dreams had been even worse than her memories.

Now, though, she was rested. Soon, she'd be well enough to resume her job. She'd worked hard to get a permanent assignment with *Events* and she would cover whatever story they asked for.

That she'd been shooting pictures yesterday testified to her recovery. Not since...then...had her camera come to hand so easily, so smoothly. She could thank Luke Brennan for that. Luke Brennan and his precious little girls.

Sarah cleaned up the darkroom, glancing often at the pictures she'd developed tonight. He wouldn't be easy to forget. His laugh was warm, his grin contagious, but the shadows in his eyes spoke of deep trouble. What could have brought such pain to his face?

She'd never know. And even if she found out, she was the last person who could help him. Daily life was as much of a challenge as she could manage these days. Until she could take charge of her own life again, she couldn't possibly solve anyone else's problems.

After sweeping up, she made sure Luke Brennan and his daughters had dried thoroughly, then closed them into a folder inside her portfolio. Tomorrow she'd get the release and send the shots to her agent. If they found a place to sell, good. If not, Sarah congratulated herself on at least taking pictures again. Six months was a long... vacation.

She tidied the kitchen area in the back of the shop, washed her cup and Chuck's and set the coffee to brew in the morning, then picked up the portfolio and her purse and left by the rear door.

The June night folded around her, not yet humid enough to cling. Screams of tourists riding the roller coasters on the boardwalk a few blocks away speared the darkness. Floodlights crisscrossed the sky from all directions—the beach attractions to the east and the giant performance halls to the west. Myrtle Beach prided itself on giving great value for an entertainment buck.

Thinking about the sleepy little town she'd visited during high school summers, Sarah whistled lightly as she walked toward her Jeep. Thanks to the tourist boom, the town had mushroomed in the last fifteen years, bringing in big-city problems without always providing the means to deal with them. Still, those little girls on the beach had been safe and happy—

Footsteps sounded behind her, running. Keys in hand, Sarah started to turn, but was too late even to scream. A man slammed into her back, taking her to her knees. Arching her body, she tried to buck, but he was too heavy. His breathing was a ragged gasp in her ear as he grabbed her shoulders and pushed her forward. She braced her arms, palms sliding against the gravel; he reached over, jerked her hands up, and shoved her down hard. Her face hit the ground, tore, burned.

She tried to twist underneath him, but his knees held her shoulders down as he sat on her back. Every other pain faded as he closed his hands around her neck and squeezed. And squeezed. Sarah stabbed at him with a key—he jerked the ring out of her fingers. She kicked with her heels, but his grip only tightened on her throat.

Weakening, she gasped, pleaded with no sound, fought the weight on her ribs and spine until a black fog clouded her vision.

And then she stopped fighting.

CHAPTER TWO

LONG PAST TIRED of his own company and fed up with self-pity, Luke checked in at the precinct station late on Sunday night.

"You're the only cop I know who has hair like that." Sergeant Baylor clapped him on the shoulder as they passed in the squad room. "Brennan, you're a disgrace to the uniform."

"The hair *is* the uniform, Sarge." He pulled up a grin, poured a cup of coffee he didn't need and propped a hip on the corner of a nearby desk. "Anything going on tonight?"

Nick Rushe, Luke's partner and frequent handball opponent, leaned back in his chair. "Just the usual—drunks and rowdies, a lost kid at the boardwalk. Oh, and a mugging."

"Yeah?"

"Not four blocks from here. Woman about to get into her car, guy knocks her down, takes her purse and what she was carrying. Beat her up pretty bad. Jordan's taking the report."

Luke glanced over at Hank Jordan's desk. A woman huddled in the chair on the aisle, eyes downcast, her face almost completely hidden by the cloth she held to her cheek.

But he recognized that curling, golden-brown hair. The part of her face he could see seemed familiar. And when she looked up to answer a question, he recognized the long-lashed, hazel gaze. This was the woman on the beach yesterday afternoon, the one taking pictures. Sarah…Sarah…something.

He was standing over her before he realized he'd moved. "Are you okay?"

She lifted her head to gaze at him, eyes dark with fright and pain. Her lips parted, but she didn't make a sound. When he put a hand over the one she held to her face, she flinched.

Luke squatted to look up at her. "Sarah? Sarah, it's okay. I won't hurt you. Can I see your face?"

She stared at him for a long time, and he thought she would refuse. Then her shoulders relaxed a fraction. She nodded, wincing, and allowed him to lift the cloth gently out of her hand.

He pulled in air through his teeth to avoid swearing. Between bruises and swelling and scrapes, the left side of her face was a mess. Luke let her put the cloth back against her skin. Her white T-shirt was torn and stained with dirt and blood, her knees nearly as battered as her cheek. "Have you seen a doctor?"

"She just walked in, if you can believe it." Hank shook his head. "Looked like death then, so she's gettin' better."

Jordan was a good cop, if a little too blunt. Luke bit back a reprimand. "Are you about finished here?"

"Yeah. I think she's given me everything she can— which ain't a hell of a lot. No motive, only one real contact in town, and no description. Big help."

"We'll work on it." Luke stood up to his full height. "I'm going to take you to the hospital, Sarah, get a doctor to check you out."

Again she shook her head, panic replacing pain in her eyes. "I don't think—" she whispered.

"You're safe with me." He pulled his ID from his back pocket and opened it in front of her. "I should have explained—I'm a cop. My partner can go with us, if you'd feel better about it." He nodded back toward Nick, who gave them a salute.

She seemed to wilt. "No. That's okay." When he put his hand under her elbow she stood and took a shaky step, then stopped. "Thank you," she said to Hank, still in that hushed voice.

Flushing, Jordan waved her away. "No problem. You take care. We'll get back to you if…when…we find something."

Luke opened doors and warded off obstacles as they worked their way slowly through the station. He could tell the effort it cost Sarah to make the trip by the sigh she gave as she relaxed onto the seat of his truck. Without asking, he pulled the seat belt over her and clicked the latch shut.

She gave him a half smile as he got behind the wheel. "Thanks. I appreciate your help."

The angle of her head and the light from the parking lot revealed what he hadn't seen before—ugly maroon finger marks on her throat.

He couldn't stifle a curse. "We'll be there in a few minutes," he said. Driving carefully, but fast, he flipped on the emergency flashers and accelerated into highway traffic.

A couple of hours later, the ER doctor came to find him. "No broken bones, no major damage. Abrasions, contusions, a couple of lacerations. She'll be sore for a while."

"He tried to strangle her."

"Yes." The doctor shook her head in disgust. "The swelling will keep her voice out of commission for a few days. Don't let her talk too much."

"Can you tell me anything else about the beating? Anything specific?"

"Besides the fact that the guy who hit her is a bastard?"

"Besides that."

The doctor cocked an eyebrow. "She's lucky he didn't kill her."

Luke found Sarah sitting on a cot in a cubicle toward the back of the emergency room, with her hands folded in her lap and bandages on the worst of her scrapes.

"Hi," she whispered. Her wide eyes were less focused than before, but the pain and panic in them had receded.

"You're not supposed to talk. Let's get you out of here." He helped her slide off the table, then braced her with his hands under her elbows as her knees buckled.

She gasped and caught at his arms. "They…they gave me a pill. I guess I'm not too steady."

"No problem." Luke put an arm around her waist. "I'll take you home and make sure you're settled."

Sarah tried to pull away, though she didn't make much progress. "I can get a cab. Really."

"I don't think so." She looked prepared to argue, but Luke simply eased her toward the doors. "You don't want to wait here another hour or two, do you? This isn't New York—cabs don't circulate in Myrtle Beach in the middle of the night." Finally convinced, she leaned wearily against him. They stepped through the automatic doors into the cool summer dark.

"All we need now is—" He thought a second and stopped.

"My keys." She closed her eyes. "But—"

"He took them." Her sigh confirmed his guess. "Do you have any friends in town? Somebody to stay with?"

"No." She seemed to lean more heavily against him at the word. Luke walked her to the truck.

"And no credit cards for a hotel room?" he asked, as he buckled her in again.

"Not anymore."

He shut the passenger door and rounded the truck bed, thinking hard. By the time he sat down, the decision was made. "Okay. I'm going to take you to my place for the night. We'll get the rest sorted out in the morning."

She tried to sit up against the seat belt. "Mr....Officer Brennan...I don't think—"

His own throat ached to hear her rasping whisper.

"Call me Luke." Backing out of the parking space, he gave her a grin. "I'm going back to work. You'll have the house to yourself. It's the easiest solution."

He didn't mention the other benefits—the fact that no one would look for her at his place. And that whoever had her keys could be inside her home by now.

Maybe he didn't need to—she suddenly stopped fighting. "Okay." The next time Luke glanced over, she was asleep.

Once parked in his own driveway, he left Sarah in the car while he went to unlock the kitchen door. Then he lifted her gently and carried her into the house. In the dining room he hesitated—where should he put her down?

The lumpy couch in the spare room, surrounded by piles of magazines? Erin and Jen's room, which usually looked as though a hurricane had hit? Or...

Luke maneuvered carefully through the doorway to his bedroom. He'd changed the sheets this morning and neat-ened up. Sarah would have enough aches to deal with tomorrow. Why not give her the best rest possible?

He lowered her to the side of the bed he didn't use and covered her with a blanket. Leaving an old football jersey nearby, with a note inviting her to help herself to anything in the house, he moved to the door, then stood for a second watching Sarah…Sarah *who?*…sleep.

She looked peaceful in the low light, almost happy. Her mouth had softened into a smile that even the bruises couldn't dim. After a night of horror, she'd fallen into sleep as easily as a child could.

But reaction would set in—Luke had no doubt of that. He'd seen victims fall apart immediately, and he'd seen them hold back until they had privacy. He figured Sarah would want to be alone when she struggled with her personal tremors.

God knew, he always had.

That thought led him to Kristin, on her honeymoon with Matt. To Jen and Erin, at Disney World with their mother and their new dad. To a family that had once been his and now belonged to another man. His brother. Forever.

The house closed in on him, airless, lightless. Breathing hard, Luke fumbled his way toward the door, fighting the need to howl. He had to get out. Get back to work, back to a reality he could handle. Back to the outside world, filled though it might be with threats and violence and agony.

At least there he didn't stand face-to-face with the total, wretched emptiness that constituted the rest of his life.

WHEN HE CAME HOME at 7:00 a.m., the only sign of Sarah's presence was a glass standing on the counter by the kitchen sink. But he could hear water running in the back bathroom. Good for her—she must be a strong woman, to be getting back on track so soon.

As he walked by the desk in the corner of the dining room, he caught the blink of the answering machine light. "You have one new message," the tinny recording announced.

"Hi, Luke." The soft Southern accent needed no introduction. "It's Kristin."

A vise gripped his gut and twisted. He braced his arms on the desktop.

"The girls wanted to call and tell you what's going on."

"Hi, Daddy! It's me!" Erin's husky voice was as unique as the girl herself. "We went to Sea World yesterday and it was so cool. They have this tunnel under the water you can walk through and the fish swim on top of you, even the sharks. And the whale splashed us with about a zillion gallons of water until we were soaked. Mommy and Daddy Matt just laughed. Jen cried 'cause it made her drop her drink. What?" Her voice died away as someone in the background spoke. "But I'm not finished! Oh, okay. Here's Jen." The phone passed, and he heard Erin's scathing whisper to her sister. "Baby!"

Luke tried to smile.

"Daddy?" His four-year-old was as quiet as her sister was talkative. "I'm Jenny. I spilled my drink. Mommy got me a new one and a dolphin hat. We're going to the Magic Kingdom now. I'll say hello to Peter Pan like you said." More background conversation, as his heart slammed against his ribs hard enough to crack cartilage. "Bye, Daddy."

"Bye, Daddy!" Erin chimed in. "I love you!"

His tears didn't wait for the end of the call.

"We thought we'd let you know that everything's just fine down here, Luke." Kristin sounded her usual sunny, in-control self. "The girls miss you, but they're having a good time. We'll be back next Saturday, and we'll call again before then. Take care." The machine clicked off.

Helpless against his own emotions, Luke hunched over the desk. He missed them so much—his daughters and his wife. How was he supposed to live with his heart ripped out?

"Luke?" Sarah's bandaged hand closed lightly on his upper arm. Her voice was barely a whisper. "Luke, what's wrong?"

A quick turn of his head shook his eyes clear. She stared up at him, her brows drawn together in concern, her face a collage of bruises and scraped skin. His football jersey swamped her.

"What's wrong?" she asked again.

He couldn't say, "nothing." And he didn't know how to explain. "My little girls—"

The grip of her fingers tightened. "Has something happened? Are they okay?"

Luke drew a deep breath. "Sure. They're great." Sarah started to relax, and he knew he should let the subject rest. Why tell her? Why go over any of it again? "They're with their mom at Disney World," he heard himself say.

Sarah smiled, then winced. "That sounds like fun."

"With my brother." Her look turned puzzled. "He married Kristin on Saturday. They're on their honeymoon."

Confusion, then horror, crossed Sarah's expressive face. She drew her hand away and stepped back.

Furious that he'd made such an obvious play for her

sympathy, Luke pushed off the desk and headed for the kitchen. "Do you want some coffee?"

The grounds were measured and the brew dripping into the pot before Sarah followed him. He glanced up as she limped stiffly into the kitchen. "Milk? Sugar?"

She lowered herself into a chair at the table, shaking her head. "Black, please. Luke—"

He held up a hand. "I'm sorry. I shouldn't have said any of that. Let's just forget it, okay? I brought some doughnuts for breakfast. Have one."

But she didn't make a move toward the box on the table, just stared at him with that serious, green-gold gaze. "You're divorced?"

Luke turned back to the coffeemaker. "Yeah."

"Because of...him?"

Carefully, he took two mugs out of the cabinet. "Yeah."

"I'm so sorry."

At that, he chuckled. "Hell, Sarah. Nobody's as sorry as I am." He brought the filled mugs to the table. "But for the record, it's not as tabloid as it sounds. She was engaged to Matt first. He went missing on a classified Army assignment and they told us he was dead. We got married and Erin and Jen were born. Then, after five years, Matt came back."

"Five years!"

"He'd been a POW the whole time, which the Army in its wisdom either didn't know or wouldn't tell us. Kristin hadn't ever stopped loving him, and...and it was tearing her apart, being with me when he was around. So there you go." Grabbing a raspberry-filled pastry, he took a sticky bite.

Sarah still hadn't touched her coffee or the doughnuts. "You're very honorable, to set her free."

"A white knight, in the flesh."

"Do the girls live here with you?"

He ran out of brittle comments. "Not full-time. Kristin and I have been sharing custody since I moved out about eighteen months ago. But now…" Luke couldn't bear to think about the change in his life. And he surely couldn't translate pure anguish into words.

The woman across the table accepted his silence and picked up her cup with the fingers and thumbs of both hands, taking a small sip of coffee. She chose a raspberry doughnut and finished it, along with the brew, in silence. Then she looked over. "I don't suppose anyone's turned in my purse."

Luke released a relieved breath at the change in subject. "I checked before I left the station. No."

She rested her unbruised temple on the back of her bandaged wrist. "I don't even know where to start. I can't get into my car without keys, and I can't get extra keys because they're in the condo." Her sigh wavered. "I can't get in there without keys and the manager doesn't know me without ID, but all my ID—"

"Hold on, Sarah. Calm down." Her rough whisper had taken on an edge of hysteria that worried him. "Don't try to solve all the problems at once. You have an extra key to the car?"

She nodded, brushing a fingertip across her marred cheek to catch a tear.

"That's good. We'll go to the condo, and I can convince the manager to let you in."

"How?"

"I'm a cop. Why shouldn't he believe me?"

"She." Her lips quivered in a near smile.

Luke grinned back. Solid ground for both of them.

"She. Once we get into your place, we'll call the credit card companies. Then—"

"Credit cards?"

"You have to cancel them, right? The guy could be running up your bill."

She stared at him, then shook her head. "That's— that's right. I totally forgot about the cards."

"Well, now you remember. So we'll cancel them and then we'll get your car."

"Wait...I'm confused." She held up a hand. "Why should you—I mean, don't you...have other things to do?"

"Sure," Luke lied, unable to pull up a laugh of any kind. "But you need some help and I've got the time to spare. We're the perfect couple."

Sarah's gaze demanded a deeper level of truth. He cleared his throat. "Look, I hate what that guy did to you. If I can't find him, at least I can help you get things back together. Any friend would do that for another. And don't ask me why, but I feel like we are. Friends." There. That was as honest as he could be.

She did smile then, for the first time since last night. "Me, too. Which is really weird, because—"

"Because I can't even remember your last name."

"Randolph. Sarah Rose Randolph."

"Well, Sarah Rose, you're as dressed as a lot of people ever get in a beach town. Find your shoes and let's start putting your life back together."

SARAH KNEW she shouldn't let herself depend on Luke. As a capable adult, she ought to be able to get herself out of any trouble she got into. Until six months ago, she wouldn't have dreamed of imposing on anyone like this.

But, oh, the comfort of having him there. With Luke

standing behind her, she found the strength to assert her identity to the condo manager, who actually believed her and let them into the house without an argument.

And with Luke around, instead of dwelling on her problems and giving up on the solutions, she felt focused enough to look through the file box she'd started for her bills, finding the credit card slips and the numbers she needed. The people on the other end of the line for each company seemed very kind. Or was that just the soothing effect of Luke's presence?

She paused between phone calls. "There's juice in the refrigerator, I think. Help yourself."

"Thanks, I will. How about you?"

"Yes, please." The first cabinet he opened contained the glasses. He chose tall ones—as she would have—and added ice, just as she liked it. She'd had the same experience last night in his kitchen—she'd known exactly where things would be, as if their minds worked in the same pattern. Sarah thought such instant closeness should be scary.

Instead, she felt grateful to have found a friend like Luke.

"That's the last of them?" he asked as she clumsily hung up the phone.

"I think so."

"Did they report any large charges since last night?"

"None for days."

"Good—we stopped him before he got started." Then he snapped his fingers. "Do you have a phone card?"

"A—" Sarah stopped herself from repeating his words, like a lost child. "I do, as a matter of fact. I'll call the phone company."

When she hung up this time, he had picked up the

framed photograph she kept on the table by the couch. "Is this your brother? Boyfriend?"

"James Daley. I...worked with him."

"James Daley, the journalist?"

"That's the one."

Luke gave her a searching look. "Daley's pretty good. I like his stuff for *Events*."

"James always told the story as he saw it."

"Told?"

Sarah braced herself to say the words she'd practiced so often. "He was killed by a stray bullet in Afghanistan, about seven months ago."

"You were there?"

"I was his photographer."

He set the frame gently back on the table. "I should know your work, too, shouldn't I?"

"Not necessarily—my name is usually in the small print at the end of the article."

"So when you took pictures of Jen and Erin, you were doing us a favor—not just out to make a quick buck." Luke's cheeks reddened. "I apologize for misunderstanding."

"Not at all." Sarah carefully carried her drink between her fingers and sat on the couch beside him. "Saturday wasn't the easiest day you've ever had."

"Still..."

"I was just glad to get the shots. And the pictures were everything I hoped. But he took them when..." Her mind's eye flashed back to last night, to a knee in her back, the sudden impact with graveled ground, rough hands dragging her portfolio out from under her body.

"Oh, damn." She put her head back, willing the tears not to fall.

Luke took her glass away, then his arms surrounded

her, nestled her against his firm chest as he stroked her hair, avoiding the bandages. "It's okay, Sarah," he whispered. "It's okay to cry."

Sarah resisted the urge to pull away. She let her cheek rest on him, breathed in the clean scent of his black T-shirt. How long had it been since anyone had put their arms around her? Longer than she could remember.

Longer, still, since being held had felt so right. For all his talent and intelligence—or maybe because of his exceptional gifts—James had never been a comforting person. He'd accepted the truth, dealt with it head-on and expected everyone around him to do the same. Sarah had prided herself on meeting that expectation, on functioning independently. Until James died.

Since then, her life seemed to consist of fragments—like the shards of a broken mirror—none of which she could fit together. And there was no one who cared enough to help her try.

So she stayed quiet for just a few minutes, soaking up the solace Luke offered. Long before she was ready, she sat up out of his arms and summoned a smile. "Thanks." She pushed her hair back with fingers that shook. "You really are a good friend to have around."

His hands lingered on her shoulders. "Are you okay?"

Sarah nodded. "I'm fine, now. Let me change clothes and get the key for the car. I'll be just a few minutes."

He toasted her with his glass of juice. "Take your time."

But she hurried through the process of dressing, avoiding her reflection as much as possible. She'd been assaulted twice before—in other countries, by people involved in activities they didn't want recorded. She knew how to survive the pain, realized that the bruises would fade, the scrapes would heal.

Ignoring the ache in her ribs and shoulders, she found dark brown linen pants to cover the bandages on her legs and a light, long-sleeved tunic which did the same for her arms.

The problem came with her hair. She couldn't lift her arms much above her waist, let alone hold a brush tight enough to pull out tangles and knots.

Did she dare...?

As she stepped back into the living room, Luke glanced up from a copy of *Events*. "You look much better."

"I'm feeling much, much better." She swallowed hard against her nerves. "I have only one more favor to ask."

"What's that?"

Sarah held out the brush. "Would you?"

"Be glad to." He stretched to his feet. "Sit in one of those tall chairs at the counter."

Standing behind her, he took the brush and picked up the weight of her hair. "You've got a handful of curls here, don't you?" His gentle tug on the ends was more delicate than she could possibly have managed. Sarah barely felt the pull on her bandages.

"I usually keep it braided and out of the way. I don't know what happened last night—how it came undone." The tension in her shoulders began melting away as he stroked her hair back from her face. She closed her eyes.

"Do you want me to braid it for you?"

"Can you?"

"I braid Erin's and Jen's all the time. It's a survival skill for fathers of little girls."

"What are they like, your girls?"

He chuckled. "Erin's the wild one—adventurous, independent, stubborn. She goes after what she wants, no matter the risk. She likes the ocean and bicycles and science books.''

''Does she take after her dad, maybe?''

He went completely still for a second, then resumed brushing. ''Sure. Jen's gentler, quieter, but just as stubborn when she wants to be. She plays dolls and has tea parties, wants to hear fairy tales and dress up like a princess.''

As she had been on her mother's wedding day. ''How old are they?''

''Erin will turn seven this summer. Jen's four.'' Luke put the brush on the counter. ''Here goes.''

He touched the crown of her head softly, gathering hair, tugging a bit against the bandage, but Sarah hardly noticed. The play of his fingers on her scalp set up small waves of pleasure, like the lap of the sun-heated ocean in a tidal pool on the beach. She took a deep breath and released it slowly. Now she knew why women enjoyed having their hair styled. So relaxing, so soothing, so...so seductive.

''Finished.'' He draped the end of the braid over her shoulder. ''Do you have a band?''

She slipped it off her fingers, struggling to stay casual. ''If you ever get tired of being a cop, you should consider braiding hair for a living. Thanks.''

When she faced him, he'd stepped back and hooked his thumbs in the front pockets of his jeans. ''You're welcome—it was my pleasure. Did you find your keys?''

He was ready to go. Much as she hated to end her time with him, she had no right to keep Luke in her life. ''They're right here in the drawer.'' She grabbed the jangle of keys and a hat off the peg by the door. ''Now, I'm all set!''

Or she could pretend she was, anyway.

CHAPTER THREE

LUKE PUT ON his sunglasses when they got into the truck, then frowned at the thought he was using them as a mask.

But the truth was, he'd enjoyed brushing Sarah's hair. Too much. The gold-brown curls were softer than they looked, like water almost, sluicing over his hands. She'd relaxed as he brushed and braided, reminding him of a kitten being stroked...and all at once he realized his body had responded to that idea with more interest than he'd have believed possible.

Since Kristin...since Kristin and Matt...he hadn't thought about sex. But the nape of Sarah's neck was soft, vulnerable. Her skin was smooth and tan, the sound of her breath like a soft wind in the trees. For just a second, he wanted...something he had no right to. Again.

He took a deep breath. "Where's your car?"

"Sawyer's Photo Shop. Not too far from the police station." She shivered as she spoke.

"He won't be there now." For just a second, Luke covered her hand with his own. "And if he is, I'll make sure he doesn't bother you or anybody else for a good long time. Okay?"

She had a sweet, sunny smile, underneath the bruises. "Okay."

He drove to the bank first, waiting while Sarah arranged to put a stop on any checks. She'd found her birth certificate and insurance papers before they left the condo and she used them to get a new driver's license, which would allow her to open another checking account when she was ready.

As they waited for a traffic light to change, Sarah shifted on the seat. "Your hair's a little long for one of Myrtle Beach's finest. Have they updated police regulations?"

Luke smiled. "I've been on special duty—hanging with the beach regulars for the past year or so, keeping an eye on their less...aquatic...activities."

"A surfer dude?"

"Nope. The word *dude* is out with serious surfers. They're proud of their life in opposition to the mainstream."

Sarah nodded. "I'll remember. Surfing for a living sounds like a good job, though. Low stress."

"Oh, yeah. Especially in January, wearing a cold wet suit and freezing my...nose...off."

"Not your idea of fun?"

"My idea of fun in January is a fireplace, a TV football game, and a bowl of popcorn." He held the picture of that scene in his mind's eye—Erin napping on the armchair, Kristin in the curve of his arm, almost dozing as she nursed Jen. Less than two years ago, he'd lived a perfect life.

"Luke? Luke!" Sarah's voice brought him back.

The brakes squealed as he automatically stomped the pedal, bringing the truck to a stop with about two inches to spare behind the Mercedes ahead.

Sarah was staring at him, her eyes wide. "She pulled right in front of you, but I didn't think you'd seen."

Luke wiped a hand over his face. "You were right. I was...my mind had—"

She nodded. "I can guess. Good thing you have quick reflexes."

A honk from behind jerked their attention to the green traffic light. Luke gritted his teeth and accelerated carefully.

They arrived at Sawyer's Photo Shop without any more stupidity on his part. Sarah directed him around the back of the painted concrete block building, where an olive-green Jeep and a full-size Cadillac shimmered in the morning sun. Luke cut the engine. "I'm betting yours is the Jeep."

She accepted his help to climb down from the truck's high seat. "Brilliant deduction, Officer Brennan."

"Corporal First Class." He grinned as she stuck out her tongue at him, then followed her to the Jeep. "I checked with Hank Jordan, the investigating officer. They dusted for prints—no results yet. But if the guy has your keys, why didn't he take the car? Jeeps are a high-return item in the stolen-car market."

"Maybe he didn't like the way it drove?"

He gave her question the chuckle it deserved. "Even if he didn't want it, I expect he knows someone who would. So…"

Using the tips of her fingers, Sarah opened the Jeep door. A wall of heat broke over them. "I'd say this car hasn't been anywhere since I parked it yesterday about three o'clock."

"And the question would be, why not?" Luke couldn't come up with an answer that made sense.

"If we don't know, I guess there's nothing we can do." Sarah stared into the interior of the Jeep for a few seconds, then seemed to shake herself free. "So life goes on. You can get some sleep and I can make some more prints. Good thing I left the negatives in the files."

"What I have to get first is a haircut. I go on regular patrol duty starting Wednesday night."

"No more surfing?"

He shook his head. "Back to real life."

She nodded. "I'll bring the pictures by your house sometime this week, okay?"

With her hat brim shading the bruises, bandages and scrapes, her face looked almost normal—sweet and calm and, as he remembered noticing on the beach, sad. Luke was suddenly reluctant to say goodbye.

But his life was too much of a mess to mix with anybody else's. "I'm home most afternoons." He stepped back, and sunlight fell on the ground between them. "Are you sure you feel like driving? Those hands have to hurt."

"I'm fine—thanks to a little white pill. Plus an automatic transmission and power steering. No problem." Her hesitation in getting up into the Jeep belied her confident statement.

Luke gave her a lift at the elbow. The bones in her arm were as light as a bird's. "I'll...be in touch if anything turns up on the case."

"Thanks." She put the key in the ignition and the Jeep puttered to life. Luke stepped back as the vehicle started to move. At the edge of the parking lot, Sarah lifted her hand and glanced at him in the rearview mirror before driving away. He waved, but wasn't sure she saw him.

Alone again, he studied the ground around him, wondering if Jordan had missed anything when he'd checked out the site of the mugging.

Fifteen minutes later, he doubted it. If the gravel had ever held any clues, they'd been scuffed away.

That left him with no theory about who'd attacked

Sarah Randolph. And with the rest of a long, hot Monday to fill.

Not to mention the rest of the summer…and the rest of his life.

THE FLORIDA SUN beat against exposed skin with an almost physical force. Kristin Brennan shifted a little on her chaise longue and prepared to sink deeper into pure indolence.

"Strawberry daiquiri for the lady?"

She peered sleepily over the top edge of her sunglasses, then woke up fast. "Just what I've been dying for! How did you know?"

Her husband sat down near her feet. "It's hot, we're in Florida, you love strawberries. Simple deduction."

"Mmm." She sipped the frozen drink gratefully. "I might just stay right here for the rest of my life, reading romances and soaking up sun and drinking daiquiris."

Matt stroked his palm along her ankle. "The hotel would probably pay you to hang around. You really improve the scenery."

His cool hand against her heated skin tightened every nerve in her body. If they weren't in public…

She gathered her wandering thoughts. "Did you get the girls settled?"

"They're safely installed in the Wee Willie Winky Center, busily finger-painting to music from every Disney movie ever made."

"I hope Erin doesn't get bored."

Matt's thumb traced a path up her calf, then circled the bend of her knee, with devastating effect. "They've got three aquariums and a library of science books. She's all set."

"So we've got…some free…time. What should we do?"

"I was thinking about a nap." He looked up suddenly, and grinned. "Or something." His hand slipped sideways to rest between her knees. "What do you think?"

"Ah…" Her thoughts puddled like an ice cube on the pool deck. "Sounds…lovely. Why don't you go on up to the room—I'll be there in just a few minutes."

His brows drew together. "Come with me."

"I need to get a shower first. I'm all sticky with lotion."

He moved his hand slightly and smiled at her ragged breath. "I don't mind."

"But I do. Let me clean up a bit and I'll be right there."

"Women." Shaking his head, Matt drew his hand slowly away from her legs and stood up. "I'll be waiting."

Kristin winked at him. "Me, too."

She watched him walk toward the hotel, straight-backed and square-shouldered, his dark hair cut in a short style that marked him right away as military. He held the door open for a woman and three children before going inside. That was just like Matt—manners were carved into his bones. Along with responsibility and a strong sense of honor.

Once he'd disappeared behind the tinted glass of the lobby windows, Kristin dropped back against her chair. She loved him so much…wanted him so desperately…her idea of paradise was a couple of hours spent in a quiet room with his arms around her. Yet she sat here, hesitating. Why?

The answer in one word—*Luke*.

No matter how much she loved Matt, Kristin couldn't

get free of the guilt her desertion of Luke had created. She didn't know if she ever would.

Leaving the pool and the bright sunshine, she took a shower in the locker room, washed and dried her hair, and put on just enough makeup to hide the circles under her eyes. Sleep didn't come easily anymore, even after a full day of walking through theme parks with the girls. Or after wonderful hours of loving with Matt, once her daughters were sound asleep in their adjoining room.

Luke's face haunted her, waking and sleeping. To remember the sacrifice he'd made for this marriage, this family, all she had to do was close her eyes.

Eight years ago, she'd betrayed Matt by marrying his brother. Then she'd broken her vows to Luke—the "until death do us part" promise. Now…

Now, everything she'd ever wanted was within her reach—the man she'd loved since junior high, and two beautiful, precious daughters. Even the possibility of more children.

Yes, she had everything…but she'd left Luke with nothing. How could she enjoy her happiness at his expense? Yet how could she have denied Matt the dream of love and family that had kept him alive through five years of imprisonment and torture?

Just outside the door to their hotel room, Kristin paused, getting herself under control. She couldn't burden Matt with her own regrets.

But the door opened before she was ready. "It's about time." Matt caught her hand and drew her inside, into his arms. "I wondered if you would make me wait forever."

His hands roamed her shoulders, slipping the straps of her tank top out of the way. He pressed kisses on her eyelids, her throat, her ears, until she was half crazy with the need to kiss him back.

Catching his lean cheeks with her palms, she held him still. "You'll never have to wait, Matt. Never again." Then she brought him close enough that she could capture his mouth with her own.

But she kept her eyes open, for fear of what—who— she'd see if she let them close.

WHEN LUKE HADN'T heard from Sarah about the pictures by Wednesday night, he considered calling. He'd thought about her for two days, hoping she'd phone or come by, disappointed when she didn't. But he didn't want to pester her. She would get to the pictures when she had time.

After a solitary dinner and a solitary movie, he went to work on the late shift—cruising the beaches and the downtown streets, looking out for trouble. The boardwalk was still busy after midnight, and the bars on the ocean-front stayed open late.

He heard the fight before he pinpointed its location— a crash of glass and the eruption of swearing gave him his first clue. As he ran toward the noise, a struggling ball of humanity rolled out of the Blue Flamingo's door. Luke radioed for backup, then joined the general chaos.

"Police! Get back—" He pulled a couple of bystanders away. "This is the police—fun's over, boys." Grabbing the tail of a T-shirt, he yanked hard. "Time to go home."

Sirens announced the approach of the backup. Luke had all the wrestlers pretty much separated by the time reinforcements arrived. The guys were too drunk to protest as they were read their rights and loaded into cars.

"You don't look like much of a cop."

Luke turned toward the voice and saw a young man

he was sure was drunk…and was equally sure wasn't old enough to drink. "You don't look like much of an adult, either. Do your parents know where you are?"

"Sure, man." But the bleary gaze slid away.

"Want to show me some ID?"

The boy shrugged. "Lost it, man."

"Sure. So give me your address."

"Aww…"

"Or spend the night in jail. You choose."

An hour later, Luke drove away from the boy's home, having awakened a mother who explained at great length how the whole problem was her ex-husband's responsibility. The rest of the night passed quietly enough, giving Luke too much time to think about how much influence a father could have on his child's life. Whether he was there or not, whether he cared or didn't…a little kid's whole world might depend on his—or her—dad.

What kind of repercussions would Erin and Jenny face because of the choices he and Kristin had made?

FRIDAY AFTERNOON, Luke remembered Sarah saying she used the darkroom at the camera shop where she'd been mugged. Maybe he would find her there. It was worth a try.

A bell jingled as he stepped into the dimness of Sawyer's Photo Shop. The walls and ceiling were painted black, the windows shuttered against sunlight. At one end of the narrow space, dusty shelves held picture frames and photo albums, equally dusty. A sales counter stretched across the other end, with cameras and film displayed in cubbyholes behind.

The long wall on either side of the door exhibited framed and signed photographs. Luke moved closer, wondering if the pictures were Sarah's. They certainly looked professional, and he found himself absorbed in unique perspectives of everyday places and things.

Behind him, cloth rustled. Hoping for Sarah, he blew out a short breath when he turned to see a man step through the black-curtained doorway.

"Can I help you?" A fairly young guy stood behind the counter, his expression polite but not exactly friendly.

"These are great pictures." Luke gestured toward the photographs.

A real smile brightened the round face. "Thank you. I take a lot of pleasure and pride in my work."

"They're yours?"

"Yes. I'm Charles Sawyer. Can I help you with something? Film? A camera?"

"No, thanks. Actually, I'm trying to track down someone who works here."

"I run the shop alone."

"But Sarah Randolph develops her photographs here, right?"

The smile on the man's face faded. "Yes."

"Is she around?"

"No. She had…an accident last week and is recuperating at home." Charles's tone didn't drip with sympathy. "Do you need some photography done? I'd be glad to assist you."

"No, thanks. I'm Luke Brennan, the cop who took her to the ER last weekend to get patched up. I just wondered how she's doing."

Sawyer's eyes narrowed. "A cop?"

"Is that a problem?"

"No. No, not at all. But as I said, I haven't seen her all week."

"Have you talked to her?"

"No."

"Aren't you worried about her?"

"Not really." Sawyer chuckled. "Sarah's a photo-journalist, you know—one tough lady." He paused, lips pursed. "Or she was, anyway. She worked for *Events* magazine until a few months ago, when she collapsed in the middle of a job and had to be shipped home. She hasn't worked since coming back to the States. Or even taken any meaningful photographs."

Oh, yes, she has. "Well, thanks. I guess I'll track her down somewhere else."

"If I do see her, I'll be sure to tell her you were here."

"I'd appreciate it." The bell on the door clanked again as Luke pulled it open. "Have a good day." A final glance at the chubby man behind the counter registered outright hostility.

For whatever reasons, Sawyer obviously had problems with Sarah. Big enough problems that he'd attack her? The guy seemed like a jerk, but was he a criminal, too?

A background check wouldn't hurt, Luke decided. Most victims of assault knew the perpetrator. Why not Sarah Rose?

Meantime, he still hadn't found her. If she didn't call tonight, he would forget his reservations about pestering her. With friends like Charles Sawyer, Sarah definitely needed a cop on her side.

SARAH SPENT the week secluded in her condo.

If asked, she could have pointed out that she needed to be there when the locksmith came. That the doctor had suggested staying out of the sun while she was taking the antibiotic. Even that the bruises on her face had gone from bad to worse, from red and blue to a horrible mottled purple, and she didn't want to scare children and animals.

Sarah recognized those reasons as excuses. Good ones, but still rationalizations. Going out would take too much effort. She simply didn't have the energy.

And so she stayed in, wearing her pajamas. Several good movies showed up on television, several times a day. She slept when she wanted, many hours at a time. Food didn't seem very important—she survived on ice cream, popcorn and buttered toast. She'd eaten much worse in Africa.

The manager sent up a locksmith to change the door locks, so she felt safer. She could check on the Jeep from her window, but those locks would have to be changed at the dealership. That would require going out.

As if cooperating with her agenda, the phone didn't ring. Her agent didn't check in—there were no deals to talk about. Her editor at *Events* only needed her if she could work. A photojournalist who refused to leave the house didn't get many job offers.

And Luke Brennan didn't call.

Not that she should expect him to. *She* was supposed to contact *him,* to bring the pictures to his house—pictures she hadn't yet developed. But going to the darkroom at the photo shop meant seeing Chuck, taking his jibes, trying not to mind his mockery. Sarah couldn't face that prospect, either, even though it meant she wouldn't see Luke.

Eventually, though, the ice cream and popcorn and bread ran out. Sarah realized she could either stay in and starve to death...or get herself together and go shopping. Saturday morning, she dredged up the will to try.

She gasped as the brightness of the day sliced at her eyes, even behind dark lenses, even under a wide-brimmed hat. The humidity was high, especially after five days in constant air-conditioning. All the usual outdoor noises—traffic, lawn mowers, sirens, birds—beat on her ears like a rock concert. Maybe she should just go back in—

"Sarah?" She wondered if she'd imagined that deep voice, that Southern accent, until she heard it again. "Sarah?"

Opening her eyes, she discovered Luke Brennan sitting astride a big Harley-Davidson parked next to the Jeep.

"What are you doing here?" She winced—her social graces had definitely deteriorated over the week alone. "I see you've had a haircut," she added lamely. "Nice."

"Thanks. I hadn't heard from you about those pictures, so I came by to see if...if you'd printed them yet."

Her photographer's eye appreciated the aesthetic potential of a gorgeous guy in a white T-shirt, worn jeans and boots on a big, black bike. Short hair only emphasized the beauty of his face, revealing his well-shaped head and the strong column of his throat. He'd make a great pinup. Or maybe without the shirt...

She halted that thought in its tracks. "No. No, I haven't. I've stayed in this week."

"You deserved a break. Your voice sounds better."

"Thanks. I guess not talking much helped."

"That's what the doctor said." He crossed his arms, and her knees went weak. "So when do you think you'll have the pictures?"

"Well..."

He looked embarrassed. "I don't mean to hassle you or anything. I'm kind of anxious to see them, that's all."

"No, it's not a hassle." She was glad of a good reason to stay out of the house. "I could go down and print them now, actually. If you wanted to come with me and wait."

"I would, but Jen and Erin are getting back from Florida this afternoon."

Disappointment weighed her down. "I'll call you, then."

"Or..." He snapped his fingers. "Or we could meet a little later. I'll go see the girls, then ride over to the shop. We can get something to eat, afterward. How does that sound?"

Tempted and yet troubled, Sarah hesitated. Luke's smile turned coaxing, a little bit teasing, and completely irresistible. "Come on, Sarah Rose, say yes."

He held out his hands, palms up, in an open, generous gesture. "How could a little dinner between friends possibly hurt?"

DADDY MATT TURNED OUT to be more fun than Erin expected.

He bought her a Goofy hat and a Minnie Mouse nightgown and cotton candy. When they went to Sea World, he let her have a Shamu cup with a curly straw, filled with strawberry punch. And he never ran out of money for the games in the kid's club room at the hotel.

Sometimes Mommy went out with Daddy Matt by herself, which was okay, because the hotel had good baby-sitters with lots of videos and snacks. Even Jenny didn't mind going to the baby-sitter's room—she got to watch *Cinderella* as many times as she wanted.

Erin knew she didn't have a real reason to be sad. She could have just about anything she wanted. What more could a kid ask for?

Like now—here she sat in the fanciest restaurant in the world, wearing a dress that she'd picked out all by herself and which didn't scratch, and she'd just eaten a whole plate of really good spaghetti. They were going to have dessert in a few minutes, just as soon as Daddy Matt and Mommy came back from dancing.

"Mommy's pretty," Jenny said. "Like a princess."

"A queen," Erin corrected. That would make Daddy Matt the king.

Erin watched them dance. Mommy's red dress swirled around her. She looked up at Daddy Matt, smiling. And he smiled down at her.

Maybe, Erin thought, she wouldn't have dessert after all. Her stomach felt funny.

Back in their hotel room, Mommy was still smiling, still humming the dance music. She stopped long enough to get Jenny undressed and read them both a story. Jenny, as usual, fell asleep before the story ended.

But Erin stayed awake, listening, even after kissing Mommy good-night. She heard Mommy and Daddy Matt talking in the other room, and then laughing. And then there was music again. She didn't have to see through the door to know they were dancing.

Erin turned over and put her pillow on top of her head. That drowned out the music. But she felt like she heard it in her head. And she saw Mommy dancing, even with her eyes closed.

In Erin's head, though, Mommy danced with the right person. She danced with Daddy.

But Erin was old enough to know that if her dream could come true, she wouldn't be crying herself to sleep.

CHAPTER FOUR

ERIN AND JEN were due back on a three-thirty flight. Luke knew his mom and dad would want a private reunion with the newlyweds and the girls, so he filled in the time baking a batch of his special cookies. At five, he headed for his parents' house on the beach.

When he arrived, Kristin's green van was parked in the driveway. Luke deliberately relaxed his grip on the handlebars. The girls were still here. He hadn't missed them.

Taking a deep breath, he switched off the bike and removed his helmet. He only wanted to see his daughters. Everybody could manage to stay cool for their sakes. Right?

Just as he put his hand on the doorknob, Luke decided to ring the bell instead of walking right in. Which was smart, he realized, when his mother opened the door.

Her blue eyes widened. "Oh…Luke. Hello. We weren't…expecting you."

"I wanted to welcome the girls home—"

A rush of footsteps sounded in the hallway behind his mother.

"Daddeee!" Jennifer launched herself into his arms. "We're home!"

"Good to see you, Jenny Penny." He hugged tight, trying to keep the bag of cookies intact, squeezing his eyes shut against tears.

Someone else tackled him at waist level. "Daddy, me, too. Me, too!"

So much for the cookies. "You, too, Bear." He stooped to lift Erin up as well. "How was Mickey Mouse?"

"He's big! This big!" Jen opened her arms wide. "I like Goofy better."

Erin stared at him, frowning. "Where's your hair, Daddy? What happened to your ponytail?"

"I got a haircut, Bear. I'm back on my regular job for a while."

"It looks funny."

Luke laughed. "Thanks. What did you do at Disney World?"

"I got my picture taken with Aladdin and the Genie, and Pinocchio and Hercules!" Erin counted on her fingers. "And Donald Duck!"

"Very cool." His mother had closed the door and disappeared. Luke carried the girls into the living room, sat down on the couch and perched one of them on each knee. "What ride did y'all like best?"

That answer involved a serious discussion of all the rides they'd taken and the high points of each. Luke studied their faces as the girls traded ideas. They were a little browner than last week. The outfits they wore looked new.

He touched a bandage on Erin's knee. "What happened here?"

Erin laughed. "We went on the teacup ride and it went 'round and 'round and 'round. And when I got off I was so dizzy I couldn't walk, and I bumped into the edge of a bench."

"You cried." Jen pointed out.

"Just a little. You cried when the whale splashed you."

"Well, you cried when—"

"Hold it." Luke squeezed them both around the waist. "I get the picture. Did you go on Peter Pan's Flight? That was your favorite when we went to the Magic Kingdom, Erin."

"We went to Disney World before?"

"Sure, you and your mom and me. Jen was still a baby, but she came, too. We have…had pictures, remember? You and me in the boat, getting ready to fly?"

She shook her blond head. "Uh-uh. But we rode it this time. Jen was scared we would fall."

Luke chuckled. "That's what you thought when we went, too."

"So there." Jennifer stuck her tongue out at her sister.

"Jennifer Irene Brennan." Kristin stood in the doorway, hands on her hips. "That's rude and unkind and you will apologize to your sister."

"I'm sorry," Jen muttered.

"Ha-ha," Erin taunted.

Luke shook her gently. "You don't hit somebody when they're down, Erin. You know that."

She hung her head. "I know, Daddy."

"I came in to tell you that Grandmother has supper just about ready." Kristin's voice was firm. "Go wash your hands."

"Oh, boy!" The girls dashed past their mother into the back of the house. Luke stood up, the meeting he'd been dreading suddenly unavoidable.

"Hi, Luke." The sun had streaked her hair and deepened her tan.

He cleared his throat. "Kristin."

"Your…haircut looks good."

"Thanks. I guess you had lots of sun in Florida."

"Not a single rainy day. Do you want to stay for supper?"

"That's okay. I just came to say hi to the girls." He held out the bag of cookies. "I brought some dessert, though they're probably mostly crumbs at this point."

Her smile flashed and was gone. "Good over ice cream." After a pause, she cleared her throat. "We've got some pictures—come and see." She almost took his hand but then, with a self-conscious blush, turned and led the way into the back of his parents' house.

Luke dragged in a breath and followed warily.

Matt and his dad sat in the family room beyond the kitchen. Their conversation stopped abruptly when Luke stepped in. The Colonel stood up. "Good to see you, son—and good to see that damn hair cut right for a change. How's the security business?" His dad thought a real man's place was in the Army. Cops were on the same level with building guards.

"We do our best," Luke answered. "Have you had a good week?" The scent of apple-laced tobacco flavored the air.

"As good as usual."

"Except that you were exhausted for several days," Elena Brennan corrected. "I'm still not sure you're up to par."

The Colonel took a deep pull on his pipe. "All the excitement of the wedding, I guess."

Luke could sympathize, though excitement wasn't exactly the word he'd use to describe his own reaction. He turned his head to meet his brother's stare. "Welcome home."

Matt nodded. "Thanks."

So much for the formalities. Luke walked back to the kitchen.

"Are you staying, Luke?" His mother turned from the counter where a baked ham and her homemade bread stood waiting. "I can make more sandwiches."

"No, thanks, Mom. I just came to say hi to Erin and Jen." He sat down at the kitchen table with the girls. "So tell me what else you did in Florida."

Kristin brought a box of pictures over and Luke listened as Erin and Jenny explained each one.

"That's me and Daddy Matt on the log ride."

"Me and Mommy with Cinderella."

"We got a lady to take this one of Mommy and Daddy Matt and me and Jen in front of Cinderella's castle. Isn't it neat?"

He agreed that it was indeed neat, wondering how each mention of "Daddy Matt" could cut deeper than the one before.

Erin looked around. "Mommy, where's the big picture?"

Elena Brennan answered. "I've already hung it on the wall, honey. Right above the television."

"Come see, Daddy. Come see." Erin took Luke by the hand and pulled him over to the wall filled with four decades of Brennan family photos. "Isn't it neat? We got all dressed up!"

"Great picture," he managed to reply, his voice rougher than he'd intended. The girls wore long dresses of white lacy stuff. Kristin's dress was a red that drew light to her hair and deepened the brown of her eyes. The three of them sat on an old-fashioned velvet sofa, with Matt in a suit and tie leaning over them. As Luke glanced down the wall he saw that the photos had been rearranged. Pictures of himself and Kristin with the girls had been moved to a bottom corner in the wide display.

"Supper's ready," his mother called.

Luke knelt in front of Erin. "I'm gonna take off and let you eat. Give me a hug."

She flung her arms around his neck. "I missed you, Daddy."

"I missed you, too, Erin Bear. I'm glad you're home."

"When can we come to your house?"

He took a deep breath. "I'll give your mom a call and we'll figure that out. Sometime this week, okay?"

"Tomorrow?"

"I'm not sure. But soon, I promise." Erin held his hand tightly as they went back into the kitchen. The rest of the family sat around the table, with Jen on the far side. "Guess I'll just wave to you, Jenny Penny. See you later, okay?"

"No, wait, Daddy!" She started sliding out of her chair.

"Why don't you just stay in your chair, Jennifer, honey." His mother, next to Jen, put a hand out. "There's really not enough room..."

But Jen solved that problem. She crawled under the table and came out in front of him. "Don't go, Daddy!"

Luke picked her up and hugged her close. "I have to, Jen. I—I have to go to work." Eventually, anyway. "But I promise I'll see you real soon." He looked over at Kristin as he spoke. She stared at her plate, with her lower lip caught tight between her teeth.

When he tried to set Jen down, she clung tighter. No words. Just a limpet clasp.

Finally, Kristin got up. "Jenny, love, let go." The little girl shook her head. Her mother put her hands around the small waist, sliding them between Jen and Luke's chest. Somehow, he stood there without moving a muscle. "Let go, Jenny."

The stranglehold released. Luke loosened his arms, and Jen and Kristin stepped away. "Thanks," he said, avoiding everybody's eyes, keeping his face as neutral as he could. "Talk to y'all later."

"Goodbye, son." His dad alone replied.

Still calm, Luke reached his bike and settled on it, pulled on his gloves, put on his helmet. Turning the key, he pressed the starter and glided into motion. But he only got around the corner before he had to stop. He couldn't see, couldn't breathe. His legs were shaking too much to be sure he kept his balance. He wondered if this kind of pain would be terminal.

And what the hell kind of life he'd have if it wasn't.

SARAH HEARD the rumble of the bike's motor despite the concrete walls of the photo shop. She smiled to herself. The last print was drying.

As she came out of the darkroom, though, she heard Chuck in the front of the shop, giving Luke a hard time.

"We don't let just anyone into the back."

"Good idea. If you'll get Sarah, she'll explain that I'm not just anyone. We have an appointment."

"She's in the darkroom. We'll have to wait for her to come out."

"And maybe I can do a fire inspection in the meantime. I'm sure all your permits and extinguishers and wiring are according to code and up to date."

Sarah laughed and stepped through the curtained doorway. "He's got you there, Chuck. When is the last time you bought a new extinguisher?"

"At least I bought one." He brushed past her in the narrow space behind the counter. "If this place had been left to your absentee management, it would have fallen apart years ago!'' The curtain swished behind him.

Sarah looked at Luke. ''That's my business partner. He doesn't—'' She registered the despair on his face. ''What's wrong? Are you okay?''

He drew a deep breath that shook. ''Sure. I'm... great.''

''You went to see your daughters, right? Did something happen?''

His hands went into his back pockets. ''No bloodshed, anyway.''

Sarah didn't insist on an explanation—he'd obviously been through enough today. ''Come into the back. I've made some tea. We can look at the pictures.''

She lifted the hinged portion of the counter, then pulled the curtain aside as Luke stepped into the back room. In contrast to this morning, he seemed almost unsteady, as if he had to concentrate to keep from falling over.

''So you got the pictures developed?'' His deep voice sounded weary.

''I did.'' Chuck had disappeared behind the closed door of his office. She and Luke downed the iced tea she poured in a thirsty silence. Then she took his glass away. ''Now, come tell me what you think.''

A step into the darkroom, he stopped dead. ''Wow.''

Sarah smiled in satisfaction. His reaction was exactly what she'd hoped for.

He moved forward to stand in front of the largest print—an eighteen-by-twenty of Erin and Jennifer bent over the bait bucket. The balance of the shot was perfect, the light on those green-and-rose dresses like something out of a storybook illustration. And just as she'd hit the shutter button, a small breeze had fluffed out the girls' lacy petticoats.

"This is…amazing. You're really good."

"Just lucky to be there when the three of you came out. All I had to do was snap pictures."

"I don't know enough about it to argue with you. But…wow." He moved down the line, studying each print in turn. "I really like that one," he said, pointing to a shot of the three of them laughing in the wind. "Could I have a copy?"

"I'll copy them all for you. And for your family."

"Nah." He glanced at the photos of himself. "Don't worry about any of those. Just the ones with the girls in them for the family. And a copy of the one with the three of us for me." Under the white light, his cheeks looked a little red.

"But your parents—"

Luke shook his head. "Nope." He went back to the first picture. "I can't believe how great these are."

Sarah propped her hip on a stool, letting him have the time he wanted. That gave her a chance to appreciate once again how solid his body was, how balanced. She'd seen models in art classes with less physique to recommend them. She'd certainly never sighed over any of them the way she wanted to sigh over Luke Brennan.

He turned around before she could. "I'm thinking I should pay you for these. Talent like yours doesn't come cheap."

"You're right." Sarah slipped to her feet. "So I'll let you buy dinner. Deal?"

He grinned for the first time since he'd come into the shop. "Deal. Let's go."

LUKE HAD PARKED the Harley next to Sarah's Jeep. "Do you want to take yours? You'd be more comfortable. I'll even let you drive, in case my mind wanders again."

She laughed. "That's a good thought. But..." Stepping up to the bike, she ran her fingertips over the leather seat, the handlebar, the dash. "This is a really fine machine."

He let out a relieved breath. Kristin had never liked his fascination with motorcycles. "Do you ride?"

Sarah nodded. "I used to. Went all the way to California from D.C. on Interstate 40 when I was eighteen."

"I took a trip like that, on I-10. There was an incredible rainstorm outside New Orleans—I thought I was going to drown."

"That happened to James and me, too. In Oklahoma City."

Luke wondered if that meant a more personal relationship than he'd realized. But Sarah continued with her story. "We waited underneath an overpass while the water climbed up our ankles. I was pretty scared. But I got some great lightning shots."

"I wasn't exactly calm, myself."

"Well, there's no rain in today's forecast." She wasn't wincing as much when she gave him a smile now, even a really wide one. "Could we take your bike?"

Luke pulled the extra helmet out of the saddlebag. "Be my guest."

In seconds she had her hair tucked neatly into the helmet. He straddled the seat and then Sarah climbed on behind him, easily and smoothly as if she'd done it every day for years. She settled like a feather, barely affecting the weight or tilt of the bike.

Luke wished he could say she didn't affect his equilibrium. But he felt every inch of her at his back. Her hands—free of bandages, though still scraped up—came to rest at his waist, and the light pressure heated his skin through his shirt like the sun at midday. He wasn't used to being so close to any woman besides Kristin.

But he could get used to having Sarah on the bike behind him. The engine purred as he pumped the gas and released the brake. "Hang on!"

They wove slowly along the main drag of Myrtle Beach restaurants, through traffic snarled with thousands of tourists out for dinner and maybe a night of playing miniature golf at one of a hundred different parks. Luke pulled in at his favorite sandwich shop to buy dinner, which he stowed with another bag of cookies in a knapsack inside the bike's right saddlebag.

Then at last they were on the long straightaway of Highway 17. The pure ecstasy of the ride—summer wind roaring around them, sight and sound blended into a blur of colorful noise—filled every need. He hadn't felt so free, so unconfined, so…so *young* in months.

Hell, it had been a year and a half since he'd enjoyed anything this much. The year and a half since Matt had come back.

They passed Murrell's Inlet, going south, and Pawley's Island, a tourist favorite. Finally, he downshifted and made a swooping turn beside the huge statue of rearing horses at the entrance to Brookgreen Sculpture Gardens.

Sarah's hands tightened on his waist. She leaned forward, and he felt her slenderness press against his spine. "The gardens are open at night now?" He could just barely hear her above the quiet roar of the engine.

"It's a fairly new program." Luke pulled out a membership card at the ticket gate and the attendant waved them through. "I thought this would be a great place for a picnic dinner."

If she said something, he didn't hear. But her hands slid up his back to his shoulders, and squeezed.

She couldn't have any idea what that did to his pulse rate.

He recovered his control during a slow ride down the curving lane lined with azaleas and tall pines. Circling the first fountain and its golden horse and rider, they finally came to a stop in the parking lot outside the visitor center. Luke let Sarah slide off first.

"You're an easy passenger." Not easy to ignore, though. "I could barely feel your weight back there."

"I guess it's like any other bike. Once you learn how to balance, you don't forget." She looked around them and drew in a deep, deep breath. "I was planning to come down here soon. I'm so glad you thought of it."

He held out a hand for her helmet and stowed it with his in the empty saddlebag, then walked to the other side to get the knapsack with dinner. They bypassed the gift shop, stopped to admire a water garden, and posed on a bench beside the life-size sculpture of a man reading the newspaper.

"I've always wanted to turn the page," Sarah commented. "Do you suppose he gets bored reading the same articles day after day?"

"I'd say so. Where are the comics? And what about the sports section?"

She laughed and led him into one of the glass-walled galleries outside the entrance to the garden. "You might like to see this."

Luke studied the photograph she'd indicated—a run-down shack in the country, weeds growing too high in front of the porch, junk piled against the steps and the walls, screen door hanging by one hinge. Almost depressing.

But by some magic he didn't understand, the first impression didn't stick. Something drew him to look *again*, to step closer, to get involved in the photograph. He found himself examining the garbage, searching for the stories of the people who'd left it there. The weeds became flowers, telling of a garden and the love that had tended it. The photographer had seen the lives behind the front of that old shack. And, somehow, had captured their essence on film.

"Amazing." Luke took a deep breath, drawing in a whiff of Sarah's sweet scent, as well. "Is this one of yours?"

"Oh, no. This is Felix Sawyer's work. He was my teacher."

"Wait—the guy in the shop is Charles Sawyer, right?"

"That's right. Felix's nephew."

"The pictures on the wall in the front of the shop look a lot like this. Charles said they were his."

"Really?" Sarah stared for a minute at the photograph. "I hadn't noticed the pictures. Charles…Chuck runs the place by himself, really—I usually go in by the back door just to use the darkroom when I'm in town, and that's not often. I've been here twice in the eighteen months since Felix died…until this week. I'll have to check those prints out." She seemed troubled by the prospect.

Luke cleared his throat. "So Felix taught you the trade. How did that happen?"

"I met him on the beach the summer I was twelve, while I was visiting my grandmother. He spent the day shooting pictures of the dunes and the sea oats, and I hung around the whole time asking questions." Her gaze was fixed on the past. "We both came back to the same spot the next afternoon and Felix handed me a camera." She sighed. "He taught me everything I know."

"He must have been proud of your career."

She sighed. "I think so. Though I didn't see him much,

once I started working for *Events*. I was always out of the country. Even when he died."

"Felix would have understood that."

"Probably. But if I had been with him more, I would have more of him to remember. I guess that's why I came here after…" She swallowed. "I feel closer to Felix when I'm developing in his darkroom. That's the place most like home."

Luke asked the next question gently. "Your parents?"

"They died in a car wreck just after I graduated from high school. My dad was Air Force, so we moved a lot. I have pictures and memories, but that's about all."

Her wistful voice called up his personal regrets. "There's more to life than memories, Sarah Rose." He squeezed her shoulder quickly, then let go. It was time to break the mood. "Do you want to eat in the official picnic area, or kinda snack as we go along?"

"Let's walk."

"Which way?"

"The sundial?"

"You got it."

STROLLING THROUGH the gardens, Sarah realized that this was another place that felt like home. The soft breeze stroked her skin, carrying scents of grass and mist, magnolias and roses. A crescent moon climbed above the trees, turning the sidewalk to silver even before the sun had completely set. Crickets hummed on every side, backed up by frogs in the rhythm section.

At the sight of a familiar sculpture, she thrust her sandwich into Luke's hand and climbed into the lap of a giant bronze bear. "Goldilocks was always my favorite fairy tale. What about your girls?"

He thought a moment. "Jen loves to pretend she's Rapunzel. Erin goes for *Hansel and Gretel*—she likes the part where the witch gets shoved in the oven.''

''Bloodthirsty child.''

''Only when it comes to witches. She's actually very tenderhearted. Especially where animals are concerned.''

''Maybe she has a future as a veterinarian.'' She slipped off the bear's knee, took back her sandwich and claimed a healthy bite. Food hadn't tasted this good in months…maybe years. ''There's the sundial— Can we still tell what time it is?''

The giant sundial, at least twenty feet across and equally high, didn't work well at twilight. They sat for a while on the surrounding wall, pointing out the emerging stars between munches on sweet-potato chips, then started their walk toward the formal areas of the garden.

''I brought dessert.'' Luke took a paper sack out of his knapsack and withdrew a cookie. ''What do you think?''

Sarah took one bite and groaned. ''I think I'd be a couple of sizes larger if I could bake like this.'' She sighed as a sinful combination of dark chocolate, pecans and oatmeal, with a hint of coconut, melted on her tongue. ''Where did you get them?''

He laughed. ''I baked them.''

''You're kidding.'' She saw that he wasn't. ''You really bake cookies?''

''I really do.''

''How wonderful. I haven't baked anything except frozen dinners in years.'' Sarah indulged herself with another cookie. ''Have Erin and Jennifer inherited your talent?''

Luke stopped at her side, and the world around them suddenly hushed. She turned to stare up at him in the almost-dark. ''What's wrong?'' All the light, all the laughter they'd been sharing had vanished from his face.

The shadow of his shoulders lifted on a deep breath. Sarah put her hand on his arm. "Luke? What did I say?"

"I guess I'd better explain, so you won't misunderstand anymore." His smooth voice had roughened.

Her mind couldn't grasp the possibilities. "Explain what?"

"I married Kristin because…" He frowned and shook his head. "Kristin was already pregnant when we got married."

Sarah shook her head, not following him.

"The baby—Erin—wasn't mine."

"Oh, Luke."

"Erin doesn't know. Only Kristin and I do, and now you."

"And the father?"

The laugh he gave was more of a moan. "Yeah. It's tough to keep secrets from the person you're married to."

In an instant, the rest of the story became obvious. "Matt?"

"Got it in one, Sarah Rose." His deep sigh trembled. "Erin's…biological…dad is my brother Matt. All along you've been feeling sorry for me as a victim, when the violation was really mine. I stole *his* wife and *his* daughter first. While he was in a foreign prison serving his country, no less."

He turned his back to her and stared off across the marsh. "So getting them back is only what Matt deserves. And losing them—living without them—is what I deserve." A moment of silence, and then his voice again, barely a whisper, ragged and dry. "Aren't you glad to know what kind of guy you're choosing to hang around with these days?"

CHAPTER FIVE

LUKE'S ARM FELT like wood to her fingertips. She stroked his shoulder a little, as she would a troubled child. "I think there's more to the story than I've heard so far. Tell me?"

He glanced down at her, his eyes shadowed by the night and his thoughts. "The benefit of the doubt? You're too generous, Sarah Rose."

"And I'm sure you're being too hard on yourself. The man who helped me pick up the pieces after I was mugged can't be all bad."

His face closed even further. Turning away, he dislodged her hand. "Is that why you're here? To pay off a debt?" Long strides took him quickly away from her, toward the back of the gardens.

Sarah wanted to follow, to explain what she'd meant. But she wanted just as much to take off in the opposite direction. This man pulled at her in ways she couldn't afford. He needed more than she could give.

Yet as he vanished under the moss-hung trees at the edge of the meadow, she started after him.

Just as she caught up, he stopped and swung around. Sarah walked straight into him. His hands closed on her shoulders. "Careful."

She could barely see his face in the gathering darkness. "I'm here because you asked me," she said, panting a little. "And because I wanted to come."

The heat of his palms warmed her shoulders. He gentled his hold, and chuckled low in his throat. "You're something else, Sarah Rose. I'm not sure what to do about you."

Somehow, the distance between them closed. She stood with her hands flat on his chest. "Don't run away."

"To be honest, that's not what I'm thinking about right now." He tilted his head, his eyes glinting silver in the night. Then he touched his mouth to hers.

His lips were firm, smooth. His kisses were careful, coaxing her along a pathway of discovery step by pleasurable step. He stroked his hands down her back and then up to rest over her shoulder blades, pulling her closer still. Melting, Sarah let herself be guided, let her body curve against his, fitting hollows and planes together like a sensuous puzzle. She breathed in his scent, the clean smell of soap, the more dangerous, masculine aura that was his alone.

Then slowly, almost lazily, he traced the seam of her mouth with the tip of his tongue.

Sarah gasped, and the kiss took fire. The hot night swirled around her, shot through with brilliant color. She parted her lips, demanding more of everything Luke offered.

And gave to him in return. A little wild, a little out of control, she closed her teeth on his lower lip. Luke groaned, then returned the favor.

She ran her hands over his shoulders, let her fingers play in his thick, shiny, short hair. An unbearable expectation filled her chest, pooled deep in her belly. She didn't know where they were going. But she wanted to get there.

The brakes in Luke's brain wouldn't function. He gave up even trying to steer. Sarah's mouth under his stopped the pain. For the first time in more than two years, he didn't have to fight against feeling. Something this good couldn't possibly hurt.

She rested against him, light, almost angular. Yet soft. Needing, not thinking, he stroked his palms over her back, trailed his fingers along her narrow spine. She made a sound like a purr, and he closed her inside the circle of his arms. Tight.

This gasp sounded like pain. Luke jerked his head back, loosening his hold. "Hell. I'm sorry—I didn't mean to hurt you. Are you okay?"

Sarah stepped backward. For the first time in…for-ever?…they weren't touching. She didn't answer his question. The night air pressed cold on his face.

He cleared his throat. "Are you all right?"

She drew a deep breath, with a hitch at the end. "I'm okay. I…you…I guess my ribs are still pretty bruised."

Luke closed his eyes, recovering reality. When he opened them again, Sarah had turned away, almost lost in the dark.

Damn. She didn't have to say a word. Only a jerk would come on to a woman who'd suffered so much, so recently. And "jerk" was practically his middle name.

"I don't know about you," he said, working to steady his voice, "but the mosquitoes have set up an all-you-can-eat buffet on my skin. Maybe we should head back to town."

"That's…that's a good idea." She turned toward him, took a few uncertain steps, then stopped. "Which way do we go?"

"This way, I think." He thumbed the direction over his shoulder. "There's a light up ahead."

"I'll follow you."

Once back in the illuminated section of the garden,

they walked quickly and quietly toward the exit. They passed the sculptures he'd wanted to share with her, but Sarah didn't linger any more than he did. Luke checked his watch by one of the lights—almost nine. He needed to get to work in a couple of hours, anyway.

The torture of the ride home didn't surprise him. Sarah's legs just behind his, her body pressed against his back, her hands braced on his ribs…if those touches unsettled him before, they unhinged him now. He gritted his teeth and pushed the bike's speed to the very limit of legal.

In the parking lot of the photo shop, he waited for her to slide off the bike first. When she hesitated, he swung his leg over and turned to face her.

"It's silly," she said, sounding even huskier than usual. "But I don't want to get in the car. I—I don't want to get off the bike."

His heart melted at the fear in her eyes. "Not silly at all. But nothing's going to happen this time. I'll make sure you get home safe and sound." He held out his hand. "I promise."

She stared at him in the darkness, then put her fingers in his. "Okay, I'll count on you."

Which was not a smart answer, considering how he'd behaved just an hour ago.

Luke took the keys and unlocked the Jeep door, checked the back seat, and the rear compartment. "Nobody here. Hop in."

She climbed in easier tonight than last week. Buckling her seat belt, she shook her head. "I'm better now. Sorry to keep you so late."

"No problem. I'll follow you home and then be on my way."

"You don't have to—"

He put up a hand. "No arguments, Sarah Rose. I'm going to make sure you get inside okay."

She sighed, but didn't protest further. Within fifteen minutes they both pulled up in the condo parking lot. Luke got off the bike as Sarah locked the Jeep.

They walked without speaking to the outside staircase of her building, and he followed her up to the second level. At her doorway, he waited until she'd unlocked the door and turned on the lights inside. He didn't follow her in.

And she didn't invite him to. "Everything's fine," she said, turning to face him.

Luke nodded. "Okay. Thanks for coming with me—I had a…good…time." How could a lie be true?

"Me, too." Her teeth flashed as she smiled. "I'll make up those prints and get them to you as soon as possible." She took hold of the door handle—his cue to leave. "Thanks for dinner."

"My pleasure." Hell, there didn't seem to be anything to say that didn't have two meanings. "Good night, Sarah Rose."

"'Night, Corporal Brennan." Before he had taken two steps backward, she closed the door. The lock clicked firmly into place.

A definite goodbye.

SUNDAY AFTERNOON, Sarah went into the shop through the front door. As Luke had noted, the pictures on display were really decent. Chuck's approach to photography had improved dramatically over the years.

Her partner came through the curtain as she studied the shots. "May I—oh, it's you. What are you doing out here?"

"Luke Brennan admired your pictures. I wanted to see them. They're good."

"Gee, thanks." He wiped not-so-imaginary dust off the counter. "They bring in a nice bit of cash, now and then."

"Have you sold many?"

"About twenty, now. There are collectors out there who appreciate my style."

"Good. I'm glad." And she was. If Chuck could find his own success, maybe he wouldn't be jealous of hers. Assuming she ever got back to work. "They remind me of Felix, but he didn't do so much with colored filters for light effects."

"Exactly." Chuck beamed. "I took what Felix taught me and expanded on it. Maybe my career took longer than yours to establish, but on the other hand, it hasn't fallen apart on me, either." He gave her a malicious grin. "Would you like a cup of coffee?"

"No." She drew a deep breath against the urge to slap him. "Thanks. I just want to use the darkroom for a while."

"You're welcome, of course. I assume that's why Felix left half the shop to you. Maybe he realized you'd be back looking for a job one day."

"Maybe." She didn't really think so at all, but she didn't have the energy to fight with Chuck. Head down, Sarah went behind the counter and scooted past him to get to the curtained doorway. Pretending to straighten the boxes of film on the shelf, he didn't move an inch to make it easier.

By the time she came out of the darkroom, he had gone for the day. And he'd left the back door unlocked, which meant any crazy—including last week's mugger—could have come in and found her alone. She locked the door, got a soda from the refrigerator, and sat down in Felix's old recliner to rest. And to think, which she'd avoided doing since about this time last night.

Luke. She could still feel his mouth on hers, still hear his rough groan of pleasure. Her experience with men wasn't vast—she'd met James right after high school, at the beginning of her job search, and hadn't been involved with anyone else.

Of course, she couldn't say the same for James. But that didn't matter much anymore.

You aren't "involved" now, either. Luke wasn't looking for a lover—he'd just lost his wife and his children. He was lonely, needing physical comfort. And Sarah had put herself within reach, practically inviting him to take whatever he wanted. If he couldn't hold the woman he loved, he could pretend, right?

The idea burned in her brain. She remembered the other women James had dallied with—beautiful ones he met in bars, fiery ones who brought him information, classy ones who gave him contacts. The first affair had injured Sarah deeply. By the third, when she broke off their engagement, she'd learned how to protect herself.

But Luke was different from James. He didn't use people, as James had. He *cared* about them, sacrificed for them. Luke hadn't explained everything about his marriage, but the facts spoke for themselves. He married Kristin *because* she was pregnant and the father—Luke's brother—was not coming back.

How could Sarah defend her heart against such an honorable, giving man?

If she let herself care too much, though, she would only be hurt when he couldn't share her feelings. And there was no reason to think Luke would ever forget his ex-wife and their life together enough to love someone else. No reason at all.

So she would mail him the prints, Sarah decided. He could distribute them as he pleased. She'd printed a copy for her agent, as well. If something came of the effort, she'd probably have to get in touch with Kristin and Matt to get their signatures on a release form, too.

But why worry until that happened?

WHEN THE PHONE RANG Thursday afternoon, Sarah's first impulse was to ignore it. Once she'd answered, her second impulse was to hang up quickly.

Her New York editor, Oliver Kerr, started without preamble. "I've got an assignment that needs your touch. Are you ready to go?"

She tried to dredge up enthusiasm, but could only find dread. "Where?"

"Central America. There's going to be a major announcement about a certain military government and what's happened to private citizens over the past eighteen years. We need to get the drop on the rest of 'em."

"Who's doing the story?"

"Len Markowitz. Are you in?"

She pictured herself leaving the beach, boarding a plane, landing in the tropical atmosphere of a third world country, camera at hand, ready to work. And shuddered.

"No, Oliver. Sorry. I don't think I've got what that takes right now."

He didn't hide his frustrated sigh. "How long is this going to last, Sarah? I've got a magazine to put out. Readers are looking for *your* pictures. Not to mention the publishers."

Was there a timetable for recovering your nerve? "I

don't know. And that doesn't do you any good, does it? Maybe you'd better hire somebody else.''

"Maybe."

Oliver didn't make empty threats. She closed her eyes. "Just let me know, okay? A pink slip or something?''

"Hell, Sarah. I don't want to do that. But I need a photographer. What options do I have?''

"None, Oliver. I understand.''

He blew a frustrated breath. "I wish you'd just get over whatever this is and get back to work. Don't you want to?''

"Of course. And I'm trying." She thought over the days since the trip with Luke to Brookgreen, most of them spent cocooned in her condo. "I'll give you a call when I'm ready. Don't feel bad if you have to get someone else. Really.''

"Okay. But I don't think I'm going to find somebody as good as you sitting on a street corner.'' From the silence on the line, she thought he'd hung up.

But then he said, "By the way, one of the mailroom guys found a couple of boxes that have your name on them.''

"Files?''

"No, letters. Looks like most of 'em came from South Carolina. Evidently arrived while you were out of the country, got put away and then just forgotten.''

"Oh." What would Felix have sent? No one else in this state—in the whole world, really—would be writing letters to her. "Could you forward them down here? I don't know what's in them, so I can't tell you just to throw the boxes out.''

"Glad to." He cleared his throat. "Call me, Sarah, when you want to come back. I'll pull all the strings I've got.''

"Thanks. I appreciate the confidence."

"You earned it." And then he did hang up.

Now what? Oliver was wonderful but, in publishing, the bottom line counted most. Stressed, depressed photographers didn't increase profits. He'd get somebody else for the assignment. That person would succeed—as she had, six years ago—and there'd be a new name on the *Events* payroll in place of hers.

Money wouldn't be an immediate concern. Traveling constantly, on expense account most of the time, had kept her bank balance healthy. The condo and the Jeep were paid for. She didn't need a job—for a while, anyway.

But work—photographic work—had been her life since she was eighteen. Who was she, if not Sarah Randolph, Photographer, *Events* magazine? Where did she fit? All the people she might have turned to were dead— her parents, Felix, James. She had no one left to care about, or to care about her.

What in the world was she going to do? Her whole life came down to a question mark.

But Luke Brennan could not be the answer.

FRIDAY MORNING, with the doorbell buzzing like a swarm of furious bees, Luke figured he might as well stop trying to sleep, since it wasn't happening anyway. Pulling on jeans and a shirt, he reached the front door just as the mail carrier turned away.

"Sorry to make you wait." Luke ran a hand over his hair. "What can I do for you?"

"Certified mail." She was young and pretty, and she gave him a bright smile. "Sign here. Hot today, isn't it?"

"Summer's definitely arrived." He handed over the yellow slip and received a large, heavy manilla envelope in return. "Thanks."

She smiled again, even wider. "Have a good day."

Luke tried for a grin. "You, too." Judging by the carrier's sudden pout, the grin wasn't much of a success. Without another word, she stalked back to the mail truck parked on the street.

He studied the envelope as he shouldered the door shut. The photographs, of course. Sarah had mailed him the pictures. She hadn't brought them herself.

No surprise. But as he dropped down on the couch and put the envelope on the coffee table, disappointment swamped him. He'd hoped to see her again.

After a few minutes, he opened the envelope and eased out the prints. Packed with layers of tissue paper between the photographs was the record of those minutes on the beach. Sarah had caught Erin's serious interest in everything scientific, Jen's penchant for fantasy and dreaming. The girls' essential beauty and innocence contrasted with the complex swirl of ocean waves.

Luke slouched against the back of the couch. From just beyond his reach, the pictures taunted him with what he'd lost. Visitation arrangements—set up to start after the wedding—gave him a weekday and every third weekend of custody. Not nearly enough to keep him an essential part of the girls' lives. Did he even belong inside the completed family circle now? With their mom and a new dad right in the house, did Erin and Jenny need him anymore?

And did he really want the answer to that question?

How to deliver the photographs was an easier issue to deal with. A phone call to his dad extracted the information that Matt, Kristin and the girls were coming to lunch on Sunday. Luke didn't bother to wonder if he would have known about the get-together if he hadn't called. He simply asked for and received permission to show up.

Carefully dressed, he arrived just as his parents' Cadillac and Kristin's van pulled into the driveway after church. His dad raised a hand in greeting, his mother nodded and bustled in the kitchen door. Matt and Kristin were busy unbuckling seat belts.

As usual, the real welcome came from the girls. "Daddy!" They screamed in unison and then ran across the grass. Luke lifted Jen against his chest and held Erin close to his side. "Well, munchkins? How was church?"

Erin hugged him back. "We talked about Daniel and the lions' den. Can you believe they didn't even eat him?"

"Pretty amazing. Not a trick I'd want to try."

"I drawed a ark," Jennifer said.

"'Cept she didn't put in two of each animal." Her sister frowned with disapproval. "Nobody draws an ark with just one bear an' one duck an' one zebra."

"Maybe their partners are already inside," Luke suggested.

"Yeah." Jennifer kicked at her older sister.

He shook his arm, and her with it. "No kicking. Arguments get settled without hitting, remember?" Jen didn't say anything, and he jogged his arm again. "Remember?"

"I 'member."

"Good." He bent over and set her on the grass just as a shadow darkened the blades. When he straightened up, Kristin stood there, close enough to touch...and completely out of reach.

"Hi, Luke." Her smile was uneasy, and he thought she looked tired. "It's good to see you."

And the right answer would be...? "Thanks." After a

few seconds of silence, he ventured a little further. "Are you getting settled after your trip?"

She nodded, watching the girls chase a seagull crazy enough to land near them. "I think Jennifer and Erin are...confused."

"I get the feeling they're a handful these days. They argue a lot?" Luke kept his focus on the children, as well. Talking was easier, without looking into her face.

"Constantly. Maybe it's the age. Erin is ready for school and Jenny's still just a baby."

"They need time." The new voice snapped Luke's head around. Matt had joined them. "Everybody needs a chance to adjust." His hand curved around the ball of Kristin's shoulder. The claim of possession came through loud and clear.

"Sure," Luke agreed, holding his brother's gaze. "You get used to anything, eventually. It's easier for some people than others, but those are the breaks, right?"

"Don't be such a jerk," Matt muttered.

"Don't be such an a—"

"Luke!" Kristin put a hand on his arm, her eyes wide.

"Erin! Jennifer!" The three of them looked toward the house, where Elena Brennan stood at the front door. "Dinner is ready!"

Luke stepped out from under Kristin's fingers. "You go on. I need to get something in the truck."

He fetched the envelope of Sarah's photographs. Holding her work like some kind of lucky charm, he followed his daughters, his ex-wife and her husband into his own personal lions' den.

CHAPTER SIX

AFTER OBSERVING the photograph in her hands during a minute of total silence, Elena Brennan sighed. "Aren't they beautiful?" Her blue eyes were soft as she looked up at her husband. "William, did you ever see such lovely little girls?"

Luke relaxed a fraction and leaned sideways against the wall of the living room. His mother, at least, approved of Sarah's pictures.

"Not since..." The Colonel cleared his throat. "Not since pictures of your girlhood, dear. Remarkable." Placing a hand on his wife's shoulder, he leaned over to examine the prints on the coffee table. "You'll need to get special frames for these."

Kristin sat on the floor with Jenny in her lap and a photograph in her hand. "I can't believe you went out on the beach, barefoot, in that dress. What if you'd fallen in the water?" Then she kissed Jen's blond head. "But you look just wonderful."

Luke's mother looked up. "You are so lucky to have daughters, Kristin. They are just the sweetest thing life can offer." Her voice sounded quavery, as if she needed to cry.

The Colonel nodded at Matt. "But sons carry on the name—give a man his place in history."

"That's true." Elena Brennan didn't sound completely convinced. "But these little blond angels..." She sighed again. "I think I'll put one of the large pictures in our room. And perhaps one in the dining room, suitably framed, of course." Carrying one of the prints, she crossed the hall to consider placement.

Erin leaned her elbows on the polished table. "Those dresses were hot. And scratchy. I thought I was gonna die of suffercation!"

Luke and Kristin laughed first, then Matt joined in. "Suff-o-cation, Erin Bear," Luke said. "But you didn't, did you?"

"Just barely not." She picked up one of the smaller prints and brought it to Luke. "Can I have this one for my room?"

"They're yours and your mom's. You can—" He focused on the picture she held up, the one of him alone that he'd asked Sarah to leave out. "Uh…sure. I guess."

Kristin leaned over. "Let me see." Erin turned the print. Her mother's eyes widened. "That's a…lovely picture, Erin. We'll get a frame and hang it on your wall so you and Jenny can both see it all the time."

Luke glanced at Matt, sitting in an armchair behind Kristin. His face was rigid and his hands, clasped together between his knees, were white with pressure.

Easing Jenny off her lap, Kristin got to her feet. "Really wonderful pictures. Let's leave them on the coffee table so they'll be safe while we eat." She put a hand on Matt's shoulder, but glanced at Luke. "Are you staying for dinner?"

Matt looked over. His blue gaze could have cut glass.

Luke straightened up. "I thought I would." He met Matt's stare. "If nobody minds."

"Of course not," Kristin said breathlessly. "Why would any of us mind?"

"I DON'T REMEMBER a lady taking pictures," Erin piped up as they ate their key lime pie for dessert. "Where was she?"

"In her chair up the beach. She had a lens on the camera that made you look closer than you really were." In his mind's eye Luke saw her again—a thin, tan woman in a copper-brown suit and straw hat, with shadows in her eyes that didn't come from that simple shade....

Then the picture changed to dusk in a sweet-smelling garden, with her brown hair curling in the humidity and her eyes sleepy as he bent his head for a kiss.

"Your father is quite pleased," Elena Brennan said, as if that settled any questions. "He's already taken several of the smaller pictures into the bedroom." The Colonel had left the table as soon as he'd eaten a few bites, saying he felt tired.

Matt looked up from the slice of pie he was mangling on his plate. "Is he okay, Mom? Seems like he's tired more than usual."

Her smooth, clear forehead wrinkled. "You know he wouldn't admit to anything. But we've scheduled a checkup for the middle of July. We'll see what the doctor says. That's after our picnic on the fourth, of course. We're expecting all of you to be here."

Just two hours at lunch was almost more than Luke could take. He felt tired at even the thought of spending a whole afternoon and evening with his family, trying to act normal, trying to pretend he didn't hurt, trying to give his brother a chance to be a father to the children he still loved.

"Can I bring something? Salad? Dessert?" Kristin always volunteered to help.

And Elena Brennan always managed to reject the offer. "No, thank you. Everything's taken care of."

Out of nowhere, Luke realized he had a question of his own. "Would you mind if I brought a friend?"

The three of them looked at him as if the idea didn't make sense. "You mean your partner, Dominick?" The reserve in his mother's voice conveyed doubt. "Would he really be comfortable?"

Nick would be comfortable anywhere, Luke figured. But his parents' guests from the country club set might not adjust so easily to the earthy cop's presence. "No. Sarah Randolph, as a matter of fact. The photographer. Y'all might like to meet her."

"Good idea." Matt's gaze had gone back to his plate. "Maybe she could make up some smaller prints of a couple of pictures. I'd like to take·them to the office."

The deciding vote had yet to be cast. "Mom?"

"I suppose that will be reasonable, Luke. She's a…presentable…sort of person?"

"Very presentable." He couldn't help a smile. "She won't offend anyone."

He glanced across the table as he spoke, and caught a flash of humor in his brother's eyes. But only a flash.

In the uneasy silence that followed, Luke realized they expected him to leave. "Well, then, I guess I'll see y'all on the fourth. Same time as always, Mom?"

She inclined her cheek for his near-kiss. "We'll be receiving after three o'clock."

"Great. We'll be here." At least, he hoped there would be a "we." "I'll say goodbye to the girls and take off. See you, Kristin. Matt."

Kristin lifted her hand. Matt nodded without meeting his eyes. Standard operating procedure for the last year and a half. Sometime they both really would have to adjust.

Erin and Jenny walked Luke to the front door. He

dropped to his knees and put an arm around each. "Gotta go, munchkins. You be good."

Jenny flung her arms around his neck. "When are you comin' home, Daddy?"

Erin opened her mouth to speak. Luke caught her eye and shook his head, and she snapped her jaw shut.

He cleared his throat. "I don't live in your house now, Jenny Penny. Remember?"

"But I want you to."

"I can't, babe. Matt lives with your mommy and you now. They're married, so they share your house."

Jen stuck out her lower lip. "But I like your stories better."

Luke gave a strangled laugh. "I've had more practice. Give Matt a little while and he'll be as good as me. Maybe even better." As usual.

She shook her head and buried her face in his shoulder. Luke held her close, cherishing her small body, her little-girl scent, while the weak patch on his heart tore open again.

He drew a deep breath. "Time for me to make like a tree and leave. Okay?"

Jenny straightened up. "Huh?"

Erin rolled her eyes. "It's a joke."

"It's not funny."

"Sure it is, if you're not a dumb four-year-old."

"I'm not!"

"Well, you don't know what it means, do you?"

"Cool it!" Luke raised his voice enough to get their attention. "Jenny, why don't you see if your grandmother has something for you to drink? Erin's gonna walk me to the truck."

"I wanna, too!"

"Nope. But I love you and I'll see you soon, okay?"

He gave her a kiss and a hug and a pat on the bottom to send her back to the kitchen.

Then he turned to her sister. "You're causing problems, Erin Bear." He stood and held out his hand. She slipped her fingers between his, and they stepped off the front porch to cross the grass. "Why are you so hard on her?"

Erin shrugged, looking down at her feet. "I don't know."

"You sure?"

She nodded, her lower lip stuck out even farther than her sister's.

Beside the truck, Luke squatted and took Erin's other hand in his as he studied her face. Her blond hair and honey skin favored Kristin. But her blue eyes told anybody who really looked the name of her dad. He was amazed that his parents and Kristin's hadn't seen the resemblance.

Back to the subject. "You're making things hard on your mom, you know. All this fighting is tough to listen to."

Hanging her head, Erin didn't answer.

"Would you do something for me?"

"What?"

"Would you be a little grown-up for me, and keep your temper around Jen? She's trying, but she's little. I have to depend on you."

To his surprise, a teardrop splashed on his thumb. He lifted Erin's chin. "What's wrong? I'm not mad. I just—"

She shook her head. "I want you to come home, too!"

He drew a shaking breath. "I explained that. You heard me."

"But I can't talk to him the way I talk to you! He doesn't know the stuff you do."

"He knows different stuff, Erin Bear. You have to find out what it is."

"But—"

Luke reached deep into his mind for any kind of pleasant memory. "When we were growing up, Matt liked to read about history—wars and exploring and all sorts of discoveries. I bet he'd share that kind of stuff with you."

She sighed.

"And he's a great baseball player. Much better than me. Get him to teach you to bat and pitch. He'd be glad to."

Her head dropped against his shoulder. "It's too hard. I don't like this. Why can't it be the way it was?"

Because... He put his arms around her. "It'll be even better, one day soon. We all have to be a little careful with each other right now. That's what I'm asking you to do with Jenny. Okay?"

She rolled her forehead back and forth on his chest. But she said, "Okay."

"Good girl." He set her back a step and stood up. "Now I'm gonna leave so you can get inside out of the sun."

"Daddy?" Her eyes, fixed on his face, were still wet. "Will you call me sometimes? I'll let Jen talk, too."

Tempted almost beyond endurance, Luke could yet see the pitfalls waiting on that road. "Tell you what." He came down to her level again. "Why don't you call me? I'm home most days until after you go to sleep. If you want to talk, I don't imagine your mom would mind. I know I wouldn't."

The little girl drew a deep breath. "Okay. I won't even call every day. Daddy Matt might get his feelings hurt."

He barely stopped himself from grabbing her up. "Good thinking, Erin Bear. I knew I could count on you. Give me a kiss."

Standing by the truck a few minutes later, he watched as she ran across the grass and into the house. When the door shut, the sound seemed to snap the wires holding him together. He fumbled his way behind the steering wheel, started the engine and sat, with the air-conditioning blowing like a storm from the northeast, breathing in gulps of wind.

Sarah, he remembered finally. Sarah would get him through this. If he behaved himself, she would feel safe. If he kept things friendly, surely she would see him occasionally. He recognized the boundary between them. He had himself under control.

He would call her as soon as he got home.

"DID YOU KNOW," Luke said as they drove toward the beach on Independence Day, "that your friend Chuck has a couple of assault charges on his record?"

Sarah's stomach did a roller-coaster flip. "Assault?"

"The cases never reached a courtroom. And the women have moved out of town."

"What does that mean?"

Luke parked the truck and turned toward her, with his arm stretched out along the back of the seat. "It means, Sarah Rose, that you should find another place to do your developing. The guy doesn't like you. He could very well be dangerous."

"You think—" She rubbed her temples, absorbing the horror. "Wouldn't I have recognized him? If he was the one who…" Somehow she still couldn't quite face that awful night.

"Not necessarily. The guy had the element of surprise

working for him.'' His warm palm covered the curve of her shoulder.

She swallowed hard, determined to ignore the tingle of that touch. "I can't believe Chuck would do that."

"You don't have to believe it. Just don't go back."

"But…" Her throat closed with tears at the thought of leaving Felix's studio and never going back. "My files are there—the whole history of what I've done."

"Go by sometime when he's not around and take your pictures out."

"Felix worked there—I worked *with* him there." Sarah stared out the windshield, seeing only a blur. "And he left me half interest in the shop—his shop. How can I walk away?"

"How can you afford not to?" Luke's other hand touched her cheek, turned her to face him. "Sawyer—if it was him—could try again. He might do more damage." His thumb wiped a tear off her cheek. "I can't let that happen."

Meeting his intense gaze with her own, Sarah fought the desire to lean into his palm, to increase the contact of skin against skin. Giving in to that feeling would only put pressure on Luke, create an obligation he couldn't afford. "Have you…talked to Chuck?" She drew away, and Luke let his hand drop to the seat between them.

"Not officially. I want you clear and safe, first."

"I—" There was no rational reason to refuse. But then, she hadn't been operating on rationality for quite some time now. "I need more proof before I jump to such a conclusion and—and disrupt my whole life."

Luke's eyes widened. "Sarah—"

She shrugged and looked away. "How do we know the charges were even true? Those women could have had their own agendas."

He drew a deep breath, obviously reaching for patience. "Sure. But let's not risk your life while we're trying to figure that out."

Having actually made a decision, Sarah wasn't inclined to back down. "I'm the one who got hurt," she said, with an attempt at decisiveness. "Felix gave me a responsibility, and I intend to fulfill it. I owe him—and myself—that."

Luke turned away, then sat silent, staring at his fingers wrapping and unwrapping the steering wheel. After a long time, he dropped his head back and relaxed his hands.

"You're an adult, Sarah Rose. I can't force you to be careful—no matter how much I want to." He drew a deep breath. "Hell, you've probably been in more tight spots, gotten yourself out of more dangerous situations, than I'll ever see even as a cop."

Her thoughts veered toward James. She dragged them back again. "A few."

"But I'm not going to quit until I know whether Sawyer attacked you, or those other women. If I get any positive results at all—"

She couldn't help putting a hand on his arm. "I'll listen. I promise."

He rolled his head to look at her, and his eyes were bleak. "I really hope you get the chance." Before she could respond, he straightened up. "So, what do you say? Are you in the mood for a party?"

KRISTIN GLANCED at the couple just arriving, then looked again. Luke had a date. Who was she?

Her brain kicked into gear. Of course—the photographer of those wonderful pictures. Practically a business contact. Luke had mentioned he'd be bringing her.

Somehow, this woman didn't fit the image Kristin had created in her mind. Under a broad hat with a brown band, she was small, slender, almost fragile-looking. A simple linen sheath covered her from shoulders to ankles, leaving only her tan arms bare. The overall impression was quiet, even a little withdrawn. Kristin had expected more...flash?

What she hadn't expected was this intense desire to...to *investigate* any new woman in Luke's life. She wanted him to find someone else, to get over the marriage of convenience they'd coaxed into a warm relationship. But she needed to be sure that woman was good enough. Luke deserved someone special, someone he could love and who would love him deeply. Only him.

Was Sarah Randolph that woman?

Clearing her throat, she called up what she hoped would be a confident smile. "Hi, Luke. Is this Miss Randolph?"

His grin was more carefree than she'd seen since... since Matt had come back. "Right the first time. Sarah Randolph, this is Kristin Brennan."

Kristin extended her hand. "I'm so glad to meet you. Your photographs of the girls are just incredible. I can't thank you enough for giving us copies."

She was surprised at the coolness in Sarah's green eyes, the absence of a smile. "You're welcome. The opportunity was too perfect to resist." Her husky voice wasn't much warmer than her gaze. "Your daughters are beautiful."

"Thanks. We think they're pretty special."

Luke glanced around at the crowd. "Where are the munchkins? Inside?"

"They're walking on the beach with Matt." Kristin hesitated, then took a risk. "Why don't you bring them back? I'll introduce Sarah to your folks and stand by as backup while they badger her for more prints.''

Eyes narrowed, he stared at her for a few seconds. Then he looked at Sarah Randolph. ''Or you could come down on the beach with me.''

''That's okay. You go. I'll be fine here.'' Sarah's sweet smile in his direction should have been reassuring, but Kristin wasn't ready to be convinced.

''Back in a few minutes.'' Luke gave Sarah's shoulder a gentle squeeze, then his long strides took him through the clusters of people on the deck to the beachfront steps.

''Well.'' Drawing a deep breath, Kristin turned back to Luke's date. ''Won't you come on inside? You can get out of the sun and have something to drink.''

Sarah stepped through the door into the kitchen. Kristin followed, her mind buzzing with questions. She only had a few minutes, she knew—a few minutes in which to make sure her ex-husband and brother-in-law wasn't making yet another huge mistake.

KEEPING ONE EYE ON Erin and Jenny at the edge of the water, Matt watched his brother cross the sand. Since coming back from Africa, he was sometimes surprised to realize that Luke had actually become an adult. A cop, no less, responsible for law and order in Myrtle Beach. The picture he'd carried in his mind for five long years was of a young daredevil with long black hair and a wide, challenging grin—a challenge usually flung in Matt's direction.

As it was now, minus the grin. ''Hi.'' The gaze meeting Matt's was the cold gray of a winter ocean.

He cleared his throat. ''Hi.''

They both looked toward the girls. ''They always find something to do out here,'' Luke said.

"The beach is magic for little kids," Matt agreed. He hated having to talk in such generalities with his own brother, but a neutral subject was hard to find. "Did you bring the photographer?"

Luke nodded. The splash of waves and the creaking calls of gulls punctuated an extended silence.

Erin looked around for the first time. "Daddy!" Both girls ran up the beach, past Matt, to fling themselves at his brother.

"Hey, Jen, Erin." Luke hauled them into his arms. "How's the party so far?"

Matt stuck his hands in the pockets of his shorts and turned to stare south along the shoreline at the hazy profiles of the hotels in town. Behind him, Jenny and Erin bubbled with news for Luke. Listening, Matt heard about a shopping trip they'd taken with their grandmother, about ice cream and pet stores with furry puppies, about a whole sand dollar found during an afternoon at the beach and dropped on the way home. Happenings daughters shared with their fathers.

Happenings Erin and Jenny hadn't shared with him.

Setting his jaw, he beat back the tide of jealousy. Major changes didn't happen overnight. The girls would come to love him, in time.

The damn word kept popping up...*time*. Matt was beginning to wonder if there would be enough *time* in the universe to get this family and its problems sorted out.

He'd thought, during their week in Florida, that he'd made progress. Now, though, he realized that the strangeness of the situation, the unreality of amusement parks and fancy meals and money showered like rain, had masked Erin's hostility, Jenny's uncertainty. Living together at home was more uncomfortable than anything had been since he came back…except for finding Kristin married, of course. To his brother.

"Matt!"

He turned to Luke and the girls.

"We're going back to the house." Erin and Jenny had already started across the soft sand.

Matt nodded. "I'll be there in a few minutes."

First, he would get his temper settled. He knew what the tension between him and Luke did to Kris—she practically absorbed it into her body. His uneasy truce with the girls didn't help. Kris looked less like a glowing bride every day, more like a woman haunted by her troubles.

Troubles she wouldn't confide. And Matt was beginning to wonder why. Once, she'd been as close to him as his own soul…and now he didn't know what went on in her head. She didn't share her thoughts with him any more than the girls did. He had no explanation for her reserve.

Unless…unless she couldn't bear to acknowledge the truth. Unless she felt she'd made a mistake ending her marriage to Luke. Regret could be putting those shadows under her eyes. Regret and despair.

With a deep breath, Matt started up the beach toward his parents' house. Since childhood, his mother had expected him to entertain at these events, talk to all her friends, listen attentively, compliment and gratify. His father encouraged him to debate politics, strategy and tactics with the men, proving his superiority as fourth-generation Army.

From the bottom of the deck steps, Matt looked up at the noisy, irreverent crowd around the pool. A hundred people, at least. By nightfall, half of them would be sedately drunk and all too eager to bend the ear of anyone who looked even remotely conscious. A dirty job...and he was the one who got to do it.

He would perform as his parents required. He would do his best to be patient with the girls, to win their affection through kindness and caring. He would continue to love Kris with all his soul—he had no choice about that.

If she saw that he could wait for her to make the first move, she might feel confident enough to trust him with her thoughts, her dreams, her expectations. In the meantime, he'd try to figure out exactly what *he* expected from his new life.

And how to get it.

CHAPTER SEVEN

THE AIR-CONDITIONING inside the Brennan house drenched Sarah with welcome coolness. She took a deep breath.

Luke's ex-wife lifted the ponytail off her neck and nodded. "How anybody managed to survive in South Carolina without AC, I'll never understand."

Sarah cooperated reluctantly with the attempt at casual conversation. "My grandmother did, for her whole life. But she lived in a small house with the windows always open." By no stretch of the imagination could this house be called small. And Sarah doubted if the windows were ever open. There wasn't a particle of dust to be seen.

"So you're originally from Myrtle Beach?" At the wide counter between the kitchen and family room, Kristin poured tea into glasses trimmed with lemon slices and mint leaves, and extended one to Sarah.

"No, but I visited most summers. I always loved the fresh air blowing through the rooms." She reflected for a second. "Then again, I was a lot younger. I might not be so comfortable now."

"We were all much younger, once." A tall man with a pipe between his teeth and Military stamped on every inch of him joined them. "Who's your guest, Kristin?"

In the next ten minutes, Colonel Brennan subjected Sarah to high-level interrogation. Her father's Air Force career, her mother's years of teaching school, her own credentials and those of her grandfathers all came under review. Sarah gave him the answers, hoping her irritation stayed hidden. She wasn't applying for security clearance…was she?

As he paused to take a breath, Sarah attempted to turn the conversational tide. "You must be very proud of your sons, Colonel."

"Indeed." The Colonel commenced a recital of Matt's extensive achievements. "He's going to put his name back on the list for a Special Forces unit any day now."

The news seemed to surprise Kristin, but not pleasantly. Her suddenly white face revealed the extent of her dismay. Having photographed the aftermath of several Special Forces actions, Sarah could empathize.

But the Colonel didn't seem to see his daughter-in-law's distress. "Matt is a man who understands the honor of serving his country. We need more like him."

"We need men like Luke, as well." Sarah held her voice steady against defensiveness. "I would have been in bad shape if he hadn't taken care of me the night I was mugged."

Kristin gasped. "What happened?"

Sarah gave a short description of that night, omitting her stay in Luke's house. "And he helped me pull things together again the next day."

"That sounds like Luke," the other woman said softly.

"We wouldn't need as much police protection if young men were called to compulsory military service," the Colonel proclaimed. "The Army teaches a man to be a man."

Before Sarah could muster the obvious arguments, the French doors onto the deck opened.

"There you are," Luke said. He stepped inside, carrying Jenny in his arms. "Hi, Dad. You've met Sarah?"

"Yes, indeed." The older man's face softened. "Hello, there, Miss Jenny. Come to Granddaddy?" He held out his arms.

But the girl in Luke's hold shook her head and tightened her grip on his neck. "Later then," her grandfather said. "Welcome, Miss Randolph. Enjoy yourself." With an old-fashioned bow, he left them and made his way toward the kitchen.

"Stiff-rumped old martinet."

Sarah nearly laughed at Luke's comment, but Kristin gave him a warning glance. "There are young ears listening. And I don't want to explain what any of those words mean."

"Sorry." He shifted the little girl until she was looking toward Sarah. "Jenny, this is the lady who took your pictures. Miss Randolph."

Sarah smiled. "Call me Sarah, Jenny. You looked like a princess in your beautiful dress."

Jenny gazed at Sarah, then at her mother. Then she buried her head in her dad's shoulder.

"Luke?" The new voice was softly Southern. Sarah turned to meet the gaze of a tall, slim woman with beautifully cut white hair. "Luke, please introduce me to your guest." Her accent conjured up the scent of gardenias, the rustle of crinoline petticoats. But her deep-blue eyes were more assessing than welcoming.

Luke cleared his throat. "Mom, this is Sarah Randolph, photographer. Sarah, my mom. Elena Brennan."

Sarah extended her hand. "I'm glad to meet you, Mrs. Brennan. Thank you for including me in your celebration."

A smooth palm barely brushed hers. "You're welcome, of course. Please make yourself at home."

In the next moment, Elena Brennan was transformed,

just as her husband had been. "Hello, Jennifer, honey.
I'm happy to see you wearing the new dress I got you."
Her smile was sweet as she brushed a hand over Jenny's
bright hair. The child jerked her head farther into the
angle of her dad's neck.

"I think this little girl needs a nap." Kristin stepped
in and put her hands on Jenny's waist. "Let's read a
story, love."

"No!" Jenny shook her head.

"Shall I read your story, Jennifer, dear?" Mrs. Brennan somehow moved Kristin out of the way to put her
own hands under Jenny's arms. "Come with Grandmom."

"No, no! I want Daddy!"

The exclamation drew glances from other guests in the
room. Lips pressed tightly together, Mrs. Brennan backed
away.

Luke sent his mother an apologetic grin, which she did
not return. "Okay, Jenny Penny. You got me. Can Sarah
come with us?"

After a long hesitation, Jenny nodded, without looking
up.

Kristin took a deep breath and stared somewhere between Luke's shoulder and Sarah's face. "Then I'll...see
you...after your nap, Jenny. I'm really pleased to meet
you, Sarah." She hurried outside again before Sarah
could respond.

"This way." With a tilt of his head, Luke indicated a
door out of the kitchen. In the gray-and-blue dining room,
he drew her notice to the picture on the wall. "Place of
honor. They really did like your work."

One of her photographs—Erin and Jenny standing together examining a shell—had been mounted in an ornate

gold frame and hung above the sideboard. Sarah couldn't help but admire the effect. "That really is a terrific shot."

"You're telling me." Luke led the way upstairs and to the end of the hallway, where an open door invited her into a colorful world of rainbows and comets.

"What a great room!" Sarah turned down the bed Luke indicated. "You must have happy dreams in here."

But Jenny just stared at her, sucking her thumb.

"She's really tired." Luke set his daughter down, covered her with the blanket, then pulled up a white rocking chair and motioned Sarah to sit. "I bet she'll be asleep before we get to the quiet old lady saying 'hush.'" He sat on the side of the bed with a book. "What do you think, Jen?"

The little girl shook her head, but her dad was correct. By page four of the storybook, her eyes closed and her breathing took on the even rhythm of sleep.

Pulling the blanket a little higher on Jenny's shoulders, Luke brushed the hair out of her eyes and stroked a finger along her cheek. "Sleeping kids are a hint of heaven," he whispered.

Sarah blinked back a burning in her eyes. "She's an angel."

He continued to gaze at his daughter. "Yeah." Then he sighed. "I guess we should join the fun outside."

His hand rested in the small of Sarah's back as they walked down the stairs again. "I'm sorry Jen wasn't too friendly. She does get cranky when she's tired. She'll be glad to talk to you when she wakes up."

His prediction proved false. Kristin brought Jenny out to the deck about six o'clock. The little girl seemed sunny enough amongst the crowd of grown-ups, sitting at a play table in front of a model castle complete with princesses in diaphanous gowns and a prince astride his white charger. While Luke fetched a cooler of ice for his mother, Sarah made her way to Jenny's side.

"That's a fantastic castle." She knelt by the girl. "Do your dolls have names?"

Jenny shook her head and rearranged the characters on their thrones.

"Does your sister play castle with you?"

"Who would want to play a baby game like that?" Erin, sturdy and disdainful, stood nearby. "I've got better things to do."

Sarah drew a deep breath. "Your dad says you like animals. What's your favorite?"

But Erin's burst of speech died as unexpectedly as it was born. With a shrug, she turned and threaded her way into the crowd, quickly becoming lost from sight.

Jenny continued with her own silent game. Sarah watched for a few minutes, made a couple of comments which received no answers, and finally stepped away.

Maybe she just didn't have the right touch with children. She hadn't been around them much, unless you counted the victims of famine in Africa, who were too sick and weak to play. The land mine survivors in Asia, missing their limbs. Or the targets of ethnic wars in Central Europe. Those were the kids she was used to seeing. Gray pictures—shots she'd taken—flashed through her brain. She closed her eyes against them.

"Sarah?" Luke's warm palm covered her cheek and tilted her head. "Something wrong?"

A shaky breath brought her back to the USA. "No, not at all. I'm fine."

"What were you thinking about?"

"Um...nothing we want to discuss right now." She smiled, and his face relaxed a bit. "I could use another drink, though."

His eyes were troubled—she hadn't reassured him. But he grinned. "That's a problem even I can solve."

MAYBE THAT Sarah-person could take good pictures. But Erin didn't like her.

There was a lot about this party Erin didn't like—the grown-ups standing too close together, talking too loud. The outfit she had to wear—a dress was bad enough, but this dress matched Jenny's and that was awful. Mommy said they had to wear them because they were a present from Grandmom Brennan.

So Erin was polite and wore the dress. And she let people pinch her cheeks and pull her braid and talk to her like she was a baby, though she'd finished the first grade. She was in the red reading group and that was the fastest. Nobody should treat her like—like Jenny.

The Sarah-person even thought she played the same games as Jenny. Didn't she know girls did stuff besides dolls?

Sitting at the bottom of the beach steps, Erin plowed her feet into the sand. Was this party going to last all night?

Someone came down the steps behind her. "What are you thinking about?"

She didn't look up, even when the Sarah-person sat down on the step just above her. "Nothin'."

"A pretty serious nothin'."

Erin shrugged.

The lady was quiet. Erin dug her feet deeper into the sand.

Then Sarah-person said, "Where do you suppose we'd get to, if we sailed straight across the ocean from here?"

Erin knew the answer to that. She talked about it all the time with her dad. "Africa."

"I guess you're right. What do you think we'd see?"

"Jungles. Animals."

"What animal would you want to see first?"

That took some thought. "Lions, maybe."

"Lions are wonderful. I saw a group of them once, sleeping in the shade. They looked really gentle and soft."

Erin turned. "You've been there?" Remembering that she didn't like this person, she whipped back around to face the ocean.

Sarah didn't comment. "I've spent a lot of time in Africa taking pictures."

"You mean like a safari?"

"Well, mostly I took pictures of people. But I've done a couple of photo safaris, too."

"Did you sleep in the trees?"

Sarah laughed—a nice sound. "I wanted to. But the tour guides brought tents along."

"Did the lions attack your camp?"

"No."

Disappointed, Erin wrapped her arms around her legs and put her chin on her knees.

"But a rhinoceros charged our van once."

"Really?" She turned around again. "Were you scared?"

"Terrified." Sarah had nice eyes, too. They smiled. "I just kept taking pictures and hoping somebody would start the engine before I got the business end of that rhino's horn!"

"Cool!"

"What's cool?" Daddy came down the steps and sat behind Erin. He handed Sarah a drink. "For you." Then he ruffled Erin's hair. "What are you two talking about?"

Sarah didn't answer, so Erin explained. "Her car got charged by a rhino. Pretty neat, huh?"

Daddy grinned. "Better her than me. I'd be climbing the nearest vine."

"They have deserts in Africa, too, you know. Mounds of sand just like this—" Sarah bent and picked up a handful, then let it trickle through her fingers "—for miles in every direction."

"Did you ride a camel?" Daddy asked.

"I rode a day out into the desert. And a day back. I was never so glad to see anything as that first date palm. No shade, no water…" She shuddered.

Above them on the deck, Daddy Matt knocked his barbecue tools against each other. "Steaks are medium rare—come and get 'em!"

Daddy got to his feet and put a hand down to Sarah. Erin frowned as the lady let him pull her up.

But then he let go and held out the same hand to Erin. "Want some food, Erin Bear?"

Erin put her hand in his. Sarah had already climbed to the deck. "Can I eat with you, Daddy?"

"There you are!" Mommy stood at the top of the steps beside Sarah. "I wondered where you'd gone. Erin, I've got your plate fixed and a place for you and Jenny. Come eat."

"But—" She looked up at her dad.

He shrugged his shoulders. "Don't worry, Erin. I'll catch you after dinner, okay?"

Erin stuck out her lip. He didn't want to eat with her. He wanted to eat with that lady.

When they reached the deck, she dropped her dad's hand and pushed between her mother and Sarah. And she didn't even say she was sorry. She found her place at the table near the door, next to Jenny. Mommy followed and sat with them. But no matter what she asked, Erin refused to talk.

She really didn't have anything she wanted to say.

LUKE FOUND a table for himself and Sarah near the edge of the deck, where they could look out over the ocean twilight as they ate. He set their plates down, Sarah arranged drinks, and a silent few minutes passed as they appreciated the food.

"Your brother cooks a wonderful steak," Sarah said. "I don't think I've eaten anything this delicious in years."

"My dad used to be the barbecue chef. But since Matt came back, he's sort of taken over. Which is okay, because he does a great job."

"Does your family have lots of parties?"

He leaned back in his chair, finally able to relax for the first time in the long afternoon. "Not so many, now. But there were always people coming over when I was growing up. Army brass, my mom's social clubs, local dignitary types. Part of the military life, I guess."

"My dad and mom entertained, too. I was supposed to stay in my room when people came."

"Were the parties wild? Military get-togethers can be."

"Oh, no. It just seemed like I always got into trouble. Without even trying."

"Boy, do I know what that's like." He sipped his cola. "Matt would stand there all day, straight as an arrow, saying 'Yes sir' and 'No ma'am', his clothes clean, his shoes shined. While I had just fallen in the fish pond."

Sarah laughed. "Or spilled strawberry punch all over the white tablecloth."

He really liked that laugh. "The dogs got away from

me once, ran through the sprinkler and then into the middle of the garden club tea.''

"What kind of dogs?"

Luke winked at her. "Springer spaniels."

"Oh, no! All that long hair!" She shook her head. "You should try the same trick with wet cats. They tend to climb up curtains and silk dresses and to perch on ladies' hats."

"Sarah Rose, I think you've got me beat. Unless…did you ever break your arm in the middle of a sit-down dinner?"

She propped her elbows on the table. "Tell me."

He shared the circumstances of his worst disgrace—worst childhood disgrace, anyway. In between the reminiscences, his mother presented the party with her traditional Fourth of July cake, topped with strawberries, blueberries, and sparklers. His dad made the yearly speech about independence and the importance of protecting the American way of life. At his parents' prompting, the whole crowd joined in to sing "It's A Grand Old Flag" and "God Bless America."

Luke listened with half an ear, more interested in watching the candlelight play over Sarah's face and hair. After three weeks, her bruises had faded enough that he couldn't see them unless he searched carefully. In the soft light she looked golden and warm, as if she'd captured some of the sun's glow before it set. He recognized a strong impulse to claim some of that heat for himself. He even made a move to cover her hand with his.

Just then, chairs scraped on the deck as people began the exodus onto the beach for the city fireworks. Sarah stood up. "I'll ask your mom if I can help clear up."

Luke winced. "You don't have to—"

But she was already on her way to the lighted doors

leading into the house. He caught up with her in time to
hear his mother's reply.

"No, thank you." That steel magnolia tone of voice
permitted no possibility of argument. "I have my own
system, and nobody else knows just what I want done."

"Oh." Sarah's voice betrayed her confused astonish-
ment. "Then let me just say thank you again. This has
been a lovely afternoon."

His mother inclined her head. "You're welcome. Now,
if you'll excuse me, I have a great deal of work to finish."

Sarah backed away, right into Luke's chest. He stead-
ied her with a hand on each shoulder, so that his palms
met smooth, bare skin. Awareness shot straight through
him. "Let's go watch the fireworks."

The crowd had gathered down on the beach. Sarah
stopped on the edge of the deck, as far from the house
as possible. "Is it just me? Or does your mother really
do all this work alone?"

"She doesn't let Kristin help much, either, if that's any
comfort. I guess she sees this as her job. Dad was an
Army colonel, she was his domestic support staff. Or
something like that."

Sarah allowed him to draw her down the steps and onto
the beach. The sand was still warm, but a light breeze
had sprung up. She shivered.

"Cold?"

"Maybe a little."

Luke put his arm around her—just a friendly gesture.
Sarah had trusted him to behave when she agreed to come
today, and he didn't intend to give her any cause to regret
that trust. "Better?" he asked.

She didn't stiffen, as he'd expected, but instead moved
a bit closer. "Much warmer, thanks."

The first fireworks blast exploded as they reached the water's edge. Red, green and blue glitter sprayed across the black sky, followed by a pounding *boom!*

Sarah looked at him and grinned. "I love fireworks."

Luke tightened his hold. "Well then, these are just for you."

SARAH SUPPOSED she should step away. A cool night breeze never hurt anyone. She could certainly survive on her own.

But Luke's warmth melted her resolve. His arm around her shoulders, his fingers playing gently with the end of her braid...the comfort of his touch was impossible to renounce. Just for tonight, just for an hour, here in the dark on the beach, she could enjoy being close.

Only a short distance away, Erin and Jenny were with their mother and Matt. Erin stood with her hands clasped behind her back, her legs firmly planted in the sand, staring skyward waiting for the next burst of light.

But Jenny huddled in her mother's arms, her face hidden from sight. With every explosion, she jumped.

After only a short time, Kristin must have decided the little girl had had enough. With a word to her husband, she started across the beach toward the house.

The fireworks display escalated as Kristin and Jenny approached the beach steps. Sparks filled the sky, each flare more brilliant than the last. And louder. One roll of thunder piled on top of another, and another, until Sarah considered covering her ears.

In a momentary pause, she heard a thin, high wail. At first, she couldn't make out the words. Then she looked toward Kristin...and understood.

Jenny was struggling against her mother's arms, fighting to get down. Kristin could barely keep her grip.

"Daddy!" Jennifer screamed. "I want my daddy!"

Luke whipped his head around. In a second he was halfway across the sand. Suddenly, he stopped dead.

Matt, too, had responded. He'd been closer, gotten there first. And he'd taken Jenny from her mother, attempting to quiet the little girl.

Still, she struggled, flinging her head back and crying hard. Luke stepped forward, then stopped again, hands fisting and opening at his sides.

Abruptly, the girl's cries changed to "Mama." Her mother took her back, and this time Jenny collapsed bonelessly into her hold. As Sarah watched, Kristin reached the steps to the deck, climbed them and vanished into the house.

Once Kristin was gone, Matt turned around. The two brothers stared at each other, and even the noise of the fireworks faded as Sarah wondered what would happen next. What would they say?

Matt shrugged, then walked into the crowd of guests, becoming indistinguishable from all the other tall, straight-backed men. Luke stood alone.

THE PARTY BROKE UP soon after the fireworks ended. Matt did his duty in the farewell process, then decided to get some fresh air while Luke said goodbye to Erin and Jenny.

Someone had sought the peace of the ocean's rumble before he could. As he crossed the deck, he recognized the slim silhouette of the woman Luke had brought to the party. She turned from the rail to face him, and he extended his hand. "I don't think we were introduced. I'm Matt Brennan. Luke's brother."

"Sarah Randolph."

"You took the pictures of the girls, right?" She nodded. "I wanted to tell you I really appreciate the prints you made. We'll be thankful to have those shots when Erin and Jenny are older."

She smiled. "I'm glad I got the opportunity."

Matt faced the sea and propped his elbows on the deck rail. "Kristin said something about my brother helping you out at the police station. You were mugged?"

"Yes. Luke took me to the hospital and helped me pull my life back together. My keys were stolen."

"He's always rescuing somebody." Although sometimes those rescues backfired. Badly. Hurting everybody involved.

After a pause, Matt cleared his throat. "I don't know if you're aware, but—"

"Kristin was married to Luke when you came back from Africa."

He glanced at her, surprised. "He told you?"

"Of course. We're friends."

"Well…great." Matt knew he should leave this alone. And he knew he couldn't. "I just wanted to say—Luke's had a pretty rough couple of years. He's not in real good shape to be going into any serious kind of relationship."

"Oh?" The warmth had left her voice.

She had a right to be offended, he supposed. But Luke always gave too much of himself, too easily. "I'd hate to see him get hurt. He's still pretty messed up about Kristin and me, and the girls. I doubt he's thinking straight."

The photographer stiffened. "I don't have any intention of hurting Luke."

"I'm sure you don't. Neither…" He hesitated over the admission. "Neither did Kristin and I. But good intentions aren't always enough."

"True." Sarah Randolph looked out to the ocean

again, then turned back. "Your family is quite...pro-
tective, when faced with outsiders. I'm sure that's an admirable quality." She drew a shaking breath. "But I
think it would be even more admirable if you considered
your brother's feelings *before* you tore his life apart.
Good night." She walked away from him—not into the
house, but through the gate leading to the front yard.

Matt leaned his elbows on the deck rail and dropped
his head into his hands. *Score one for the photographer.*

LUKE CUT the engine in the parking lot of Sarah's condo
and dropped his head back against the seat. "Whew...
quite a night."

"Is Jenny okay?"

"Kristin calmed her down, I finished the story we
started, and she went to sleep. She'll be her usual cheerful
self in the morning." He wrapped his hands around the
steering wheel, unwrapped them and stretched his fingers
wide, wrapped the wheel again. "This was her first time
outside with fireworks. We...they should have realized
she'd be scared."

Sarah's hand covered one of his. "You're doing your
best, Luke."

Quick as lightning, her touch set up a rumble inside
him. A deep breath drew in her scent—not perfume, but
an essence he recognized simply as Sarah Rose. If he
looked at her, if she moved any closer, he'd forget his
good intentions and take what he couldn't help wanting.

But Sarah drew back before he made any more mistakes. "It's been a long day. Do you have to go to work
now?"

Luke released his breath and nodded. "In an hour or
so."

"This will be a pretty rough night, I guess."

It already had been. He opened his door. "Let me walk you upstairs." By the time he rounded the hood, though, she'd gotten out of the truck. "You're an independent woman, Sarah Rose."

She sighed. "I used to be." After a silent walk up the steps, she turned in her doorway. "Thanks, Luke. I enjoyed the party and the chance to see more of Erin and Jenny."

"Thank *you*—I don't know if I would have stayed without you."

"So…" She drew a deep breath. "I'll say goodnight."

"'Night." His hand cupped her cheek before he realized what he was doing. Sarah's eyes widened, but she didn't pull away. He needed to taste her, to lose himself in this woman who gave so much, so freely. She could heal him, if he let her. If she wanted to…

And why would she? He was just about the worst bargain on the planet these days. Luke flicked the tip of her nose with his thumb and stepped back, shoving his hands into his pockets. "Sleep well, Sarah Rose."

She started to say something, then stopped with a soft sigh. "You, too."

Yeah, right. "Can I call you sometime?" She hesitated, and he found a reasonable excuse. "I'd like to keep tabs on how you and Sawyer are getting along."

"Oh. Okay…sure." She took a step backward, into the glowing protection of her home. "Leave a message if I don't answer."

"I will." He lifted his hand in a farewell salute. She did the same, then quietly shut the door, leaving him once again in the dark.

CHAPTER EIGHT

DIRTY, SWEATY and in a lousy mood, Sarah jerked the Jeep to a stop in the photo shop's parking lot late on Sunday afternoon. She squished across the hot asphalt in sneakers wet with marsh water and heavy with mud, pulled the door open, and stepped into chilly darkness.

When her eyes adjusted, she saw that one low lamp was on. "Chuck? Are you here?"

He didn't answer, which only meant he could be playing another of his games with her. He got a big kick out of practical jokes, like hiding his car and pretending to be gone, then sneaking up on her while she was concentrating. But he wouldn't deliberately hurt her. What would be the point? What could he gain?

With you out of the way, he would have the entire shop to himself.

Goose bumps covered her arms as Sarah eased her gear bag onto a chair and toed off her shoes. With her as a partner, Chuck had the best of both worlds. He pretty much ran the shop as he pleased. On the rare times she was here, she made a point of not interfering with his decisions. Yet he had someone to share the liabilities. In a beach town, during hurricane season, that could be very useful.

Rationalization did nothing to ease the chill she felt, the sense of unease. Was Luke right? Was she being stupid to stay?

The most frustrating, infuriating part of the dilemma was that she simply couldn't decide. James would have expected her to take the risk. Luke urged her to be safe. And there was a part of Sarah agreeing with each of them. Where was the part that would say what *she* wanted, what *her* choice was?

She stood paralyzed in the darkness for an eternity. Nothing happened—no sound except her own rushed breathing, no movement but her own pulse. Still she stood, listening.

Until, with a sudden snap, her temper broke. "This is absurd," she muttered aloud. "Leave or stay. But don't huddle like a rabbit caught in an open field!"

Since Chuck wasn't making himself obvious, she decided to stay. A few minutes of working with Felix's equipment, imagining his hands as he set up and demonstrated and instructed, was enough to distract Sarah from her fears. The challenge of creating and improving pictures absorbed her completely.

At the end of three hours, though, she was far from satisfied. She'd spent the morning in the marshlands shooting animals and plants, water and sky. And they were nice enough pictures...for an amateur. But they didn't connect, somehow. A crane perched in a live oak was pretty, but what did it mean?

With a sigh, she crossed the darkroom, thinking about a drink and some food. Maybe her perspective would improve—

She pulled the door open, and a man's shadow confronted her. Sarah gasped, her muscles flooded with terror. In the next second, she recognized Chuck.

The fright did not fade.

"I didn't know you were here," he said, pushing past

her into the darkroom. He examined the drying prints, then turned to face her. "Postcards?"

His grin was malicious, superior. She clenched her jaw. "No. Just some experiments."

"Not terribly successful, are they?"

"Not terribly." Sarah left him to his gloating and went to get a glass of tea.

Chuck followed. "Could be you require dead or maimed bodies in your shots to work up any real emotion."

She kept her back to him and made herself finish half of the glass before answering. "What a lousy thing to say—as if I enjoyed those kinds of assignments."

He shrugged. "Just a suggestion. Maybe death is what gets your juices flowing. That would explain hanging around with a cop, too."

Sarah jerked around. "What are you talking about?"

"The guy who was in here harassing me. Brennan. Being a cop isn't one of your safer jobs these days. I'm just guessing that the risk turns you on. You could sleep with him tonight...and tomorrow he's dead."

Sarah had a sudden vision of James, sliding down a rock wall with a hole in his chest...and then Luke, the same way.

The floor seemed to tilt underneath her feet. She leaned back against the kitchen counter with her eyes closed, fighting for balance, clutching the cold, wet glass with both hands.

"What's your problem, Chuck?" she whispered over the bile in her throat. "Do you really hate me?"

He chuckled. "How could I hate you? You provide me with so much entertainment." His heavy footsteps receded, the back door squeaked open, closed. In another few seconds the Cadillac engine grumbled to life, then died away.

Setting the glass on the counter, Sarah ran water over her wrists and wiped her face with a damp paper towel. Luke was only partially right—Chuck was abusive. But he used words instead of his fists.

And he got the results he wanted. She'd spent the past six months learning to resist the horrors her mind recalled too easily. With one malicious sentence, Chuck had disabled her control. Once again, she was part of that scene...the smell of gunsmoke and fire and dead bodies, blown down her throat by a frigid winter wind. The sound of children crying, women moaning, men cursing. And the sight of James—energetic, vital James—as still as the stone he slumped against. The darkness closed in....

Beside the chair, the phone rang. Sarah clamped her hands over her mouth, blocking a pitiful squeak of fear. After two short peals, the answering machine picked up with Chuck's cute message. Then the beep.

And then a voice. "This is Luke Brennan, trying to reach—"

She fumbled desperately for the receiver. "Hello? Hello?"

"Sarah, it's Luke. Are you okay?"

She dropped into a nearby chair, still light-headed, but now with relief. "Um...not really."

"What happened? Is Sawyer there? Did he hurt you?"

Tears sprang to her eyes at the concern and anger in his rich voice, while a warm, fluid sensation welled up deep inside her body. She wasn't sure which reaction to worry about most.

"Nothing happened...well, I did have a run-in with Chuck. Just words," she added as Luke started to swear.

"But mostly I guess I'm just tired." The world settled safely around her again and she tried to lighten up. "Let's forget about Chuck. Have you seen Erin and Jenny since the party?"

"They came over Wednesday afternoon. We spent some time on the beach, grilled burgers for dinner. I took them back...home...before bedtime."

"I know you all enjoyed the day."

"Yeah. We set up a date for next Wednesday." After a pause, he said, "Would you like to join us?"

"I—"

"I don't know what we're going to do, yet. But I'd...we'd like it if you came along."

The invitation threw her back into conflict. She wasn't used to being worried about, checked up on, included— she hadn't known a relationship like this since her folks died. Luke and his daughters could restore the *normal* to her life. They could balance the horrors she remembered with images of fun and family, laughter and love.

But her answer should be no. Seeing Luke again would push her ability to stay friends to the very limit. She stood in danger of coming to care for this man—depend on him—far too deeply for her peace of mind. Or his. She recalled Matt Brennan's words: *Luke's not in real good shape to be going into a serious relationship.*

"I'm sorry, Luke—I've got something already set up for Wednesday." The lie tightened inside her like a slipping noose. "Maybe some other time?"

"Sure. A Saturday might be better—I'm going to talk to Kristin about letting the girls stay next weekend during my long break."

"That sounds great. I hope you all have a good week."

After a stunned silence, Luke cleared his throat. "You, too, Sarah Rose. Take care of yourself."

"I will." She hung up quickly, before she could retract her words. She'd done the right thing—made a rational decision and stuck by it.

Why had she never realized how badly doing right could hurt?

"DO YOU THINK you should give Sarah Randolph a call?"

Kristin looked up from mending the latest rip in Erin's favorite jean shorts. Matt sat in the recliner nearby with the newspaper. "I'm sorry—what did you say?"

"I wonder if you should get in touch with Sarah Randolph—Luke brought her to the party last week."

"I remember. Why?"

He folded the sports section carefully. "I got the feeling they might be...involved. And I think she should know what she's getting into."

"Which is what, exactly?"

Matt sent her a patient look. "He's still on the rebound. He's not going to be much use to any woman until he gets over...you."

Kristin folded a leg of Erin's shorts into careful pleats. "That's Sarah and Luke's business, isn't it? She seemed like a very smart, perceptive lady to me."

"I don't know about that. I tried to give her a little warning, but—"

"You *warned* her?" She felt as if the breath had been sucked out of her lungs. "What in the world did you say?"

"What I just said to you—that he's had a hard couple of knocks and probably isn't ready for any kind of solid relationship."

Kristin closed her eyes, struggling to hold her temper.

Matt meant well. She knew he meant well. "How could you have done that?"

"What? What did I do?"

"Talked about your brother behind his back, and as if he was some sort of…of defective person!"

Anger flashed in her husband's blue eyes. "I don't want to see Luke wreak any more damage, that's all."

"Luke doesn't wreak damage."

Matt just stared at her. His face looked as it had the day he came back into her life and found her married to Luke.

Kristin clung to her point. "He didn't marry me to hurt you. You know that."

Her husband shook out the business section of the paper. "I lived with him a lot longer than you did. Maybe I've had more experience with what he does and doesn't do."

"And maybe you—"

"Mommy! Mooommmyyy!" Coming from the direction of the backyard, Jenny's voice quavered with panic.

Kristin dropped the sewing and met her daughter at the door. "What's wrong, Jen?"

"Erin fell off the swings."

When they arrived, Erin lay on her back under the play set, so still that Kristin's heart stopped beating. She fell to her knees, bending over her daughter as Matt pulled the swing out of her way. "Erin? Erin, can you hear me?"

The bright blue eyes opened, remaining unfocused for a few seconds. Then, with a cough and a huge, rasping breath, Erin sat up.

Tears pricked at Kristin's eyes. She put a shaking hand on Erin's back. "You okay, honey?"

The little girl nodded. "That was…weird." Her voice sounded hoarse, breathy. "I couldn't breathe."

Kristin got to her feet and helped Erin to stand. "You must have knocked the breath out of your lungs. What were you doing?"

"She climbed on the bar," Jenny volunteered, pointing to the top support of the swings.

Erin cast her sister a disgusted glance. "Tattletale."

Jenny stuck her tongue out.

Kristin sighed. All systems normal. "Let's go on inside. It's hot and you need a drink." The girls raced ahead of her as she started toward the house. When she realized Matt hadn't followed, she turned around. "Matt?"

He looked up, his face whiter than Erin's had been. "What the hell was she doing up there? She could have been seriously hurt!"

"But she wasn't." Kristin walked back and took his hand. His other arm curved around her waist. "Be thankful for what didn't happen, and put this behind you. Kids fall, they get hurt. We can't control the whole world, can't protect them against everything. We can only love them with all we've got and hope that's enough."

He drew a deep breath and pulled her closer. "This parenting stuff—it's tough to get the hang of."

She nodded against his chest. "It's easier if you get to start from the beginning. But you'll catch on. I promise."

When she lifted her face, he accepted the invitation with a sweet kiss. They held hands as they went into the house.

But Kristin wondered how long her reprieve from disaster—with the girls and with Matt—could possibly last.

LUKE HAD JUST stepped out of the shower when the doorbell rang. He pulled on a T-shirt and jeans and raked his hands through his hair as he rushed across the house.

Expecting the pizza he'd ordered for dinner, he stood speechless in the open doorway staring at Sarah on the front step.

She looked up at him. "Hi?"

"Uh...hi." The setting sun haloed her hair with gold, deepened the tan on her bare arms and legs. But the light in her greenish eyes seemed to come from inside, and her mouth kept slipping into a smile. Watching that smile, he barely remembered his manners. "How are you?"

"Really good. I'm sorry I just dropped by, but I have some terrific news and I wanted to tell you."

"Yeah? Come on in." He shut the door behind her, appreciating the straight line of her spine and that long, soft braid before she turned around. "What's the news?"

When she turned, the smile had conquered her face. "My agent called. We've got an offer for the pictures."

"The girls' pictures?"

She nodded. "A very upscale travel and life-style magazine is running an article on the romance of southern beaches. The girls' shots fit perfectly with their theme."

The pleasure she took in the achievement was enough for him. "That's great, Sarah Rose. I don't know how these things work—are they planning to pay you?"

"Definitely." She grinned widely. "Quite well, as a matter of fact. That's another part of the good news."

"Even better! I've got some wine...want to share a toast?" The invitation came off the top of his head, before he'd taken time to think. Why should he expect her to accept, after she'd frozen him out on the phone last week?

But she nodded. "I'd love to."

The pizza arrived as he poured the wine. They took their glasses, the bottle and the box out to the small back porch overlooking a tiny square of grass and the flower beds he and the girls worked on when they got the chance.

Sarah surveyed the yard. "This is great. You grow your own tomatoes?"

"One of the best parts of summer is fresh, ripe tomatoes."

"My grandmother used to make BLTs for supper."

"I do that for the girls a lot. And I learned to throw together a gazpacho recipe a couple of years ago. Really tastes like summer."

"Mmm." She sat down on the porch swing. "I love gazpacho. What else do you make, besides sinful chocolate chip cookies?"

Luke leaned over to clink glasses. "First, a toast—to my little girls and your talent. An unforgettable combination."

Sarah smiled. "I'll drink to that."

He held her gaze as they sipped the wine. The shadows in her eyes had almost vanished, replaced with a glow that seemed intended for him alone.

But acting on the feelings she stirred in him would bring those shadows back. Luke propped a shoulder against the wall and deliberately broke the mood. "So now what happens? Do you have all the details?"

"The beach issue is set for next September—a farewell to summer piece, I gather. The only hitch is…they want me to get a release from everyone involved."

"You mean Kristin." Sarah nodded. "I guess you'll have to talk to her. I can't predict what she'll say, but I can't think of a reason for her to refuse, either."

"Would it help if you were there when I asked? If she knew you approved?"

Luke shrugged. "Maybe. We can try. What's your time frame?"

"I'd like to get back to them by the first of next week."

"Kristin is probably running in circles this week getting ready for Erin's birthday bash. She makes a big deal out of birthdays."

"I'm sure the girls love that."

"Always. In fact—" he hesitated, then decided to take the risk "—one chance to see Kristin before next week would be at the party Friday afternoon. Want to come?"

"Your family might not like—"

"What's not to like? I'm going, and I'm inviting you."

"But Erin—"

"I'll ask her, if you want. But I'm sure she'll say yes. The more, the merrier at a birthday party, right?"

"Right." This time Sarah leaned forward to clink glasses. "A toast to Erin's birthday."

"Definitely. And should we eat this pizza before it's too cold?"

"Definitely."

"COME ON, Jen—gotta brush those teeth." Matt waved the sparkly pink toothbrush. "One minute and we'll be done."

She shook her head again.

"You know, when your mom left to go to her cousin's party, she made me promise you'd brush your teeth before you went to bed. I can't break my promise to your mom."

No change. "How about an extra story? Will you brush your teeth for that?"

Another refusal. He couldn't force a kid to brush her teeth, especially not when he was still on probation as a father figure. Matt rinsed off the brush and put it back in the cup. "You win, Jen. Let's get into bed."

When he picked her up, she didn't cuddle, as she did with Kristin, but sat up straight and stiff.

Time, he told himself. *It's gonna take time.*

As he set Jenny down on her own bed, Erin came into the room. "I need to talk to my dad."

Matt swallowed an Army word for that idea. *Her* dad was in the room with her. "Uh...how about tomorrow, Erin? Your mom did say bed by nine."

"I can't sleep unless I talk with my dad."

"Me, too." Jenny stood up. "I want to talk to Daddy, too."

He recognized a no-win situation when he saw one. "Okay. We'll call your...dad. Then we'll read a story and get to sleep. Right?"

"Oh, goody!" Jenny clapped her hands. "I get to talk to Daddy!"

Setting his teeth, Matt crossed the hall to the bedroom he shared with Kristin, picked up the cordless phone, punched the memory button, and then the number one—after all, who would be listed first on Kristin's autodial, if not her ex-husband?

SARAH INSISTED that Luke sit besider her on the swing. They'd polished off half the pizza and most of the wine. The heat of the day faded and the moon rose over the back fence as they sat silent, listening to frogs and crickets and the distant buzz of traffic on the main drag. Sarah set her glass on the low table beside the swing, leaned back and closed her eyes. "I always forget about Southern nights."

"Pretty special." The swing swayed gently. "I'd probably have taken off by now to see more of the country, except for the girls and the fact that I really do love this place."

"Believe me, travel isn't all it's made out to be. I've hardly been in one place for more than a couple of months in the past eight years."

"Balance is important, I guess."

"I think so." Though she was having a little trouble with the concept tonight. Luke's warmth beside her, the drift of his clean soap scent, set up wavelets of excitement she couldn't ignore. His hair had dried as they talked, to fall lightly over his forehead with a softness she longed to explore with her fingertips. His T-shirt had dried, too—but she remembered the first glimpse of damp cotton that revealed more than it hid of the muscles in his shoulders and chest.

Sarah swallowed hard. She should go, before... "I should go."

"Okay." Luke stopped the swing with the whisper of his bare foot dragging over concrete. He stood and offered his hand to help her stand. "I'm really glad you came over."

She gazed up at him, at the glint of moonlight in his black hair, while the strong warmth of his fingers cradled hers. "Me, too."

"Sarah, I—" He looked away, and gave a sort of shrug. Sarah prepared to let him go.

But then he looked back into her face...and with a slide of hands over skin, a coupling of arms and thighs and mouths, they came to hold each other, joined by a kiss that had no beginning and couldn't possibly ever end.

Sarah ran her fingers through his hair, feeling each

individual strand as soft as silk thread. The back of his neck was warm, textured yet smooth, the skin of his shoulders firm and smoother still. She could have touched him forever.

And been touched *by* him. His hands under her top stroked lightning along her spine. He defined the arch of her ribs with his thumbs, and she lifted toward him, intoxicated with pleasure. The kiss went fathoms deeper.

When his palm covered her bare breast, Sarah realized the moans she heard were hers. But she didn't care, couldn't think past the moment, past the need to have him closer still, to lift his shirt and let the skin of their bodies touch. She wanted his mouth on her shoulders, her throat, moving, always moving until...

Inside the house, the phone rang.

CHAPTER NINE

THEY BOTH JUMPED, and separated. Luke ran his hands over his hair, turned away, and then turned back.

"You should answer," Sarah whispered. He went into the house. She pressed her fingertips against her eyes and waited for the quivering in her knees to stop.

When at last she joined him inside, blinking against the bright light, she found Luke sitting at the desk in the dining room, the phone held to his ear.

"Sounds like it's gonna be a cool party, Erin. Rain? No way. Of course I did—don't I always get you a birthday present? No, I won't tell you what it is. You'll just have to wait three days to find out." He rolled his eyes as Sarah went by. "Hey, Erin Bear, is it okay if I bring my friend Sarah to your party? Yeah, the one who took the pictures. Maybe she could take some pictures of your birthday. I'll ask."

When he looked up, eyebrows lifted in question, Sarah smiled and nodded, then went into the kitchen with the wineglasses she carried. Another commitment to spend time with Luke, a chance to get herself in even deeper trouble. She hardly knew whether to laugh or cry.

After a short pause, his voice changed abruptly. "Sure, I'll be glad to talk to...Matt...a second." He sounded anything but glad.

The conversation was muffled by the running water she used to wash the glasses. When she could hear again, there was an unfamiliar edge in Luke's tone. "I know you have a real problem with this, but do you want her to go to sleep tonight or not? Then just let me tell her a story. We'll figure out the rest some other time."

After a long pause, he said, his voice back to normal, "Hi, Jenny Penny. Ready for bed? I bet I can tell you one of your favorite stories without even looking at the book. Sure I can—listen."

Sarah listened, certain that her heart would break as Luke recited a bedtime story to his little girl over the phone. A man of extraordinary gentleness and compelling passion, he tempted her in ways she'd never expected to know.

But Luke had no place in his life for another woman. His daughters needed as much of him as he could give. An outside relationship would shortchange Erin and Jenny.

And where would *they* fit into Sarah's life? She expected to return to the career she'd built, the only life she'd known for years. Could she leave them all here, and visit occasionally? How would that be fair to anyone? Luke had lost so much…a part-time relationship was the last thing he needed in his life.

The best she could do—for herself, for Luke and for his daughters—was to retreat *now,* before the situation got much more complicated, and every one of them got hurt. They all had suffered enough.

She'd left her purse in her locked car. Carrying her keys, she caught Luke's eye and mouthed a silent "Good night" on her way to the front door.

He stood up, still talking to Jenny, but with a hand raised as if to stay "Stop."

Sarah didn't stop. She smiled, waved, then got into the Jeep and drove away before he could possibly catch her.

LUKE HOPED for a quiet shift on the night before Erin's birthday party. At 2:00 a.m., he was beginning to think he'd get his wish.

Then he noticed the car ahead of him—dark blue, reasonably new, with local plates. The driver wasn't speeding. In fact, the Volvo crawled along well under the posted limit. That was odd enough. As Luke followed, the car slowed down at every side street leading toward the beach. Sometimes the turn signal blinked, sometimes it didn't. But at each intersection, the vehicle hesitated, then continued straight down the highway.

Luke decided this behavior was erratic enough to warrant a drunk driving check. He flipped on his flashers and moved close enough to read the bumper sticker—Vanderbilt: *The* University of the South.

The driver didn't pull over. As if he hadn't noticed the police cruiser on his tail, he drove on, still slow, still debating whether or not to turn. Luke triggered the siren, then added the spotlight. Neither warning got the driver's attention. The Volvo didn't stop, didn't speed up. It just rolled through the night.

As they approached a corner with vacant lots on each side and an empty road between, Luke pulled up beside the Volvo and rolled down his passenger window. The man drove with his hands clutched around the top of the steering wheel, his shoulders hunched. Even with the siren right beside him, he didn't seem to notice.

Finally, Luke drew ahead, moved over into the same lane ahead of the Volvo, and lightly put on his brakes. He was thankful to see the driver straighten up and slow down. In another minute, both cars were stopped on the shoulder of the side road.

As Luke walked back, the Volvo window opened. "Something wrong, officer?"

"You're driving strangely, sir. Is there a problem?"

"N-no." The guy looked bad—glassy-eyed and pale. Beyond him, the inside of the car was a mess—fast-food bags and drink cans, newspapers and magazines littered the seats, front and back.

"Could I see your license, sir?"

"Sure." He lifted his hip and pulled out his wallet. "There you go."

Luke took the license. "Have you had anything to drink tonight?"

"Not since about six. I had a beer with my supper. I can walk a straight line, if you want me to."

Drunks often offered to prove they weren't. "Just wait in the car, sir. I'll be right back."

A computer check on the license brought up no prior arrests. Luke returned to the Volvo. The driver looked up at him. This time, the guy had tears in his eyes and on his cheeks.

Luke softened up. "Look, Mr. Craven, you're not safe out here, driving a car when you're this upset. Why don't you go home and get some sleep?" He handed back the driver's license.

Craven choked. "I can't."

Without asking, Luke could guess the rest. Domestic problems. "Well, then, get a room somewhere—"

"She's leaving. My wife wants to leave me."

Luke winced. "I'm sorry about that, sir. But you're a danger to other people on the roads. I'll take you—"

"I knew she wasn't happy. I work too much—always have. It's the only way to stay ahead. And we wanted the kids to have good schools, a chance at college."

"Mr. Craven—"

"I thought we could settle our problems once we got the kids out of the house. Our youngest just moved to

Washington for a job. And now…" He put the license back in his wallet and stowed the wallet in his pocket again. As he shifted in the seat, something clunked onto the floor of the car. "What can I do? How can I keep her if she doesn't want to stay?"

Luke knew the answer to that question. But Craven didn't want to hear it. He leaned down and put a hand on the man's shoulder. "You can't solve anything tonight, Mr. Craven. Or by yourself. Let me take you to—"

He glanced into the space under the steering wheel, and his hair stood on end. Half hidden by Craven's leg, the barrel of a gun gleamed in the dim interior light.

"Mr. Craven?" Luke moved to stand slightly behind the driver's window. "Do you have a permit for that weapon?"

Craven lifted his head to stare dully at Luke, then shifted his knee to look down at the gun. "Uh… somewhere."

"You don't have the permit with you?"

"N-no."

"Hand me the weapon, Mr. Craven. Butt first."

"No." Craven straightened up in his seat, looking totally alert for the first time. "I don't have to do that."

"Yes, you do, sir. I'm asking you to give me the weapon. Now." Luke held out his hand near Craven's shoulder.

Craven sat stone still, his hands remaining in sight on the steering wheel. Luke waited a long time. Several cars whizzed by on the main highway.

"Look, Mr. Craven." Luke leaned an arm on the roof of the car, praying he wasn't being stupid. "I'm not a family counselor. But…I've been where you are. It's a very bad place. That doesn't mean you can't survive."

After a long minute, Craven said, "What would I do without her?"

"Hurt. A lot." Luke could recall the pain very easily. "But hurting won't kill you—unless you let it."

Craven glanced at the gun. "Why not?"

Luke had asked himself that question more than once. "You said you have kids."

"But they're grown. They don't need me."

"Yeah, they do. And their kids will need a granddad. Think about what the grandkids will miss if you…check out."

For what seemed like forever, Craven debated within himself. Luke stood motionless, afraid to unbalance the situation by moving. He thought about Erin and Jen, about whether they still needed *him*. He thought about Sarah Rose and how much he was coming to need her.

Finally, the man in the car reached toward the floor. Luke tensed.

Craven brought up his hand, holding the gun by the barrel, and extended it out the window. "Here. Keep it away from me."

With a sigh of relief, Luke obliged. Half an hour later, he had Craven registered at a nearby motel. They parted at the door to the room.

"Thanks, Officer." Craven shook his hand. "I guess you've done me a favor."

"I think so, Mr. Craven. Get somebody to talk to—a minister, a counselor, or just a friend. That card I gave you has some numbers, if you need them. You *can* feel better."

The other man sighed. "Maybe." He looked over at the bed. "God, I'm tired."

"I'll leave your gun in the evidence locker at the precinct—claim it when you're sure you're ready. Good night, sir.'' Luke closed the door between them.

Back in his cruiser, he rested his head on his hands, as Craven had earlier. This last hour had taken more effort, more energy, than most shifts required during the whole night.

He hoped Craven would be okay. Sometimes just letting another person know about the pain helped. Telling Sarah about his troubles—receiving her compassion and understanding—had radically changed Luke's life. She'd become his personal guide through the darkness.

And he groaned at the thought of waiting ten more hours to see her again.

The rest of the night passed without a single incident. Luke was at his locker after the end of the shift, changing out of his uniform, when Hank Jordan came by.

''Hey, Brennan, I thought you'd want to know—we received a report on another mugging like Sarah Randolph's. Monday night.''

Luke pulled his shirt over his head. ''Where?''

''At one of the outlet malls, in a back parking lot. Woman walked to her car, got hit from behind and beat up. He took her keys and her purse, but didn't take the car. Another Jeep.''

''And didn't get caught, either?''

Jordan shook his head. ''Nah. But we're beefing up mall security and drive-bys. We'll get lucky.''

The cop sauntered out of the locker room. Luke shook his head. Police work should not have to depend on getting ''lucky.'' But this guy was smart enough not to leave evidence. Until he did, luck was all they had to go on.

As he closed his locker door, he wondered where Chuck Sawyer had been during the second attack.

LUKE KNOCKED ON Sarah's door with about eight minutes to spare before Erin's party. "I'm sorry I'm late," he said as she waved him inside. "I can't believe it, but I slept through the alarm."

"That's okay." She smiled, but it seemed to take effort. "I'll be right back. Just let me get a hat."

Before he could say anything, she vanished into the bedroom. Luke glanced around while he waited and caught sight of a photographic proof sheet on the counter—a series of pictures featuring marsh birds and deer. The shot of a frog clinging to the arch of a reed made him smile.

"Ignore those." Sarah came out in a wide-brimmed straw hat. "Nature shots have never been my specialty." She gathered her keys and purse with the air of a person facing a dental appointment.

She wasn't her usual sunny self today. Luke tried to think of something cheerful to talk about. "You're great with people, though. I went to the library and looked through some back issues of *Events*." He waited while she locked the door and then double-checked it. "I noticed the pictures this time, as well as the writing. You've worked in the world's worst trouble spots."

She was silent for a moment, then replied, "Most of them, I think."

Following her down the steps, Luke decided he didn't like the hat—he couldn't read her face, couldn't gauge her reactions. He tried to tread carefully. "Cops—especially in really big cities like L.A., New York, Miami—see such brutality that burn-out gets to be a real possibility. Looking at your pictures, I wondered whether reporters might face the same problem. And photographers."

Sarah's answer came only after he'd started the engine.

"James didn't. He never slowed down, never fal-
tered...until that very last instant."

"It could be hard to keep up with a guy like that."
The conversation wasn't turning out as cheerfully as he'd
hoped. Luke glanced across the truck seat when he
stopped at a traffic light, but the hat was in the way again.

"It was all part of the job." Her tone was anything
but encouraging.

He decided to ignore the hint. "You must have some
wild stories to tell."

"What seems exciting at the time often looks only
stupid in hindsight. James would still be alive if he hadn't
taken one more chance."

"Were you close...friends?" He hadn't intended to
ask that question—though he definitely wanted to know
the answer.

Her laugh was rueful. "James and I went through the
whole spectrum. Friends, lovers, enemies...we did it
all."

A blackness grew inside him that Luke recognized as
jealousy. And dread. "Which were you at the end?" He
tried to sound casual.

She took a long, long time to answer. "Not lovers. I
broke that off years ago, when I realized he wasn't—
wouldn't ever be—faithful."

Luke let out a breath he hadn't realized he was holding.

"Not enemies. James was a hard man to hate, especially when our work turned out so well. But not friends,
either. I was impatient with his tricks and his constant
push to beat everybody to the punch. But I admired what
he wrote and his dedication to the story."

After another long pause, she said, "And now...I don't
know...how I'm ever going to go back."

Her voice was small, but he heard the pain. Luke parked the truck on the curb at the edge of Kristin's front lawn, turned in the seat and removed the damn hat.

Then he wiped her wet cheek with his fingertips. "I'm sorry, Sarah Rose. I know it hurts."

She shook her head, and tears flew into the air like tiny diamonds. "It's not...I mean, I am...it was horrible that James died."

"You know he wouldn't want you to suffer over him." He spoke softly. "James would expect you to get on with your life and with your career. For your sake, and his."

"That's pretty much the problem." Sarah drew a shuddering breath. "I tried to go on. I managed for about a week. And then, one day...I just...couldn't, anymore."

"Everyone needs a break—"

"Not a break," she interrupted. "A breakdown. I couldn't function. Couldn't think or drive or get to a hotel, couldn't make my own plane reservations or figure out where to go. A couple of reporter friends sent me to New York. My editor got me to a therapist. I'm more or less in control, and I'm getting better with day-to-day details. But—"

When she looked up, the lurking shadows had completely dimmed the light in her eyes. "The pictures of your girls was the first time I've used a camera since...then. The only decent work I've done in almost a year. My career is probably over. I can't even think about going back—or I fall apart, like this."

She glanced out the window. Erin was running toward them across the grass. They were almost out of time.

Sarah knew it, too. Putting her hand on the door handle, she attempted a shaky smile. "Don't worry—I'm not dangerous. Just..." The smile died. "Just totally useless."

MATT STOOD on the threshold of the outside door to the kitchen, watching controlled chaos. In the hours he'd been at work, Kristin had draped the deck rails with rainbow streamers anchored by bunches of balloons in each corner. A long table covered by a cartoon character tablecloth was set for a feast. No doubt the pizza she'd ordered was on its way.

Out in the grass beyond the deck, ten little girls were lined up for a relay race, each carrying an egg in a spoon. Knowing Kris, Matt was sure the eggs had been boiled first.

He spotted Erin at the head of the line. The birthday girl had consented to dress up and have her hair braided. Matt was glad to see her so excited. She often seemed too somber, as if life wasn't as much fun as it should be for a seven-year-old.

Of course, Erin's life was a little more complicated than the average. Having two dads was hard enough. When they were brothers...

White-hot jealousy poured through him, like a fire blazing just under his skin. *Luke* had seen Erin born, had held her as a baby, watched her first steps and taught her the alphabet.

For five years Matt hadn't even known his daughter existed. Kristin had finally told him—*after* Luke moved out of their house. Sometimes Matt wondered if he ever would have found out, otherwise.

"Matthew!" His mother climbed the steps onto the deck. "I wondered where you were." She came close and offered her cheek. Matt leaned over to give her the kiss and a hug, careful not to disturb her neat outfit and precise hair.

"Hey, Mom." He drew a deep breath to calm down. "Looks like the party's going well."

"Well enough, though I think races are a bit rambunctious for a little girl's birthday party."

"Kids need to move." He looked for his father, found him seated under a tree in a lawn chair. "How's Dad?"

"Tired." Her voice trembled. "He's always tired. I'm very worried."

"He went to the doctor this week, right? What happened?"

"Your father refused to allow me in the room, so I don't know what was said. He reported that the doctor talked about a good diet, exercise, plenty of rest."

"Sounds kind of superficial."

"Yes. I called the doctor myself, and spoke with him about the fatigue. But he said basically the same things to me as your father did."

"Does he have another appointment?"

"In the middle of August."

"Meanwhile, you'll be taking care of him—he couldn't ask for better."

His mother didn't reply. Matt followed her gaze…to Luke, with Jenny in his arms and Sarah Randolph beside him. "Don't worry, Mom. We'll just have to be careful to keep things quiet and peaceful. No upsets. We're all adults." Was he reassuring her, or himself? "And we can act like adults, for Dad's sake. Right?"

"I hope so." She sighed, her eyes still on Luke. "I do hope so."

WHILE THE KIDS got some free time to play, Sarah presented the details of the picture offer. "There's no marketing attached to the article, no selling of any kind. Just a photo essay on southern beaches. Erin and Jenny certainly show Myrtle Beach at its very best."

Six pairs of eyes stared at her—Kristin and Matt, Colo-

nel and Mrs. Brennan, and Kristin's parents, Joe and
Irene Jennings. Luke sat in a chair on Sarah's right, looking back at the rest of the family. Nobody said a word
for what seemed a very long time.

Kristin finally stirred. "I don't see any reason why we
shouldn't sign the release. After all, this isn't much different from being pictured in a newspaper at a parade."

"A newspaper," Mrs. Brennan said, "does not go all
over the country. You would be inviting all sorts
of...people...to come looking for children in Myrtle
Beach."

"I don't think—" Sarah began.

"What sorts of advertisements are in this magazine?"
Kristin's mother looked only slightly older than her
daughter. Her hair was still a shiny blond, her face
smooth and her figure trim. "Liquor? Cigarettes? I don't
think the girls should be part of that type of promotion."

"Mother, Sarah said they wouldn't be personally ad-
vertising anything."

"But being in a magazine promoting such things ef-
fectively supports them, Kristy."

Matt shook his head. "I don't like the idea, either. The
girls don't need that kind of exposure. Maybe perverts
won't read this kind of magazine. But producers and
agents might. We don't want the hassle."

Luke straightened up in his chair. "The chances of
modeling agents or Hollywood producers showing up on
your doorstep are pretty remote."

The glance Matt threw toward his brother held no humor. "Principles, bro. Principles."

"I think it's up to the girls' parents to decide," Elena
Brennan said decisively. Kristin's mother nodded in
agreement.

"Great," Matt said.

"Sounds good," Luke said at the same time, standing up. "Kristin and I will talk it over and let you all know what we decide."

Sarah caught back her own gasp. Mrs. Brennan's jaw dropped—obviously, this had not been her plan. Kristin's mother stared at her daughter with a confused expression. Matt looked simply murderous.

And Kristin went pale. But after a second's pause, she got to her feet and recaptured control of the situation. "That's right. Matt and Luke and I will decide what to do." Her mouth relaxed into a smile. "Would it be okay if we let you know Monday or Tuesday, Sarah?"

"That will be fine. Just give me a call." Sarah breathed a sigh of relief. Kristin had salvaged the situation. Sarah couldn't help admiring Luke's ex-wife, even though her desertion had hurt him badly.

But perhaps she'd had no choice. The thought came to Sarah that Kristin had been as much a victim of circumstance as Luke. The weariness in Kristin's face confirmed that explanation. This was a predicament from which no one—not Luke nor Matt nor the wife caught between them—could emerge unscathed.

As Erin's party continued, Sarah stepped into her role as official birthday photographer, observing activities from the outside. She caught the Brennan parents' obvious devotion to each other, and to their granddaughters. Elena Brennan's eyes followed both girls as they played, her expression tender, gentle, vulnerable. The Colonel seemed pale, and he rarely left his chair, but his gaze, too, was on Erin and Jenny.

Late in the afternoon, Sarah's pleasure in the relaxed and happy family mood died as she framed an encounter between Matt and Luke. Through her lens, she watched the two men confront each other, their body language antagonistic, even challenging. Then Luke said something, turned on his heel and walked away. Matt merely stared after him, with an expression that clearly said, "Go to hell."

Sarah lowered the camera and glanced around to find that Kristin had witnessed the scene, too. When their gazes met, she lifted her eyebrows, then shrugged. Sarah shrugged back. Surely the brothers would behave the rest of the night. How much longer could this party possibly last?

When the time came for Erin to open her gifts, Luke ended up leaning against the deck rail beside his ex-wife. Sarah, on his other side with the camera, considered somehow easing between them, just in case.

Before she could make a move, Matt showed up on Kristin's left. He kept his eyes on the children, but his comment was for his wife. "You two seem to have a lot to talk about."

Kristin opened her mouth, but Luke answered. "Deal with it, Matt. Kristin and I have children to consider, to discuss."

"Child. A child."

Frigid silence greeted Matt's remark. Kristin thawed first. "Matt, please. You know things are more complicated than that."

He shook his head. "Actually, I don't. What I do know is that they won't get simpler as long as we don't tell the truth."

"You agreed to wait." Luke's soft voice sliced through the children's excited chatter. "You said Kristin and I could decide when the girls were ready. And we promised we'd do that as soon as we possibly could."

Matt gave a caustic laugh. "I get the feeling that promise may turn out to be worthless."

Kristin straightened up. "Matt!"

Luke stiffened. "You b—"

"Mommy, Daddy look!" Erin stood up in the circle of her friends. "An aquarium!"

With a reproachful glance that included Matt and Luke, Kristin hurried to Erin's side. "That's wonderful, sweetie. Who got you the aquarium?"

"Um…" She thrashed through the paper around the box and came up with a blue envelope. Taking out the card, she opened it and read aloud. "For a special girl's special birthday. Love always, Daddy…" She raised her face. "Daddy Matt."

The dimming of her excitement was painfully obvious. "Happy Birthday, Erin." Matt's voice sounded forced. "I thought we'd pick out some fish when we get everything set up."

"That'll be cool." Erin looked at her mother, then at Matt again. "Thank you, Daddy Matt. I really like it."

He nodded and stepped back to prop his hips against the rail of the deck. Arms crossed over his chest, he appeared to have closed himself off from the rest of the crowd.

Luke's face was an expressionless mask. Sarah put her hand on his bicep. "Are you okay?"

He came back slowly from whatever frozen place held him. Finally, he shook his head and met her eyes. "Sure. Sorry you had to witness that."

"You're all in a tough situation." She slipped her hand down his bare arm to close their palms and join their fingers. "Everyone's doing their best."

Luke squeezed her hand. "Generous Sarah Rose."

Erin opened Luke's present last. "Wow, Daddy." She twirled the large, multicolored globe. "And a whole set of books on animals of the world. Cool!" Stepping through the crowd, she crossed the deck and put her arms around his waist. "Thanks! I love you!"

Luke released Sarah's hand to hug Erin. "You're welcome, Erin Bear. Happy Birthday."

Sarah caught a movement in the shadows on the edge of the deck. She turned her head in time to see Matt bolt down the steps, cross the grass, and disappear around the corner of the house.

CHAPTER TEN

KRISTIN COULDN'T take the time to find Matt until the last of the children had been picked up by their parents. Leaving Erin and Jenny on the deck with a dozen new toys and six adult supervisors, she tracked her husband down.

He sat in their bedroom, in the window bay they'd furnished with two armchairs and a small table so they could have a place all to themselves to read and to talk. Matt wasn't talking, he wasn't reading. Slumped in his chair, he stared at the blinds closed against the hot afternoon sun.

She cleared her throat. "Now that the hordes are gone, the rest of us were thinking about hamburgers for dinner. But we couldn't find the chef."

"Sure." He didn't turn his head. "Be right out."

"Matt…" She crouched by his knee, putting her hand on his thigh. "You know I meant what I said. We *will* tell Erin."

"Sure," he said again. His palm covered the backs of her fingers. "I'm sorry I blew up. I just have to be more patient. Everybody's doing their best." He squeezed her hand and helped her up as he stood. "Now I guess we'd better get some real food cooking."

He started for the door, but glanced back when she didn't follow. "Are you going to make me do it all by myself?" He grinned, just like his usual self.

She wasn't fooled—and his misery broke her heart. Becoming a family wasn't supposed to *hurt*. "I'm tempted, but I'll let you off the hook. I'll be out just as soon as I brush my hair."

Matt nodded, and left the room.

Standing alone, Kristin looked around *their* space, hers and Matt's. She almost expected to see a small shadow searching the corners of the ceiling for a crack to slip through. Or a delicate white bird fluttering near the windows, seeking escape. A symbol of the soul—the essential spirit—she'd just sensed leaving her marriage. She didn't find anything.

But she felt its absence.

JENNY FELL ASLEEP on Luke's lap after supper as they watched Erin practice cartwheels, with Sarah coaching and snapping pictures. Across the lawn, Kristin and Matt lingered over coffee on the deck with her parents and his. Luke acknowledged the symbolic grouping with a rueful shrug.

Just before dark, Sarah stowed her camera and came to sit beside him in the grass while Erin ran toward the house. "She's worn me out." She pushed loose curls back from her flushed face. "Where does she get all that energy?"

"I think she drinks rocket fuel for breakfast." Luke shifted his arm and Jenny relaxed a little more into his hold, nestling with her thumb just touching her full lower lip.

Sarah glanced over and smiled. "A sweet little girl."

He couldn't help smiling, himself. "More than I deserve."

She started to say something, but the group on the deck broke apart. Kristin's parents hugged her and Matt, then disappeared into the house with their daughter and grand-daughter following.

"They didn't say goodbye," Sarah said, in a stunned voice. "Not even a wave."

Luke brushed a beetle off of Jenny's shoulder. "As far as they're concerned, I hit on Kristin when she was vulnerable and took advantage of Matt's disappearance for my own...gratification. Once he came back, I pretty much disappeared from their horizon."

Sarah stared at him, a line drawn between her straight eyebrows. "How could they misunderstand you so totally?"

Her assumption warmed him deep inside. "Matt sets a pretty tall standard. I knew early on I couldn't measure up. I guess I went too far to let everybody know I wasn't about to try."

"But—"

They both glanced toward the deck as his dad came down the steps, leaning heavily on the rail. The deck lights silhouetted a slight bend in the Colonel's usually straight shoulders, a general impression of weariness in the lines of his body.

Shifting Jenny, Luke looked at Sarah. "Can you take her?"

"Of course." She held out her arms. Jen didn't wake as they made the transfer.

He got to his feet and met his dad halfway. "Are you leaving?"

"Your mother thinks it's time I got to bed." The Colonel gave a laugh that turned into a cough. "She worries too much."

Judging by the lack of color in his father's austere face, Luke didn't think so. "That's what retirement is all about, right? Early to bed, early to rise?"

"Hmph." The Colonel lifted a hand and nodded to Sarah where she sat under a tree. "It was nice to see you again, Miss Randolph."

She smiled. "Thank you, sir. Take care."

On the short way back to the deck, Luke barely kept himself from offering his dad an arm to lean on. He knew what kind of reaction he'd get. At the foot of the steps, though, the older man paused, as if gathering strength to make the climb.

Finally, he took the first step, and two more. On the fourth, he stopped with a gasp.

"Dad?" Luke put an arm around the narrow waist. "You okay?" The Colonel didn't answer. He seemed to sag into Luke's hold. Luke lifted his head and raised his voice. "Hey, Matt. Give me a hand, here."

His mother looked their way. "Oh, my God."

Matt took hold on the colonel's other side. "Just relax, Dad." Together he and Luke lifted their father completely off his feet, took him across the deck and into the house to lie down on the family room sofa.

Luke headed into the kitchen. "I'm calling the doctor."

"Stop right there." Weak or not, his dad commanded attention when he gave an order. Reluctantly, Luke turned back.

The Colonel had propped himself up on an elbow. "I don't need the damn doctor."

"Of course you do." Sitting beside her husband, Elena Brennan took his hand. "Something is obviously not right."

"Everything is just fine." After just a few minutes, Colonel Brennan drew his free hand out of his wife's hold. He moved to sit up, forcing her to stand. Swinging his legs around, he got to his feet, once again the strong, controlled officer they'd known all their lives. His face was still paper-white.

"We'll be going now." He ushered his wife toward the front of the house. "We'll see you all tomorrow for dinner."

"Granddaddy?" No one had even noticed Erin, standing in the doorway to the hall. "Are you all right, Granddaddy?"

The Colonel stopped in front of her and bent over to even out their heights. "I'm fine, sweetheart. Just a little tired. I really enjoyed your birthday party. Give me a hug."

Elena hugged her granddaughter as well, and then her husband swept her out the door.

In the house behind them, Luke and Kristin and Matt stared at each other. But it was Erin who broke the silence. "Where's Jenny?"

"Right here." Luke turned and found Sarah in the kitchen, with a very rumpled, very grumpy Jenny at her side. Sarah made a wry face. "She wasn't happy when she woke up in the dark with just me."

"Mama—" Jenny held out her arms.

Kristin picked her up. "Okay, sweetie. I think it's bath and bedtime for both my girls. Give your dad a kiss, Erin…" She drew a deep breath. "And give Daddy Matt one, too. I'll take Jenny in to help me run the water."

Erin ran to Luke. "Can you read me a story, Daddy? Before you leave?"

He tweaked her nose. "You're gonna fall asleep the second your head hits the pillow, Erin Bear. Another night, okay?"

She pouted but turned away. Then, with a glance at Matt, she said, "Would *you* read me a story?"

Matt, of course, didn't hesitate. "I definitely will. Go

pick out the book and I'll be there as soon as you're tucked in.''

Luke waited to speak until he was sure Erin would have reached her room. "Way to score points, *bro*."

"This isn't a game, Luke. There's no reason I can't read her a story."

"Except she's exhausted and needs to be asleep."

"So she falls asleep while I read. What's the deal?"

"The story isn't the issue, here. The deal is we're supposed to cooperate, not undercut each other at the first opportunity."

His brother rolled his eyes. "Yeah, sure. That's why you're always butting in, right? So we can cooperate?"

Behind him, Sarah gasped. Luke clenched his fists and his jaw. "'Butting in' is not the way to describe taking care of my children."

Matt took a step forward. "*My* children, now. And *my* wife."

After a blank second, Luke found himself standing with a hand pressed flat against Matt's broad chest. "Only because I let you, *brother*. Remember that, when you're enjoying *your* children. When you're making love to *your* wife. I stepped out of the way. If I hadn't, *you* wouldn't have a damn thing." He pushed with the flat of his hand. Matt swayed, but didn't step back.

Luke turned on his heel and found Sarah standing frozen, her fingers pressed against her lips. "I'm sorry, Sarah Rose. I guess we're ready to go." He took her out the back door, through gathering darkness to the gate in the fence, and across the front lawn to his truck. She trembled under his hand.

Or was it his own shaking he felt?

The ride to her condo was silent. She didn't argue

when he got out to walk her upstairs, didn't say a word until she'd unlocked the door. "Coffee?"

He drew a relieved breath. "Juice?"

She nodded. "Come in."

They sat side by side on the sofa, still without speaking, until they'd each drained half a glass. Then Luke let his head drop back against the cushion. "I really do apologize. You shouldn't have had to hear us beating each other up."

Sarah shook her head. "Don't worry about me. The girls, though…"

"God, I know." He closed his eyes. "This could tear them apart. There's only one solution I can think of…and I can't face it."

She shifted next to him, took his glass out of his hand and put it on the coffee table with hers. "What solution is that?"

"I could leave town." Even saying it hurt.

"Luke—"

"I mean, the situation might resolve faster if we lived far enough apart that the girls didn't see me as often, as easily."

"They would miss you terribly."

"They'd get used to depending on Matt. Kristin and he could build their life together without having me around to remind them of the past."

Sarah's hand lighted on his arm. "They could relocate, as easily as you could. Matt could get a transfer."

"But then the girls would miss out on two sets of grandparents. The friends they've made, the schools they're used to. Why put them through that? I'm the one without ties, without roots. I could live…anywhere."

"Do you want to?"

"Hell, no." He rubbed his eyes. "I can barely get

through a week without seeing them. How would I survive months? I'd go crazy, wondering. And then there's
my dad. Obviously, he's not well. He had a heart attack
when I was eleven—that's when he retired from the
Army and settled in Myrtle Beach. I want to be close by,
if he's sick.''

She nodded, and they were quiet again. Luke hadn't
realized he was cold until he felt the warmth of Sarah's
palm on the skin of his inner arm. Covering the back of
her hand with his, he pressed her comfort closer. ''You're
a good friend, Sarah Rose. Thanks for putting up with
me.''

When he rolled his head over the cushion to look at
her, she was blushing. ''I like being friends with you,''
she murmured. ''You care so much about other people.''
She lifted her face, and her eyes glistened in the low
light.

''Don't cry.'' She blinked and a tear dropped, rolling
down her cheek to linger at the corner of her mouth. Luke
wiped it away. ''I don't want to make you cry.''

The skin of her face felt like velvet against his thumb.
He curled his fingers and skimmed his knuckles along
the line of her jaw.

Sarah tilted her head against his touch. She whispered
his name on a drawn-out breath.

Opening his hand, Luke fitted the column of her throat
into the span. Her pulse hammered on his fingertips. Her
lips separated with a sigh. The muscles in his arm tightened...or she leaned forward...or both, because then her
mouth, sweet with the taste of orange, fused with his.

The next clear thought he assembled was how small
she felt in his arms. Running his palms along her back,
he could trace the bones, the play of muscles as she
moved closer, lifting her arms to put them around his

neck. Her fingers in his hair, on the skin of his shoulders, drove desire deep into his bones.

Desire…without despair. He'd forgotten how passion felt, how hot, how wild, how formidable the intimate contact between man and woman could be.

And to be wanted…to be needed, as Sarah's small sounds said she needed, was a blessing he'd never expected to regain. Stopping now would tear him to pieces. He'd renounced almost everything in his life that mattered—couldn't he claim this moment, this woman, for himself?

Luke's kisses stole Sarah's breath; his hands stroked her body into a fever of wanting. Yet she nearly wept at the restraint she could still sense between them. The man in her arms asked so little, yet gave all of himself to those he loved. Someone—*someone*—should repay his generosity. Without thought for themselves. Without reckoning the future, or remembering the past…

Suddenly, his hands stilled. He took a deep breath and drew back, tucking her head in to his shoulder. "Sarah," he said then. His whisper was rough. "I'm not carrying protection."

She burrowed deeper against him. "I don't have any."

"Then I should go—"

She shook her head against him. "Please, no."

He actually chuckled. "Please, yes. I can go out to buy what…we need. Or—" his hand brushed back her hair "—or I can go home."

Sarah sat completely still. This was a chance to rethink a risky decision. If she let Luke come back, she was practically asking him to break her heart.

But maybe his heart would heal, just a bit. Not because she was anything special, some kind of magic worker. Only because she wanted him and needed him for exactly

who and what he was. Sarah wasn't sure he'd received
that gift often in his life. And now it was hers to present.

She drew back far enough to meet his gaze. His gray
eyes shimmered with the clashing forces of passion and
self-control. The promise she read in his face sent a
shiver down her spine.

"Hurry back," she whispered, watching his mouth
widen into a grin. "I'll be waiting."

LUKE TOOK A KEY when he left, let himself in on return-
ing, then relocked the door. The front rooms were dark,
but candlelight flickered in the doorway to the left.

Sarah turned from the window as he entered the bedroom. "Welcome back."

"Thank you." Dropping the box by the bed, he
crossed the room. "You're beautiful." She'd taken out
her braid and combed the long length of her golden hair
down her back. She wore a straight gown of something
white and soft that skimmed her collarbones, the tips of
her breasts, the bones of her hips. "So damn beautiful."
He threaded his fingers into that hair and brought Sarah's
mouth up to his.

"Mmm." Her hands slipped under the hem of his shirt.

He caught his breath as her fingers traced over his ribs,
the swell of his chest, the hollow of his throat. "Any
second thoughts?" he whispered, as Sarah's lips brushed
his ear.

She shook her head. Her teeth closed over the cord of
his neck, and he groaned.

Smiling, Sarah lifted her gaze to watch the meld of
gold and silver in Luke's eyes. "Is there anything else
you want to talk about?"

He smiled in return. "Maybe later." His hands were
relaxed, his breathing slow. Sarah shivered—at the deep

note of desire in his voice, at the play of his fingers inside the neckline of her gown. Luke seemed intent on taking his time.

And she could hardly wait.

But he didn't hurry. Instead, he carefully learned her curves, her angles, her secrets. She had never been loved like this, never been taken so far out of herself. She wanted him *now,* wanted to tear his clothes off and discover his body as he was discovering hers.

At last they were both trembling, his hands less sure, less controlled, her kisses wild. He let her take off his shirt, let her run her hands and lips over his beautiful chest while he fought with the buttons on his jeans.

Then, finally, he entered her embrace completely, his skin hot and smooth against hers, his muscles taut, his breathing fractured. And Sarah took him inside, opening all of herself, giving everything she had, in return for the rapture of hearing Luke cry out her name.

LUKE OPENED his eyes to a dim room, though the glare sneaking through slits in the blinds advertised a sunny morning outside.

Inside him, there was a new ease. A sort of lightness, where for so long a coiled spring had existed. Whatever time it was, this was a day he didn't have to dread, didn't have to simply endure until sleep eased the pain. Today was Sarah Rose.

He turned his head. She slept beside him, curled under his arm with her cheek pillowed on her hands. As he watched, her eyelashes fluttered, lifted, then closed again. But he knew she was awake.

"I love dreams like this," she murmured, still with her eyes closed.

Luke rolled onto his side to face her. "Like what?"

He let his hand stroke the curve of her hip, the smooth skin of her thigh, savoring without shame his body's reaction to her nearness.

Sarah stretched and moved a little closer. "The dream where I'm with a really special man." Her drowsy voice stirred ideas he didn't try to ignore. "And when we make love, the connection between us is so strong that I can still feel it when I wake up."

His pulse was racing, but Luke managed a smile. "Do you get to dream like that often?"

Sarah opened her eyes, and her gaze gleamed gold with desire. "I hope so." Her head dropped back as he pressed his mouth against the pulse beating in her throat. Her hands claimed him. "I really do hope so."

LUKE AND SARAH spent the entire weekend together, at her place and his. Saturday night they rode back to Brookgreen Gardens on the Harley, where he kissed her under the live oak trees at dusk, kissed her until her knees collapsed and his hands shook, and a gardener coming around the corner had to cough discreetly before they noticed him. They saw the sculptures this time, then found an inn on the way home and spent the night listening to the creaks of an old house as they made love on lavender-scented sheets.

Sunday evening, they lay tangled together in his bed, still catching their breath, when the phone rang. Sarah started to move away, but Luke's arm held her close to his side as he felt for the receiver.

"H'lo." His voice was even richer, deeper after sex. Sarah smiled, hearing the word rumble in his chest under her ear.

And then he stiffened. "Hey, Kristin." Sarah moved

away again; he let her go and sat up himself. "What's up?"

The air in the room cooled, as if a breeze had blown through. Luke turned completely away, giving Sarah a view of the lean lines of his back, the elegant shape of his shoulders and head. As she dressed, she couldn't avoid hearing his side of the conversation.

"Good. I think it's reasonable. I'll let Sarah know. Sure. Are the girls okay? Ice cream, huh? That'll win some points. No...okay, I believe you. He's trying. I'm trying, too." He listened for a minute. "Well, you're the only one. Yeah, I know. We all need time. Right. Bye."

Luke put the phone down and sat still for a few seconds on the edge of the bed. Then, with a deep breath, he reached down to pull on his shorts, pick up his shirt. Once dressed, he turned to Sarah.

"Kristin says she talked Matt into signing the release. You've got your pictures published, Sarah Rose." He grinned, but she could see the effort he made. The tension had come back to his eyes, his mouth.

Her own smile wasn't easy. "That's wonderful. I'll get the releases to all of you in the next couple of days." With Kristin's image between them once again, Sarah felt awkward for the first time since Friday night. "Um...I'm hungry. Can I take you out for a seafood dinner?"

And Luke understood the problem. The apology in his gaze twisted her heart. "Sounds like a great idea."

The evening fell short of that assessment, as they carefully worked their way through the meal with conversation that avoided anything really important. An even more difficult moment came afterward, when he took her home. She didn't know if she should invite him in. She didn't know what he wanted...or even what *she* wanted.

But that was nothing new.

As she sat paralyzed, Luke reached for her hand. "What do you say to a good night's sleep?"

Was he having second thoughts? Drawing back? "I've been sleeping okay."

He grinned. "I seem to remember differently. I figure you might be ready for a night alone. I don't want to crowd you."

"You haven't." But maybe he felt crowded? Maybe *he* needed some time to get his balance back? "Still, I've got chores to do, bills to pay and stuff. I could use some time to catch up."

Luke nodded. "Okay." He came around the truck and opened the door. "I'll give you a call tomorrow morning, see how things are going. Sound good?"

It sounded like twelve lonely hours. "Fine. Just fine."

He walked her up the stairs and to her door. Another goodbye at the threshold. Sarah blinked against the tears in her eyes.

Luke glanced over his shoulder, at a couple of kids running down one side of the open-air walkway, then stepped into her condo and pushed the door shut. "I don't want an audience."

His arms came around her, hard and tight, and his mouth took hers. Sarah felt herself dissolving. She didn't want him to leave, didn't want to spend this night alone. Could she convince him, without words, to stay?

"Sarah." His whisper shook, as did every breath he drew. "You're making this tough."

"Good." Her own voice sounded fierce. She slipped her hands under his shirt, warming her palms on the heat of his smooth, bare back. "I'm trying."

Luke chuckled. "If that's the case..." He let her go suddenly, turned and put the chain lock on the door. When he came back to her, his fingers reached for the top button of her shirt. "Let's just see how tough you really are, Sarah Rose."

SOMETHING HAD CHANGED.

Sarah lay awake deep in the night, eyes wide-open as Luke slept with his head on her breast. Physically, they couldn't have been closer. The passion between them only increased each time they made love.

But the connection between them was broken. Or at least frayed. Kristin had come back into his mind—if, in fact, she'd ever left. Sarah had known before making love with Luke for the first time that his heart belonged to Kristin and the girls. She thought she'd accepted the risk such commitment incurred.

Now, when it was too late to reconsider, she was surprised and dismayed to find that going in with her eyes wide-open did absolutely nothing to heal the hurt.

CHAPTER ELEVEN

As soon as Kristin opened the door on Wednesday, she realized Luke had changed.

After staring at him a few seconds too long, she gathered her wits. "Come on in. The girls are just finishing their lunch."

"Thanks. How was dinner Sunday?" He stepped inside with an ease of movement she hadn't seen in him for a long time.

"Fine. Just fine." She couldn't bring herself to ask why *he* hadn't been there.

"How was Dad feeling?"

Leading the way to the kitchen, Kristin shook her head. "Not so great, although he wouldn't say anything, of course. He has another appointment next week to see the doctor. Your mother insisted."

"That's good."

As they entered the kitchen, Jenny looked up. "Daddy!" She slipped from her booster chair and ran into Luke's arms. "Can we play golf? Can we?"

Erin joined them for a group hug. "Can we, Daddy? We haven't been to the dragon course in a long time."

Luke laughed—a genuine, free sound. "I'm all for it. Maybe we'll take a boat ride, too. You guys get your hats, and we're ready to roll."

They ran to their rooms, leaving Kristin alone with her ex-husband.

But the awkwardness she expected didn't evolve. Hands in his pockets, Luke leaned against the frame of the doorway into the family room. "Sarah's bringing copies of the release forms with her this afternoon. You can sign them when I bring the girls back."

With that one word—*Sarah*—the pieces fell into place. His tone, the softening of his eyes, and that sense of relaxation...Luke and Sarah Randolph were involved. Sleeping together, Kristin was sure. She'd lived with him for five years. She could still read his mood.

A bolt of emotion shot through her—loss, relief, or happiness for him, she couldn't tell which. Maybe all three. "Sarah's going with you today?"

"I'd like the girls to get to know her. And vice versa."

"That's...great. She's a nice person—as well as a wonderful photographer."

"Yeah, she is." There it was again—that extra richness in his voice. She'd heard it on Sunday when she called him, but hadn't realized exactly what the difference was. Now, the idea made her blush. Kristin scrubbed at the clean counter, hoping to avoid both her thoughts and Luke's eyes.

Erin and Jenny dashed into the family room, their baseball caps askew, excitement blazing in their faces. "Let's go, Daddy!" Erin grabbed his hand.

"Let's go," Jenny echoed. "Bye, Mommy!" Without even a hug, she started for the front door. Erin followed, pulling Luke with her. Gratefully, Kristin brought up the rear.

"I'll have them back by eight," Luke promised. "You have a nice, quiet afternoon."

And then, for the first time in over a year, he touched her—reached over and put a hand on her shoulder, squeezing lightly. While she absorbed the implications, he turned and jogged across the grass. "Let's go, munch-kins!" The girls waved as they drove off in Luke's truck. Kristin lifted her hand in return.

When they were out of sight, she closed the door behind her and leaned against it, listening to the empty house.

Luke had cut himself free. Sometime between Erin's birthday last week and today, he'd realized he could live again. He now knew there should be someone else in his life, a love to replace the careful relationship he and Kristin had built together. She was happy for him. Truly happy.

At the same time, she feared that Luke's rescue might have come just a little too late to keep his relationship with his brother from crumbling into sand.

Not to mention her own.

ERIN THOUGHT the top of her head might come off, like one of the people in a TV cartoon who got so mad that they just exploded, with all this fire and smoke rushing out like a volcano erupting.

Why was *she* here?

That lady—Sarah—climbed into Daddy's truck and turned around to smile at Erin and Jenny. "Hi. I hear we're going to play miniature golf."

Jenny stuck her thumb in her mouth.

All at once, Erin felt really cold. "You're coming with us?"

"Isn't that great?" Daddy opened his door and climbed in. "Sarah says she can't putt worth anything. I thought you two could give her some lessons."

Erin didn't believe it. "But—"

He looked at her through the mirror. "What's that, Erin Bear?"

"Nothin'."

Daddy frowned, but didn't say anything else.

Erin hit her head against the back of the seat and stared up at the ceiling of the truck. She was getting tired of all the different people she kept having to be nice to.

First, there had been Daddy Matt. He wasn't *Daddy* Matt in the beginning—he was Uncle Matt when he first came back. He'd been away somewhere for a long time. Everybody cried when he came back—even Granddaddy Brennan. Erin hadn't known that granddaddies ever cried.

Then weird things started happening at home. Mommy cried—not like she did when you gave her a handprint plate for a present, or made her breakfast for Mother's Day. Sad crying. It had scared Erin a lot, to see her mom cry.

Daddy got quiet, about the same time. Mommy and Daddy didn't talk much anymore, except late at night. They thought Erin was asleep, but she heard them, sometimes. Listening to what they said had made her stomach hurt.

And then there was the day when she and Jen and Mommy and Daddy all sat down at the kitchen table with milk and cookies—Daddy's special cookies.

Mommy had started talking first. She said people who were married sometimes couldn't keep living together. That things happened and they needed to think about what they wanted to do.

Daddy said that had happened to him and to Mommy. And so...

Erin squeezed her eyes shut. She hated remembering this part. But it had happened whether she wanted to remember or not.

So Daddy left. He packed his clothes and went away to a different house—the little house he lived in now.

That was bad enough. But then Uncle Matt started coming over. He would take them all places—to the movies, to the beach, to play crazy golf. He took Mommy places alone, too. Sometimes Erin and Jen got to stay with Daddy those nights. Sometimes, a baby-sitter stayed with them at home.

The week after Jenny's birthday on January 13, Mommy had told them that she was going to marry Uncle Matt. Erin refused to remember how she felt that day. It was too bad to think about.

And now Daddy was bringing this Sarah-person along on their adventures. Was he going to marry her? Was Erin going to have two daddies *and* two mommies?

How could they do that? Didn't anybody see how hard this was to understand? When you were seven, you could handle stuff. But Jenny was still a baby. She didn't know what was going on. That wasn't fair—didn't they *see?*

Why couldn't things just be the way they were?

"Here we are!" Daddy stopped the truck. "I see the dragon up there waiting for us—are we ready?" He lifted Jenny out of the car seat.

Sarah held out her hand to help Erin out, but Erin ignored it. Holding hands was for people you liked. She had to hold Daddy Matt's hand, because he was Mommy's husband now.

But she wasn't going to be friendly to anybody else.

Especially not this Sarah-person.

THEIR AFTERNOON together should have been a success. Everyone managed to get a hole in one. They followed up the game with ice cream cones, a boat ride on the lake, and the purchase of small stuffed dragons to take home.

But Erin and Jenny remained polite and distant. They

spoke directly to Sarah only if she spoke first. Otherwise, all their attention and conversation was for their dad. Caught in the middle, Luke gradually lost the relaxed grin he'd worn at the start of the afternoon. Sarah didn't feel much like smiling, herself.

Because she'd brought the release forms with her, she went with Luke to take the girls home. Kristin opened the front door as they all climbed out of the truck and dropped to her knees on the porch to welcome her daughters with hugs and kisses.

She looked up, laughing and blushing, as Sarah came close, with Luke behind her. "It sounds like you had a good afternoon. Hello again, Sarah. Come on in."

With a daughter under each arm, Kristin led them to the dining room, where Matt sat at the table. His eyes widened as the group came in. "Hey, Erin, what's that you're carrying?"

"A dragon." She held the stuffed toy up, but didn't go closer.

"I got one, too," Jenny said. "Mine's purple."

Matt grinned. "I can see that. What will you do with a purple dragon?"

"I'm gonna sleep with it."

"Wow." He looked impressed. "Sleeping with a dragon? You're braver than I am!"

Jenny giggled, but Erin slipped away from her mother. "Can I get something to drink, Mommy?"

"Of course—there are box drinks in the fridge."

"Me too, me too!" Jenny hurried after her sister, leaving the adults in a tense silence.

Kristin made the first move. "You brought the release forms, didn't you, Sarah? Let me get a pen." When she left the room, the temperature dropped at least ten degrees.

Sarah decided to ignore the hostility in the air. "I understand you're working in the recruiting office, Matt. Do you get a lot of volunteers?"

He drew his eyes away from Luke and gave her a smile that recognized her effort. "In the summer, around graduation time. And then again in the fall, when college gets tough and the kids decide they'd rather get paid for taking orders."

"What's the proportion of women to men applying for the Army?"

"In this area, very low. I've probably seen ten female applicants in the past year or so. Other parts of the country have a higher rate."

"A pen," Kristin commented as she returned, holding it up. "Rescued from the crayon box. I'm going to have to hide the writing utensils from those girls if I want to have one!" She glanced from Matt to Luke and back again, but didn't comment. "Where do I sign?"

Sarah pointed out the signature spaces. Luke had already filled in his name with the small, neat letters he used. Above that line, Kristin added her name with a rounded, flourishing script. The only space left for Matt to write was underneath Luke's name. His mouth tightened as he signed in a style not so different from his brother's.

"Great." Sarah breathed a sigh of relief. This whole difficult day would soon be over. "I'll send you copies of these. And when the magazine comes out, I'll get as many of those as I can for you. I really do appreciate your cooperation."

"You're welcome." Kristin replied, with another glance at her husband. Sarah recognized the chiding message conveyed. She had a similar urge to shake Luke out of his stubborn silence.

Only as Kristin opened the front door did Luke finally speak. "I need to tell the girls goodbye. I'll be right back."

As his brother went toward the kitchen, Matt stood up. "I've got some work to do, so I'll say good-night now."

"Thanks again," Sarah said.

He nodded, unsmiling, and headed in the opposite direction from the one Luke had taken.

With an audible sigh, Kristin leaned her forehead against the edge of the door. "This is not working," she said, almost under her breath.

Sarah didn't know whether or not to respond. Before she could decide, Kristin continued. "I expect the girls to act like children." She straightened up with a sad smile. "Somehow, I thought Matt and Luke would be more mature."

"They both...love you." She swallowed hard against the urge to deny that truth.

Kristin's brown eyes glistened in the twilight. "And I love them. Amazing, isn't it, that with so much love around, we're all so unhappy? I took what I wanted," she continued, in a near whisper. "And ruined everybody's life."

Sarah put out a hand. "I don't think—"

Luke came down the hall. "They're practically asleep on the kitchen table. I doubt you'll have much trouble getting them to bed tonight."

Kristin squared her shoulders. "That'll be a first. I hope they stay awake for their baths."

"Skipping their baths wouldn't kill them."

She glanced at him, one eyebrow lifted. "We've had this discussion before. Baths are not optional."

He grinned and lifted his hands. "Okay, okay. We'll get out of the way. 'Night."

But in the truck, the grin had disappeared. "I'm sorry, Sarah Rose. This day didn't turn out anything like I planned."

She sighed. "That's okay."

"I should have checked with the girls before I asked you along." One side of his mouth quirked up, and he winked at her. "I guess I haven't been thinking like a dad for the past few days."

Sarah couldn't help a small smile. "It's okay. They're still working everything out."

"And I imagine at some point Matt and I will stop behaving like spoiled brats ourselves."

"You recognize that, do you?"

"Oh, yeah. So does he. One day we might even admit that to each other...but probably not any time soon."

"Soon would be better for both of you...and Kristin."

"She looks tired." His voice had gentled. "Stressed."

Sarah swallowed hard. "She's caught in the middle. And she cares."

"Yeah." He drew a deep breath and started the truck. They didn't say anything on the drive home. But Luke reached for her hand and twined his fingers between hers. The pleasure and pain of that simple contact drove Sarah to the edge of tears.

In front of her building, he turned to face her, keeping hold of her hand. "I go on duty in a couple of hours. You're going to get another good night's sleep."

"You won't."

"I'll sleep tomorrow morning. Can I call you in the afternoon? I don't have anything planned, but..."

She wasn't wise enough to protect herself. "That's okay. We can think of something."

His eyes glittered in the light from the street lamp. "You're right about that, Sarah Rose." He brought her hand to his mouth. She felt his breath, his lips, his tongue, on her skin, and shivered. "We can definitely think of something to do."

She almost leaned into him, almost closed the distance between their bodies for a kiss, at least. At the last second, she pulled her hand back instead. "Don't walk me up, okay? I'll see you tomorrow." He sighed, but let her go.

Sarah waved through the window when she got into the house and watched as his truck turned out of the parking lot.

Then she switched off the light again. Her whole body prickled, in the way her leg did as it awoke from being "asleep." She sat on the couch, staring into the darkness, and thought about Kristin. About the despair in Matt's eyes, and the tension in Luke's hands. About the confusion in two little girls' faces.

Sarah was afraid—afraid for all of the Brennans, and for herself. She was beginning to want so much more than Luke had to give. And wanting…needing…what she could never have was a sure recipe for heartache.

OLIVER KERR CALLED the next morning. "Sarah, you have to be ready to work by now. The refugee crisis is a big story. You're the only one who can get the pictures I want. Please, come back."

After a mostly sleepless night, she reacted badly. "I can't." No qualifications, no excuses.

The phone line seemed to go dead. Then Oliver said, "Okay. You can't. I'm sorry, because you're the best photographer I ever had. But I can't keep you on the payroll if you're not working. I'll get somebody to box up your stuff."

Sarah closed her eyes and propped her forehead on the heel of her hand. "Thanks, Oliver."

"Give me a call sometime." He disconnected without a goodbye.

LUKE SLEPT WELL into Thursday afternoon—later than he'd slept in years. And better than he'd slept in years.

He called Sarah after his shower. "Sorry. I didn't wake up until three o'clock."

"No problem. You needed the rest." Her voice was flat, strained.

"What's wrong?"

After a pause, she sighed. "I got fired today."

"From the magazine? Why?"

"Because I wouldn't take a job."

"You wouldn't—" The picture clarified, suddenly. To go back to work, Sarah would leave Myrtle Beach. The idea froze his blood. Thank God he didn't have to face the possibility. Not today, anyway. "Can't they give you extra time off?"

"My editor has fudged for me more than six months now. But he couldn't hold off the suits forever. No work, no pay."

"Damn. I'm really sorry." About everything except the fact she wouldn't be going away.

"Me, too."

"Do you want some company? We could go for a walk on the beach, get some dinner."

Another long pause. Then she sighed. "That sounds lovely. But I'm in a pretty lousy mood right now. Maybe tomorrow?"

Luke bit back his own disappointment, and the urge to coax. "Okay. I'll give you a call. Take care of yourself."

"Thanks. Stay safe tonight."

"I always do."

About 1:00 a.m. Friday morning, though, that promise proved a little too cocky to keep.

Luke stopped at the speaker of a drive-through fast-food place to get coffee. When no one asked for his order, he drove to the delivery window, which was empty and stayed that way. Yet the lights were on inside. He could smell the vented steam from the grill.

Easing the cruiser past the wall-to-wall windows in the front of the restaurant, he saw only one customer standing at the counter, partially concealing one clerk. There were no cooks, managers, or other workers visible.

The whole picture looked very, very wrong.

He radioed for backup, then reversed the car into the shadows behind the restaurant. The back door would be locked from the inside. A cop couldn't get in. But a suspect could get out. Luke flipped off the safety on his revolver, crouched behind his open door and waited.

An approaching siren flushed the robber out that back door, as he'd hoped. Luke jumped to his feet. "Police. Stop where you are."

Wide, panicked eyes glanced his way. "Screw you," the guy said, raising a pistol. A shot whizzed by Luke's ear. He flinched. Then the robber took off running.

Luke followed. Their terrain didn't favor the escapee—the wide-open parking lot of a mall left nowhere to hide. Slowly, Luke gained ground.

"Stop!" he shouted again. "Police!" His quarry disappeared around the corner of the department store on the end of the building.

Luke stopped just before that corner. "Look," he panted. "You're not going anywhere. There are cops all over the place. Just give it up before somebody gets hurt and you're looking at charges more serious than robbery.'' Holstering his gun, he crouched low against the wall.

There was no sound for about ten seconds, then the sudden scrape of shoes on concrete. The guy popped around the corner, gun pointed and already firing at exactly the place Luke's head would have been.

With a yell, Luke took him out at the knees. The gun clattered to the pavement as they crashed to the ground, rolled over and off the curb into the street. Luke grabbed for a secure hold, but his hands kept slipping on clothes and sweat-slick skin. Once, he came up on top, but an agonizing jab stole his breath and sent him crashing to the side. He managed to hang on, wondering where the hell his backup was.

He was down on his back, with two hundred pounds on his chest and a pair of hands squeezing his throat, when the click of a pistol hammer pulling back shut the situation down.

''Put your hands in the air and stand up. Now.'' Nick's voice sounded deadly. The fingers around Luke's neck loosened and he opened his eyes, blinking away black spots, to see the barrel of a service revolver propped against the perp's ear.

In the next second, the pressure on his chest eased as the guy stood up. Luke lay where he was, getting his breath back, until Nick had marched the assailant into custody and returned to bend over Luke.

''You okay, Brennan?''

''Yeah. Just winded.'' He sat up and propped his elbows on his knees. Rubbing the heels of his hands in his eyes, he fought back an urge to be sick. ''Anybody in the restaurant hurt?''

''Nah. He scared 'em, but he's not really a killer. Now get yourself over there and let the EMTs check you out.''

Nick put a hand under Luke's elbow to help with the standing up part. "You got blood running down both sides of your head."

The medics patched up the scrapes across his forehead, on his elbows and the backs of his hands, and the graze where that one bullet had scratched his ear, while Luke dictated a report to Nick on the whole episode. He argued when the captain ordered him home, but eventually gave in.

Nick shoved him gently toward the cruiser. "Go get some sleep. We can handle this town for one night without you."

"Oh, sure. That's why I'm the one all scraped up. Tell the truth, Rushe."

"The truth, Brennan, is that you're such a hotdogger, nobody else gets any action unless you're out of commission."

Luke grinned at the familiar ribbing. The sick feeling left him as shock and reaction receded. "Well, if the rest of you lazy bums would just do the job..."

MATT PUT Jenny in the seat in the grocery cart and strapped her in. "You get to ride. Neat, huh?" She only stared at him and sucked her thumb.

"Right. Let's hunt down your sister." He wheeled up and down the aisles without seeing Erin. Kids got taken from grocery stores every day, he thought, with a thud of his pulse. And they never came back...

He found her, as he should have expected, in the toy and book aisle. She jumped as he approached, and put the book she'd been reading back on the rack.

Matt took a deep breath. This didn't have to be a big issue. "What are you reading? Something scary?"

Erin shook her head. "Just a book about training dogs."

"You like dogs?" She nodded. "Have you ever had one?"

"No. Mommy says we're not old enough."

"Well…maybe we could talk to her about that. I miss having a dog."

His daughter—*his* daughter—looked him straight in the eye for once. "Really?"

He grinned. "Really."

She almost smiled back. "That would be neat."

Matt rolled the cart past her, toward the end of the aisle. "Let's get this done, then. The sooner we get home, the sooner we can ask your mom."

They finished up the shopping in relative harmony, with Matt reading out Kristin's list, Erin fetching the items from the shelf, and Jenny munching on animal crackers. As he loaded bags into the back of the van, Matt congratulated himself on a fairly successful outing.

Instead of resting, as he'd hoped she would, Kristin had used the time without the girls to do laundry, mop floors and clean the oven. The girls went to their rooms to play, while Matt brought in the groceries.

"You work too hard, Mrs. Brennan. You were supposed to take a nap." God knew she needed the rest. When she came to bed, she couldn't ever seem to settle. More often than not, if he woke up in the middle of the night, he'd find her sitting in the kitchen with a cup of tea. "Just thinking," she would say.

"I did rest. Honest." She carried cans to the pantry.

"Five whole minutes?"

She flashed him a smile. "Ten, at least."

Jenny trundled into the kitchen. "Mommy, Erin won't share her new book."

"What new book, sweetie?"

"The one she got at the store."

Kristin looked at Matt with a question in her eyes.

"I didn't buy a book," he countered. "Or else I would have gotten them each one."

She nodded in approval. "Let's go see this book, Jenny."

Matt followed. Erin was sitting on her bed, flipping through the pages of a book about oceans.

Kristin sat down next to her. "Jenny says you have a new book."

Erin shook her head without looking up. "This is mine, Mommy. 'Member—you bought it for me at Sea World?"

"I remember." She looked at her other daughter. "Was this the book you saw, Jenny?"

The little girl stuck out her lower lip. "It was a book about dogs an' I wanted to see the pictures an' she wouldn't let me."

Matt straightened up from the door frame. Before he could speak, Kristin put a hand on the girl's knee. "Erin, do you have a new dog book?"

Erin stuck her tongue out at her sister. "Tattletale." Then she reached under her pillow and showed Kristin the dog training book she'd been reading in the grocery store.

"Where'd you get the book, Erin?" Kristin flashed him a warning glance, but Matt ignored it. "That's the book we talked about at the store. Where did it come from?"

"Matt—"

The answer was clear. So was Kristin's protest. But Erin was his daughter, damn it. "Tell us how you got the book, Erin."

She flipped it onto the bed. "I took it, okay?"

"Erin..." Kristin stared at their daughter. "You took the book and didn't pay for it?"

Matt cleared his throat. "You know what that's called?"

"Stealing," Erin said in a low voice, gazing into her lap.

"I *stole* the book." She looked up, her eyes bright with defiance. "So what?"

CHAPTER TWELVE

KRISTIN SAT speechless, staring at her daughter. Where had this come from? Lying? Defiance? *Stealing—Erin?*

"Erin, you're confined to your room." Matt stepped forward. "Your mom and I need to talk. Give me the book."

Before Kristin could reach out, Erin grabbed up the book and tossed it at Matt. Then she flung herself over on the bed, her back to them, and lay perfectly still.

"Come on, Kris." Matt put a hand under her elbow and lifted her to her feet. "Jenny, go play in your room for a little while."

"I wanna stay with Erin."

"I don't think that's a good idea right now." Again, before Kristin could react, he picked up Jenny and carried her out. Jenny started crying. Matt put her in her room, still crying, and shut the door.

He waited for Kristin to walk out of Erin's room. He closed that door, too, then led her to their bedroom.

"Now what?" He leaned backward against their closed door. "Has she done this before?"

"Of course not!" She dropped into a chair by the bay window. "I can't believe she did it at all. Are you sure you didn't buy the book?"

"I'm sure, Kris. She put it back on the shelf. But she must have picked it up again when I didn't see. We did not pay for that book."

"Well, I'll have to talk to her. She needs to understand—"

"I think I should handle this."

"Why?"

"I'm her father."

"But—" Kristin could only imagine the results. "I know you mean well, Matt. But this situation is so complicated. If you think I'm too easy on her, maybe... maybe Luke—"

He slapped his hands against the door panel. "I was waiting for that. But I really hoped you wouldn't bring him into this."

"He knows Erin better than anybody. He can get through to her."

"There is not enough room in this family for two fathers...or two husbands. You'd better decide—" He stopped and ran a hand over his face.

Slowly, Kristin got to her feet. "We've been married two months and you're ready to walk out?"

"Hell, no. I'm being kicked out!"

She stared at him, and he stared back. Hurt blazed in his blue eyes, so like Erin's. Catching her breath, Kristin swallowed everything she wanted to say, all the protests, the arguments, the accusations. She'd ruined one marriage. She would not destroy this one as well.

"I'm sorry." And she was. "Of course, you should be the one to deal with Erin. She did this under your supervision. That makes it your responsibility."

Matt eyed her warily. "That's a quick turnaround."

Kristin shrugged. "I was wrong." She crossed the room to stand in front of him and put her shaking hands on his chest. "*You* are my husband, and *you* are the head of this household."

His arms came around her, pulling her close, and his

chest lifted on a deep breath. Under her ear, his heart
beat strongly…for her. He'd survived to come back
home…to *her* and to the child he hadn't known about.
What else could she ask for in life?

She vowed to deserve the gift. Matt should never doubt
again that she loved him, that they belonged together.
And the girls would learn that same lesson. She would
help them…teach them. The health and strength of her
marriage—and her family—was up to her.

From now on, she wouldn't let anything or anyone get
in the way.

IT WAS just a dumb book. Erin didn't really want it. She
didn't know why she'd taken it. Except…

Except that being with Daddy Matt made her want to
do things like that—bad things. Made her want to get in
trouble, any way she could. If she got in trouble enough
when she was with him, maybe Mommy would change
her mind. Maybe Daddy—her real daddy—would come
back.

If Mommy could get unmarried once, she could get
unmarried again, right?

LUKE GAVE UP on sleep Monday morning when an attempt to roll over goaded awake the monster pain in
every muscle of his body. He must be getting old—three
days after the fight in the parking lot, he still hurt. With
a groan, he headed for the shower. Hot water could only
improve the situation.

Standing under the spray, he thought about Sarah.
She'd lost her job because she wasn't ready to work
again. Did *he* have something to do with her decision?
They hadn't made any plans, hadn't defined their connection at all. Luke wasn't sure he knew what to say.

Sarah made his days worth living. She was a reason to go on. What else mattered?

He shoved that question to the back of his head until he'd dressed, downed coffee and a bagel and called Sarah at home.

Her machine picked up, but he didn't leave a message.

On impulse, he dialed Kristin's number next. "What's going on with the Brennan girls today?"

Her hesitation surprised him. "Um…not much. Jenny and I might hit the library after her nap."

"What's Erin doing?"

Kristin sighed. "Erin's grounded, since Friday."

"You grounded a seven-year-old? For what?" The details sucker-punched him. "Erin stole a book? Why?"

"She won't say. But I think she's angry. At everybody."

They'd gone through some counseling sessions. He didn't have to ask what she would be angry about. "We talked to them about telling us how they feel."

"That was before…before Matt moved in. I don't think she feels comfortable talking to him."

"And I haven't been around." Because of Sarah. Or because he'd been too caught up in his own misery to really see what his daughter was going through. "So you set up a consequence for breaking the rules. That's reasonable."

"Actually, Luke—" He heard her deep breath. "Matt handled the whole situation. She took the book while she was out with him. I thought it was right for him to discipline her."

"Oh." His first impulse was a loud protest. He swallowed his pride. "That sounds…okay. Is she allowed to talk on the phone?"

"Only to you. I'll get her."

He only had to wait a few seconds. "Daddy?"

"Hey, Erin Bear. I hear there's been some trouble."
She didn't reply. "You know stealing isn't right. Don't
you?"

He heard a low mumble. "What'd you say, Erin?"

The words came more distinctly. "He made me."

"Who made you?"

"Daddy Matt."

Luke almost laughed. He gentled his voice in time.
"How do you figure that?"

"If you lived here, everything would be okay."

"Erin, if I lived there we'd be fussing about cleaning
up your room and being nice to your little sister. Nothing's perfect, honey. And you know I love you, wherever
I live. Right?"

Her only reply was a snuffle and a sob.

Fifteen minutes later, he hung up the phone. He'd
calmed Erin down, told her she could be mad at him, her
mom, Matt, anybody, but breaking the rules wouldn't ac-
complish anything.

He certainly had the experience to back up that piece
of advice. He'd broken the rules often enough. Marrying
his brother's fiancée had definitely been against the rules,
though he'd done it for the right reasons—because he
cared about Kristin and wanted to give her baby a father.

Which brought him back to the original question on
his mind. He knew exactly what mattered between a man
and a woman who cared about each other. Commitments
and weddings, marriage and family. All the things he'd
thought he had with Kristin—the plans and dreams and
feelings that had crumbled into dust with her first look
at Matt's face after five years.

Now Kristin was, well, fading as a source of pain.
Sarah Rose was a necessary part of his day. A source of

laughter and comfort and desire he'd never expected to find again and was pretty sure he didn't deserve.

That realization only increased his worry about what was going on with Sarah now. She'd called on Friday while he'd still been asleep, too groggy to answer the phone. Her message said she'd be in touch, but she needed some time to think first.

Luke wasn't sure what that meant. Was she reconsidering her job situation? Maybe she'd decided she couldn't afford to give up the career she'd worked toward since high school. Would she have taken off for an assignment on the other side of the world without even saying goodbye?

And what would he do if she had?

No DEADLINES. No pressure. No guilt. After spending twenty-four hours feeling lost and confused, Sarah discovered that life without a job was more comfortable than she'd anticipated. It took her a couple of days to fully realize the truth—for the first time in years, she felt free.

Monday morning, she decided to celebrate at the boardwalk on the beach. Crowded, noisy, garish to the point of bad taste, the oceanfront district in downtown Myrtle Beach was *alive*. Tourists and locals went there for fun and for profit. Why not join the show?

Since she didn't have to, she took her camera along. She snapped babies with their wet diapers dragging in the sand and caught a surfer in midcurl. Two lithe young girls leaning on the rail gave her an interesting shot from the back, their neon bikinis barely covering the essentials. She found a little boy covered head to toe in drips of chocolate ice cream, and an older couple in wide-brimmed hats strolling arm in arm, each one carrying a pink flamingo lawn ornament.

The two rolls of film she'd brought along were used up before she even thought to check how many frames remained.

Back home, she whistled as she climbed the steps. Rounding the corner, she glanced at her doorway. A large, brown paper-wrapped box sat in front of her door.

Sarah slowed down, stopped, a good distance away from the package. Had someone sent her a gift? But who? Most of the people she knew in the world lived right here in Myrtle Beach. Why would they *send* anything? And if not...

Unattended packages often meant death in other parts of the world. She'd covered stories about mailroom terrorism, even gotten an award for her pictures of an embassy secretary blown to bits while slitting open an envelope.

The bright morning turned ice-cold. Could this be a bomb? Was the crazy who'd attacked her before trying a new approach? Should she call the police?

It might have been seconds, or minutes, or an hour she stood frozen, trying to decide what to do. Then, without warning, quick footsteps thudded up the stairs at her back. Sarah spun around, choking back a cry as a shadow fell across the walkway.

"Sarah, I'm sorry." Luke said. "I know you wanted time alone...but I needed to make sure—"

She flung out a hand to stop him. "Don't move. There's a—"

But he'd already seen. His eyes narrowed. He came close and put a hand on her arm—a warm, dry, comforting hand. "Do you know who sent it?"

Sarah shook her head. With a deep breath she turned back to the box and edged a few inches closer, trying to read the label. Squinting, she recognized the logo on the return address sticker before she'd deciphered the words—a capital *E* superimposed on a circle representing the world. *Events* magazine, New York, New York.

She sagged against the nearest wall, embarrassed and relieved. "It's from the magazine. My editor. I—I forgot he was sending a package. Some letters they'd been saving for me."

"Whew." Beside her, Luke propped his hands on his hips and dropped his chin to his chest, rolling his head from side to side. "Getting a box in the mail used to be so much fun—now, unless you're sure you know who it's from, it's just scary."

Sarah stared at him, seeing him clearly for the first time. "Speaking of scary—what happened to you?"

"I ran down a guy robbing a fast-food place." He shrugged, and winced. "The hazards of the job."

She stepped close enough to see all the damage. A bandage across his forehead, another over his ear. Fingerprints on his neck that sent a shudder through her entire body.

Without warning, a picture flashed into her mind—James, in the last five seconds of his life, chasing after a young man who had volunteered information and then chickened out. A burst of gunfire, and the jerk of James's body. Her own high-pitched scream.

"Sarah?" Luke's hands caught her shoulders as she swayed. "You need to sit down." He guided her to her door, shoved the box out of the way with his foot, and then took her keys to open the lock. With an arm around her waist, he eased her inside, toward the couch.

But she recovered enough to move away. "I'm okay. I just—" She couldn't explain.

Behind her, the door shut. "Okay. *I* need to sit." He

went past her to the sofa and eased down with a sigh,
then patted the cushion to his left. "Join me?"

She needed to calm down, first. "In a few minutes?
I've been out in the sun all morning and I'm dying of
thirst. Can I pour you some juice?"

"That would be great." She felt his stare as she bustled in the kitchen. "Where have you been?"

"I went to the boardwalk." After giving him a drink,
she went back for her own, then leaned against the
counter, hating herself for avoiding him. "I shot a couple
of rolls. I haven't got a clue how they'll turn out, of
course."

His gray gaze pinned her down. "What's the problem,
Sarah Rose? What did I do?"

"Nothing!" Oh, God, now she was treating him the
way his family did. Making Luke feel responsible for her
problems.

Still, she couldn't shake the feeling that his life was
really no different than the one James had led. Just as
dangerous—just as deadly.

"Then what's bothering you?"

"I—" She put down her glass and pressed her cool
fingertips to her eyes. "I just didn't expect... You look
so..."

"Rotten? They're just scrapes."

She didn't look up. "How often does this happen to
you?"

"Getting scraped up?"

"Getting choked and beaten."

"I'm a cop, Sarah Rose. The job poses certain physical
risks." She lifted her head to stare at him, and he
shrugged, with another wince. "Every year or so. Or less.
I don't keep count. Most of the time I'm just handing out

traffic tickets and finding misplaced kids.'' He held his hands out wide, grinning a little.

Sarah couldn't return the smile. "And James was supposed to stand on the sidelines taking notes."

His hands dropped. "That's what you're thinking? I'm going to end up like James?"

"No...I don't know." Sarah sighed and put her head back in her hands. "Maybe I'm just afraid that I won't ever get past the fear that you might."

He got to his feet and started across the room. "Sarah—"

The phone rang, and she sidestepped him to answer. "Hi, Kristin. As a matter of fact, he is. Just a second." She extended the phone. "For you."

He managed to take the receiver and get hold of her hand at the same time. "Don't run away," he said quietly. And then, "Hi, Kristin. Everything okay?"

As he listened, his fingers tightened around her wrist until she couldn't have slipped free if she wanted to. But the sudden stillness in his face held Sarah motionless anyway.

"Right. I'll be there in a few minutes. Just hang on." He clicked off, then stood gazing at the handset as if he weren't sure what it was.

"Luke?" Sarah put a hand along his jaw, feeling the heat of scraped, inflamed skin. "Tell me."

"My dad..." He closed his eyes. "My dad got up from his nap this afternoon...and had a heart attack."

WHEN THEY ARRIVED at the hospital, Elena Brennan had found a chair in the crowded waiting room, but both Matt and Kristin were standing.

"How is he?" Luke's hold on her hand brought Sarah

into the family circle with him, though she tried to hang back. "What do you know?"

Mrs. Brennan didn't look up from her hands, held tightly together in her lap.

Matt answered. "Nothing. We haven't heard yet."

"How long has he been here?"

"A couple of hours."

"Have y'all tried to find somebody?"

For the first time, the brothers connected, eye to eye. Matt frowned. "You see what a zoo this place is. Can you do better?"

Sarah felt the tension in Luke's body increase ten-fold. "No. Probably not." He shrugged, then winced. "I just wondered."

"What happened to you?" Kristin, on Matt's other side, peered at her ex-husband. "Did you fall off that crazy bike of yours?" She was teasing, by the glint in her eye...and yet her voice held a note of real concern.

When Luke didn't explain, Sarah did. "He chased down a robbery suspect a few days ago."

Kristin put her hand to her throat. "Are you...are you okay?"

"Yeah. Bruised and scraped mostly."

"The last time something like this happened, you ignored cracked ribs for three weeks and nearly ended up in the hospital with pneumonia."

Sarah glanced at Matt, saw his mouth press into a thin, straight line. His blue eyes, fixed on his wife's face, were dark with pain.

Luke didn't notice. He waved away Kristin's concern. "That was years ago."

"Three."

"I'm smarter now."

Kristin looked him up and down. "I can see that."

"Mrs. Brennan?" They turned in unison to confront a man in surgical scrubs and a white lab coat, with tired eyes and a kind smile. Elena rose and stepped in front of Matt. "Yes? How is my husband?" Her voice was flat with her effort at control.

"We've got him stabilized and resting comfortably. I expect him to recover, though I'm concerned about the damage to his heart muscle."

Matt caught his mother's shoulders as she fell back a step. Elena took a deep breath. "Can I see him?"

"Of course."

Once she'd disappeared, Kristin waved Luke into the vacant chair. "Why don't you sit down before you fall down?"

He shook his head. "You've been here longer."

"I need to call my mother. I threw the girls at her and ran off."

"I'll go with you." Without acknowledging Luke at all, Matt put an arm around his wife's shoulders as they wound their way through the crowd. The possessive message came through loud and clear.

But Luke wasn't watching. Sarah turned to find his gaze on her face. "Then you can sit."

"Not likely. You get the chair, Corporal Brennan. Or else we'll give it to somebody else."

To her surprise, he surrendered. "Okay. I'll sit." But he kept hold of her hand and pulled her to stand between his knees. "Happy?"

"Yes." She gave in to the urge to brush the shiny black hair from his forehead. "It sounds like your dad will be okay."

"Yeah." On a long breath, he dropped his head back against the wall. "One more complication this family didn't need."

"You're strong. You'll all get through this."

"That's just it, Sarah Rose. Each of us is strong enough, alone. But as a family..." He took a deep, broken breath. "As a family, I think we're falling apart. And I don't seem to do anything but make it worse."

"No!" Her denial drew stares from other people in the room. Sarah glanced around and then knelt between his knees, her hands still held in his. "This is not your fault," she whispered fiercely. "Any more than it's Matt's. Or Kristin's. Or your mother's."

"Like I said—maybe everything would get easier if I left."

Sarah opened her mouth to protest, but before she could answer, Luke looked beyond her, toward the door of the waiting room. Mrs. Brennan had returned, white-faced and tight-lipped and looking about a minute from falling down. "Where is Matt?"

Luke helped Sarah up, then stood. "He and Kristin went to call her mom and check on the girls. Is everything okay?"

Elena's stare questioned her son's sanity. "Your father's had a heart attack. No, everything is not okay."

At the harsh reply, Sarah stiffened. Beside her, Luke took another deep breath. "I know that, Mom. I mean, is there something I can do? Can we drive you somewhere?"

Mrs. Brennan looked from Luke to Sarah, and back again. "I need to go home and get your father's things." Her voice suddenly faded.

"We'll take you home and bring you back." Sarah nodded when Luke glanced her way. "Are you ready to leave?"

His mother pressed her lips together. "Yes," she said tightly.

Luke squeezed Sarah's hand. "I'll go get the truck and pick you two up at the front entrance. Give me ten minutes." He made his way to the door with his head held high and energy in his step—as if being allowed to assist his mother were a great honor.

Without really acknowledging Sarah's presence, Mrs. Brennan turned toward the door. Sarah followed in silence.

Out in the hallway, they met Matt and Kristin. Mrs. Brennan explained the situation.

"We can take you home, Mom." Matt put his arm around her shoulders. "On our way to get the girls."

Sarah ached for Luke.

But Kristin intervened. "If Luke's gone to get his truck, that'll be better. The girls would get restless, waiting while you pack the Colonel's bag. Nobody needs to hear Jenny whining today."

Matt and his mother both stared at Kristin with varying degrees of confusion and anger. Sarah could have hugged her.

"I guess you're right," Matt said at last. "Mom, I'll meet you back here when the girls are home."

"Thank you, son." She presented her cheek to be kissed, then made her way to the elevator, leaning on Matt's arm, with Sarah and Kristin in her wake.

Sarah let the distance lengthen. "You handled that well," she told the woman beside her.

Kristin sighed. "I thought I was walking a tightrope before, trying to keep everybody happy. Now I'm... I can't think of a picture scary enough."

"Walking a tightrope over a shark tank? With no net?"

"And somebody's tossed a raw steak into the water." Kristin laughed. "That sounds about right."

Still smiling, they joined Matt and his mother on the elevator. Even Mrs. Brennan's sharp glance couldn't dim Sarah's amusement.

Luke's truck waited at the front door. Sarah climbed into the small rear seat, then Matt helped his mother into the front. "Dad's going to be fine." He put a hand on her shoulder. "Try not to worry."

His mother didn't bend. "Of course." She didn't say a word on the drive across town. Luke didn't initiate a conversation, and Sarah wouldn't have dared.

At the Brennan house, Luke unlocked the door for his mother, then stepped back as she and Sarah entered the foyer. Mrs. Brennan stood still, looking around as if she didn't recognize her own home.

Luke put a hand lightly on her shoulder. "Do you need some help packing? Is there something we can do?"

The narrow shoulders straightened. She lifted her chin. "Not at all. I'll be finished in a few minutes."

She walked toward the back of the house. Her son stared after her. Sarah heard his sigh. "We'll wait for you on the deck."

Outside, Luke was quiet for so long Sarah thought he might have fallen asleep in his lounge chair. She turned her head to study him. Despite the bandages, the ugly bruises and raw skin, he was beautiful. His poor hands were swollen and scraped from fighting, but she didn't doubt their gentleness. This had to be the most caring man she'd ever met.

He turned his head and opened his eyes. "Hi."

She had to smile. "Hi, yourself."

"What are you thinking?"

Sarah felt a blush rise in her cheeks. "Nothing, much. How about you?"

Luke propped his elbow on the arm of the chair and

held out his hand for hers. "Thinking some more about leaving town."

She joined her palm to his. "What about it?"

"How much easier that would be if you came with me."

CHAPTER THIRTEEN

"Luke." Sarah's heart leaped. Then it fell back into her chest with a dull thud. "I don't think—"

He sat up and leaned closer. "We can go wherever you want. Eastern mountains, California beaches, anyplace in between. A cop can always get a job."

That was the first problem. He would expect to remain on the police force. But what kind of partner could she be to a man who risked his life on a regular basis? Whatever nerve she'd possessed had died with James.

He interrupted her silence. "Maybe there's somewhere you need to be for your career. New York? L.A.?"

Problem two. Sarah laughed. "I don't have a career, remember?"

Luke shook her hand gently. "No—I remember that you don't have a job at the moment. You carry your career with you. As long as you're taking pictures—"

"That's just it!" His eyes widened and she lowered her voice. "I'm not taking pictures."

"Sure you are. This morning, you said—"

"Was just…just fluff. Eye candy. Not real photography."

"And what is *real* photography?"

She pulled her hand away from his and went to the deck rail. "Real photography has heart and soul and art, all combined. Like Felix's pictures. Like the pictures

Chuck's been selling. Photographs have to mean something.''

Luke followed to stand behind her, not touching and yet, somehow, she felt his concern like a living current between them. ''Why have you lost faith in yourself? Sarah, your pictures of the girls captured their hearts and souls beautifully.''

Tears stung her eyes. She faced into the wind for an excuse. ''There used to be this—this click inside me, an instinct for the perfect shot. My best pictures weren't posed, or composed. They—they happened. I always knew when I had a good shot. I didn't have to think.''

''And now?''

''Now I have to think. Only…I can't. When I try to compose, analyze, consider…I get nothing. Or else shots anyone who can point a camera could take. I've lost my instinct. And I can't take pictures—can't have a career in photography—without it.''

In the long silence that followed, the pounding of her pulse was louder than the crash of waves on the beach.

Finally, Luke stirred. ''So you can do something else. Teach. Repair cars. Run a Fortune Five Hundred company.''

Sarah looked over her shoulder and saw his eyes laughing, but kind.

''You can do anything you want to do, anywhere…with me.'' He wrapped his arms over her shoulders from behind, surrounding her with his warmth. ''You and I…we're special together.'' His mouth moved against her temple. ''For the first time in two years, I look forward to waking up. I'm actually a human being again. Because of you. I need you in my life.''

Problem three. Not *I love you,* but *I need you.* She

made him feel good and that was enough. Luke wasn't asking for—or offering—love.

Just days ago, feeling good might have been enough for her, too. Enough to make her agree with his crazy plan to leave town together.

But now she had fallen completely in love.

And suddenly, feeling good wasn't nearly enough.

As soon as Sarah stepped away, Luke realized her answer.

"I think…" She ran a finger along the rail of the deck. "I think it's too early to make decisions like this. We haven't known each other very long."

"We knew each other the moment we met."

Sarah shook her head, not looking at him. "Matt said…I mean, you've just lost your family, Luke. You don't need to rush into another…situation."

He barely heard anything after that first word. "What's Matt got to do with this?"

"He suggested—"

Luke turned her around with a hand on her shoulder. "To you?"

"Well, yes—"

"Damn him. He had no right to talk to you about me."

"Luke?" His mother called from the house. "I'm ready to go to the hospital."

"Be right there, Mom." When he looked back at Sarah, she'd started toward the door. If he hadn't known her answer before, he certainly knew it now.

The ride to the hospital was as quiet as the ride home had been. Matt and Kristin were waiting for them outside his dad's room.

"He's resting comfortably. But he wanted to see you as soon as you came back, Mom."

"Of course." His mother brushed a fingertip across her bangs, squared her shoulders, and slipped into the dimness beyond the door.

"We'll take her home," Kristin said. "You both look like you could use some rest and something to eat."

Sarah smiled. "Sounds good."

Luke agreed. "First, I need to talk to Matt a minute. Privately."

His brother raised his eyebrows, then shrugged. "Okay."

"Luke—" Sarah's eyes were wide with apprehension. "Don't you think...another time?"

"No, this is the time." He put a hand on her shoulder. "I'll be back to get you in a few minutes."

The hospital had emptied out since the afternoon. Luke turned into a vacant waiting room at the other end of the hall and closed the door after Matt followed him in.

His brother turned to face him. "So?"

"Just one question— What the hell right do you have to interfere in my life?"

Matt's eyes narrowed. "What the hell kind of question is that?"

"You warned Sarah to stay away from me."

"I thought she should know what she was getting into, yeah."

"It didn't occur to you I might have told her myself? That I had already made sure she knew the score?"

"This is not the usual stuff you share with a woman you're dating." Matt had moved into a defensive position, arms loose, eyes wary.

"And Sarah's not the usual date." Luke balanced on the balls of his feet, bent his knees a little and relaxed his hands. "You've caused enough trouble in my life. From now on, just stay out of my business."

"I'd be glad to—if you didn't keep getting in *my* face. Get a life of your own, why don't you, instead of scavenging around mine?"

Without thinking, Luke drove his fist into his brother's jaw. Matt came back just as fast with his own hit, then grabbed Luke around the shoulders. Locked together, they crashed into a row of chairs. Luke grunted as he fell across the edge of a seat and his bruised ribs took the impact. That pain blended with other hurts as Matt rolled him onto the floor, straddled his chest, and punched him again. Heels digging into the carpet, arms taut, Luke pushed and twisted, but Matt's weight didn't budge.

Matt had always won their fights, won any contest Luke offered. Including their personal family feud.

"Get up!" Kristin's voice was hoarse. "Get off of him, Matt. Now!"

The weight eased off his ribs, and the pain came back. Luke propped himself on an elbow. "I don't need your help, Kristin."

Sarah knelt beside him. "You don't need mine, either. But you two can't do this, not in a hospital with your dad sick down the hall."

As if to prove her point, a security guard stepped in. "Problems, here?"

Luke sat up with a groan. "Not anymore. Sorry. We'll straighten the place up."

"Damn right you will," the guard said. "And you'll pay for breakages, too."

Like little boys, they cleaned up under adult supervision. The damage turned out to be minor—one chair broken and a pile of magazines ripped to shreds. Not even any blood to wipe up.

Then the guard took names, addresses, phone numbers,

occupations. ''The cops versus the Army, huh? Wouldn't like to give odds on that fight.''

Nobody else smiled.

Things went from lousy to miserable when a new voice said, ''What in the world is happening here?''

Luke looked toward the far end of the room to see his mother standing in the doorway. He swore under his breath.

Matt walked over and put his arm around her shoulders. ''Nothing to worry about, Mom. Are you ready to go home?''

She stepped out of his hold. ''You've been fighting. With your father so ill...'' Catching her breath, she looked at Matt. ''Are you hurt?''

''No.''

Then she looked across the room, at Luke. ''Don't I have enough to worry about?''

His whole body must have gone a little numb, Luke decided. The words barely hurt at all. ''I'm sorry, Mom. I hope Dad wasn't upset.''

''Fortunately, your father was asleep when I left. I hate to think how he would feel, if he knew—'' She shook her head. ''I certainly won't make things worse by telling him. But if this is the way you intend to behave, I think it would be best if you didn't visit again until your father is much, much stronger.''

He'd never been officially kicked out before. ''If that's what you want, Mom. Let me know if there's anything I can do.'' He glanced at Sarah's horrified face. ''Are you ready to go?''

Out in the hallway again, Luke headed for the elevator without another word. He concentrated on walking easily and steadily, though his ribs and his hip were killing him and his jaw ached like hell.

Sarah stepped in beside him, and the doors closed. "Are you all right? We can go to the emergency room."

He shook his head, and staggered a little as the walls circled. "I'm fine."

When she didn't answer, he opened his eyes. Her frown was skeptical, angry. But her gaze was worried.

"I'll drive," she said in the parking lot. "Give me the keys." Luke didn't argue, because he simply didn't have any words left.

MATT SPOKE as soon as they pulled out of his parents' driveway. "You might as well comment, before you explode."

Kristin tightened her hands on the steering wheel. "I don't have anything to say."

He eased around in his seat. "You're mad that we were fighting. He punched first, Kris."

"Well, you landed your fair share." She let the subject drop while she concentrated on changing lanes. "What I've never understood is why your mother is so hard on Luke."

Matt stared at her in silence for an uncomfortable moment. "I'm not sure even she knows." His head dropped back against the seat. "He was always a handful, even as a baby. I remember him crying for what seemed like days without stopping. My dad was in Southeast Asia when Luke was born. Mom hired a nanny to take care of Luke, because she couldn't manage both of us on her own."

"Still, he was her son."

"Yeah. But he was so…different, growing up. She never understood what he wanted."

"Did you?" She used every ounce of control she had to sound fair. To *be* fair.

"Not really. I didn't understand why his grades were only average—he's a smart guy. I didn't understand why he always seemed to be in the principal's office for some stunt or the other. And I never understood where he wanted to go with his life."

Kristin stopped the van in their driveway and killed the engine. "Could you...talk to her? She can't keep Luke from seeing your dad."

Matt shook his head. "Nothing I can say will help."

Turning her head, she stared at her husband across the dark car. "Why not? You're his brother—you could defend him."

He gave a short, harsh laugh. "I'm not exactly on his side, Kris. He comes around as often as possible, making sure my daughter never gets a chance to see me as anything more than the man who drove her daddy away. To be honest, I think Mom has some points in her favor."

Everything inside of her urged Kristin to defend Luke. But the risk was too great. If she pushed too hard, this marriage could fail. Losing Matt—*again*—would kill her. She loved him deeply. And she couldn't bear to think of what would happen to the girls. Erin and Jenny had borne so much.

So she sighed and pulled the key free. "We're going to have to get this worked out. For the girls' sakes, if nothing else. They won't understand why Luke can't come to Grandmom's house anymore."

Matt joined her as she walked to the door. "Mom will back down, eventually. She always has. When Dad's feeling better, they'll settle everything."

His arm slipped around her waist, and he pulled her close against him in the shadow of the front porch. "In the meantime, how about a good-night kiss?"

Kristin looked up into her husband's face. His words

and his tone were light. But even in the darkness, his face showed the strain this situation imposed on all of them.

"Only one?" She fought to bring up a smile.

Matt's blue gaze sparked with desire. His grin gleamed white in the night, and he bent closer. "One to start with, anyway."

WHILE LUKE SHOWERED, Sarah made peanut-butter-and-jelly sandwiches for dinner and set them on the table with glasses of milk.

He stopped on the threshold of the kitchen. "Not much food around, is there?"

"Not much. But this beats popcorn and orange juice— my standard diet."

"So if we lived together, maybe we'd eat better?"

Sarah gazed up at him, unable to decide if he was joking or not.

After a look at her face, he raised a hand in surrender. "I take it back. I don't have to be hit over the head, despite what my brother thinks." He sat down at the table, but just stared at the food as if too tired to pick it up.

Sarah played with the crust on her own sandwich. "Your mom will change her mind, won't she?"

Luke shrugged. "Who knows? She's been mad before, but this is a first for me—getting kicked out of the family." He thought a second, then laughed. "What am I talking about? Was I ever really part of the family? Maybe once you kick me out, too, Sarah Rose, I'll really stay gone."

"You have a right to be bitter." She took her hand away from the sandwich—she couldn't possibly put food into her churning stomach. "But *I'm* not kicking you out."

"Not letting me in, either. Did you notice that?" Luke pushed his chair away from the table. "I think we were more in touch *before* we made love."

She couldn't deny the truth. "I'm trying."

"What's there to try? Either you want to be with me or you don't. But you don't have to stay out of pity, or because you want to protect me from my family, or because you think you owe me, somehow. You should be here because that's what you *want,* Sarah. Plain and simple."

It would be simple, if he loved her. "Everything I've done, I *wanted* to do, Luke. I don't pity you, or owe you, and I can't protect you. Maybe we made a mistake in getting so…involved. We could have—*should* have—waited until we knew where we were going."

"Or where we weren't going." He laughed again, completely without humor. "No, I can't go that far, Sarah Rose. I wouldn't have missed being with you even…even if I'd known it would hurt this much."

Sarah would've made the same choice. But that knowledge didn't make anything easier. "I don't have my car," she said, finally. "We left my place in your truck."

"And that answers my other question." Luke stood up slowly. "I'll take you home."

BACK TO the sleepless night routine.

Luke lay on his bed in the dark with the radio on, hoping the noise would drown out his thoughts. Especially his thoughts of Sarah in the dark, her slim, eager body holding his, giving him a glimpse of heaven.

Instead he thought about Kristin, but without pain for a change. Being with Sarah had taken the hurt and melted it into a sweet sadness. Kristin had been a friend, a lover, a wife. Sarah was more, in every way. A true friend, who understood him better than anyone ever had. A lover who seemed to be the other half of himself. So much more than a wife—a mind and a soul he could meet without fear, without pretending, without hiding anything at all.

He'd thought… Hell, he wasn't sure he'd thought at all, when he asked her to move away with him. She'd been through a bad time; he knew she was fragile. And yet he would have sworn Sarah cared about him, cared a great deal. He'd offered her as much of himself as he could…as much as was left. Maybe that just wasn't enough.

Music wasn't helping him get to sleep. He tuned the radio to a talk station, locking on to a weather report. "Tropical Storm Daniel," the announcer said, "located 460 miles southeast of Bermuda, traveling north-northwest at thirty-five miles an hour, with winds expected to be at hurricane force by late tomorrow…"

Oh, good. Just what they needed—a brush with a hurricane. The last few had been predicted to hit dead on in Myrtle Beach, yet had somehow deflected to the beaches in North Carolina. No reason to think this one would be any different.

Except there would be a certain convenience to getting taken out by a storm. At least nobody could claim it was Luke Brennan's fault.

"I THOUGHT you'd skipped town."

"Hello to you, too, Chuck." Sarah stepped into the rear of the photo shop on Thursday and leaned back against the door. "I can't believe this heat."

"It'll break for a while when the hurricane hits."

"What hurricane?"

"Daniel. Headed right for Myrtle Beach." For the first time he looked up from the book in his lap, squinting at her. "What planet are you on that you haven't heard the warnings?"

Good question. "I haven't caught the weather lately." Especially not the past three days, sitting alone in her condo wondering why she didn't simply accept what Luke offered—an intimate, exciting relationship with a really good man, the closest friend she'd ever known. Why couldn't that be enough?

"Been taking pictures?"

Chuck's question brought her back to reality, such as it was. "A few. I thought I'd see what they looked like this afternoon. It's too hot for the beach."

He nodded and turned a page. "I put those last prints you made—the ones from the marsh—on the end of the counter."

"Thanks. I appreciate it." Sarah stepped into the darkroom, clicked on the light, and swung her satchel off her shoulder onto a chair. She pulled out the two rolls she'd shot on the boardwalk and turned toward the workbench, already thinking about filters and framing.

As Chuck had said, her proofs were stacked on the end of the bench. Above them, a chemical bottle lay on its side in an acrid-smelling puddle.

The rest of the puddle had dripped down on the prints. And on the envelope of negatives, placed on top.

"Damn it, Chuck!" She surveyed the mess. "What did you do?"

He bustled in. "What? What are you talking about?"

Sarah presented the pile of ruined photos. "How could this have happened?"

Hands in his pockets, he stepped closer, investigating.

"I guess the top wasn't put back tight on the bottle, and it got knocked over somehow."

"Somehow?" Her face felt hot, her hands were cold. She couldn't remember being this angry in years.

"I haven't used that bottle since I don't know when."

"It just fell by itself?"

"Maybe it did—when a door slammed or a plane flew over or...who knows? If you'd had the presence of mind to take care of your own equipment, there wouldn't be a problem." He muttered under his breath as he turned to leave.

"What did you say?"

"Just that the pictures weren't all that great—you said so yourself. Why make such a big deal?"

Why, indeed? Did it matter what happened to mediocre photographs?

With a sigh, she put on heavy rubber gloves, drew the garbage can over to the bench, and brushed the ruined pictures into it. She picked up the bottle of acid—and stopped, surprised by its weight. More specifically, the lack of weight. When she tipped the bottle over the garbage, not a drop came out. The container had been deliberately emptied.

Sarah let the bottle fall into the trash can. She sponged off the counter and the floor, dried the surfaces with paper towels, and sponged again. With the trash can back in place, she made sure her two rolls of film went back into the satchel, and checked that the negatives of Erin and Jenny at the beach were still in their pocket. She'd left her cameras at home, so the satchel was largely empty. There was room for most of the prints and negatives she'd stored over the years in the file drawers Felix had given her. She took them all, and the tab with her name in his handwriting.

Then she stepped out of the darkroom, the bag heavy on her shoulder, extra files held in her arms.

Chuck glanced up from his magazine, then looked again. His forehead furrowed. "What are those?"

"My pictures, from Felix's files. I'm taking them with me."

"Oh. Okay."

"I won't be working here anymore, Chuck. You deliberately poured acid over my pictures." And maybe Luke was right—maybe Chuck had attacked her, too.

"Are you paranoid, as well as depressed?" He rose out of the chair. "Why would I do something like that?"

"I don't know—I gave up a long time ago trying to figure out what goes on in your mind." She was so furious she didn't have room for fear. "But even using Felix's lab is not worth having you destroy any more of my work."

He gave a snort. "Such as it is."

She might have hit him, if her arms weren't so full—and if Luke's warnings hadn't suddenly taken hold of her mind. "W-whatever." She drew a deep steadying breath. "Send my profit checks to my post office box. If they don't arrive, I'll be sending a lawyer to find out why."

Arms crossed over his chest, he grinned—a satisfied, victorious grin. "Have a nice life."

Sarah looked at him with contempt, and left without another word.

CHAPTER FOURTEEN

AT THE BEGINNING of his Saturday shift, Sergeant Baylor handed Luke an incident report. "Another mugging, same M.O."

"Great." Luke skimmed the report, then rubbed his weary eyes. "Does he have to kill a woman before we get on the ball?"

Baylor laughed. "Hold your horses, son. Criminal Investigations is putting together a sting operation. Women cops with Jeeps, set out as decoys in different parking lots. We'll draw him out."

Luke thought of Sarah's face the night she was mugged. "I hope to hell I'm on duty." Then he pictured Chuck Sawyer's malicious grin. "I'd love to be the one who takes that bastard down."

KRISTIN CALLED Luke on Saturday afternoon. "Your dad's out of the hospital."

She heard him let out a long breath. "That's good. How is he?"

"Pretty strong, actually. His heart recovered much better than the doctor expected. They've sent him back home with instructions for a low-fat diet, exercise and no smoking. I'm sure you can imagine exactly what he says about that."

"Oh, yeah." Luke's laugh was rueful.

Gathering her courage, Kristin prepared to deliver the

real message. "He asked me to call and tell you to come see him."

"That won't make Mom very happy."

"She'll be at church Sunday morning. He wants you to get there about ten." Should she tell him why? The Colonel had taken her into his confidence, told her his plans. And asked her not to tell Luke ahead of time. Or Matt. But what his father had to say would be so difficult to accept… Didn't Luke deserve to be warned?

"I can do that. Thanks for playing go-between. I hope you don't get caught."

"Your mother…" She couldn't find a way to tell him. The Colonel would have to break the news. "You know your mom will change her mind soon. All the worry and stress just—"

"Don't fool yourself. She'd be just as glad if I didn't come back. And I'm thinking about it."

Dismay drove every other thought out of her head. "What does that mean?"

"Just that Matt's probably right. I should get out of the way, let you four get your life started."

"Luke, the girls would be crushed if they lost you!"

"They'd…recover. It's not like I'm leaving them in an orphanage. They've got you. And Matt will do okay, with me gone."

"Please, please reconsider. I don't think—" She hesitated. As the one who had ruined his life, what right did she have to protest if he left? "I—I don't know if I could bear knowing I'd driven you away."

When he spoke, his voice was gentle. "Kristin, you're not driving me anywhere. I'm trying to make some decisions that will be good for us all—you and Jen and Erin and me. And Matt. I'll keep thinking. But that's the way I'm leaning."

After a pause, she said, "What about Sarah?"

"What about her?" He sounded wary, and weary.

"Will she...go with you?"

Luke took a while to answer. "I don't think so."

"She cares about you."

"Yeah, well—"

"You care about her. And I like her. Don't throw Sarah away. Please."

Luke laughed. "It's a little weird, don't you think— managing your ex-husband's love life?"

"Not if he's a good friend."

"Kristin..." He cleared his throat. "Are things working out between you and Matt?"

"They're going to. I'll do whatever I have to as long as Matt's happy."

"What about you?"

Kristin gave him the right answer, the one thing she was certain of. "That's what makes me happy, too."

SNEAKING OVER to his parents' house on a Sunday morning was one of the stranger stunts Luke had pulled in his lifetime. But, in accordance with the orders Kristin had conveyed, he timed his arrival to coincide with church services. An encounter with his mother wouldn't make any of them feel better.

His dad met him at the front door. "Good to see you, son. Come on in." He led the way toward the den, moving better than he had in months. They settled into the pair of recliners at the end of the room. The Colonel eased his chair back.

Luke stayed on the front edge of his seat, with his elbows propped on his knees. "You're looking good, Dad. How do you feel?"

"Much better. Miracles of modern medicine, and all

that.'' He put a hand out, searching over the surface of the table between them. But his fingers found the tabletop empty, and with a sigh he dropped his hand on the arm of the chair. ''Except for the damn pipe. A man shouldn't have to give up his pipe.''

''Better than giving up his life.'' Luke got a steely glance for that one. ''So, what did you want to see me about? Something special?''

The Colonel nodded. ''Go into my study, open the bottom right-hand drawer of the desk, and bring out the book in there.'' He handed over a small brass key. ''Unlock the middle drawer first.''

The bottom right drawer was designed to store hanging files but its only content was one book, resting spine up. Drawing out the volume, Luke realized he held a photograph album. The calico cat-gingham dog design on the cover predicted baby pictures. Ones he'd never seen?

He relocked the desk and carried the book back to the den. But when he tried to hand it over, his father shook his head. ''Sit down.''

Luke sat, feeling his hair stand on end. ''What's going on, Dad?''

''Look at the pictures.''

His chest tightened as he opened the cover. The title page, including date of birth and baby's name, had been left blank. Luke flipped to the first photo sheet and studied the pictures.

After a minute, he got his bearings. ''That's Matt?'' His father nodded. ''And...Mom?''

''Yes.''

He stared at the shots of a young woman with Jennifer's silvery-blond hair worn in bangs across her forehead and curls flipped up on her shoulders. She and Matt were obviously posing at his birthday party—there were pictures of Matt with a cake, pictures of him blowing out the candles, pictures of him on the back of a rocking horse Luke remembered riding himself.

"This is cool, Dad." But what was so important about a trip down memory lane? "How old is Matt in these? Three?"

"Two. Look closely."

Wondering if the heart attack had shorted out his dad's brain circuits, Luke gazed at the photos again. Matt wore a white cowboy hat, boots, chaps and a blue-checked shirt. He'd been a chubby little cherub, for sure. Elena Brennan wore orange—a loose, sleeveless top, since Matt's birthday was at the beginning of September, and shorts in an orange-and-yellow check. An average mom from the early seventies, she looked tan and fit and—

Pregnant. Not a lot, but enough to show. He glanced at his father. "How old did you say Matt is here?"

The Colonel drew a deep breath. "Turn the pages."

More pictures. Matt standing beside a jack-o'-lantern. Matt and his mother at a Thanksgiving dinner with other relatives. "You were deployed for the holidays that year?" Luke didn't look up from the pictures.

"Came home for New Year."

Christmas shots came next, showing Matt as a sturdy toddler with a doll of some kind. "G.I. Joe," Luke wondered aloud. "Cool."

And through all the photos, his mother glowed—beautiful, poised, graceful, even in the last weeks of pregnancy. "Mom sure was gorgeous."

William Brennan's face was grim. "Still is. Keep going."

The baby arrived in winter. Hospital portraits of a scrunched-up face brought back memories of Erin and Jen. A couple of pictures showed his mother standing on the steps of Army post housing, with snow piled up at the sides, Matt in a snowsuit, and a bundle of blanket in her arms that Luke assumed was the baby. Two pages of indoor pictures featured a munchkin dressed in pink for Valentine's Day. Wide dark eyes surveyed the world with serious consideration, and there were dark curls appearing on the bald little head.

But...pink?

Luke glanced at his father, then turned the page. The photos ended with Valentine's Day. The remaining sheets of the album were empty.

He flipped back to the last picture. The print had a year stamped in the margin. Luke focused on the tiny numbers—1965. Three years before his own birth.

He stared at his father. "This is Matt." He tapped the chubby face. "Who..." He cleared his throat and moved his finger over the baby. "Who is this?"

His dad's eyes were clouded with emotions Luke had never seen there before—sorrow and tenderness and deep, aching regret.

"Melody," the Colonel said, barely above a whisper. "Your sister, Melody Ann Brennan."

KRISTIN HAD MADE A Sunday afternoon run to the grocery store, so Matt checked to be sure the girls were safe in the backyard before answering the ring of the front bell. When he opened the door, he wished he'd ignored the summons. "Luke."

His brother looked sick. "We need to talk."

Matt stepped back in silent invitation. Luke went into the living room and turned. "I spent some time with Dad this morning."

"I thought Mom said—"

"He asked me to come."

"Okay, he asked." Standing just on the edge of the room, Matt crossed his arms over his chest. "And?"

"He told me what everybody neglected to mention all these years."

"Which is…?"

"That I was the third child, not the second."

Matt's stomach went hollow, as though he'd been punched. "What the hell are you talking about?"

Luke nodded. "There was a baby between you and me, born in January of '65. She died."

Matt held up a hand. "Wait—Dad told you that?"

"There's a photo album with pictures. I'm wondering why you never mentioned it."

"Because I didn't know!"

"Right." Luke's expression bordered on contempt. "You just missed the whole thing?"

"I guess I did. How old was I, two?" Matt shook his head. "You said—a girl?"

"Melody Ann."

"What happened?"

"Mom went in to wake the baby one morning, and she wasn't breathing."

"Dear God. She must have been devastated."

"According to Dad, she was seriously depressed for over a year. Almost nonfunctional. You had a nanny."

Matt started to shake his head again, then stopped. A face came into his mind—a woman with dark eyebrows, exotic eyes, a faint scent of spices. "I don't know what I remember. Where were we living?"

"Fort Campbell."

He tried to picture the house. "A complete blank. But what difference does this make, anyway? Thirty-five years is a long time ago."

"That's the point." Luke put his hands in his rear

pockets. "Dad was trying to explain why I've been cast as the family scapegoat my whole life."

Matt didn't like the conclusions he was drawing. "A baby died. That's really sad. But what's it got to do with you?"

Luke shrugged. "Mom wanted a girl. Very, very much. And when she got another boy...she went back into depression. I had a nanny, too."

"Oh, come on. We're talking about a rational person, here. She wouldn't...be hard on you just because you carry a Y chromosome."

"According to Dad, she could and did. Do you have another explanation?"

"Hell, I don't know!" Matt had asked himself the question often enough, when he was living at home and trying to figure out his family. "You were always in trouble, always fighting with me or somebody else. Maybe she just couldn't handle that kind of hassle on her own without getting mad. Especially after losing a baby."

"Yeah, well, it's been a long time since I caused any major problems in her life." Luke raised his eyebrows. "What's the explanation now?"

Matt snorted. "A long time? When did you ever stop? You ditched college to take that cross-country bike ride, then entered the police academy, when you knew the parents wanted you in the Army. Two years out of high school, you married *my* fiancée. Had babies with her— not one but two, as far as Mom's concerned. And you haven't stopped causing problems since I got back. I can see reasons for her to be mad."

With Matt's last words, the temperature around them dropped to absolute zero. After an endless silence, Luke took a deep breath. "You really are a narrow-minded bastard, aren't you?"

KRISTIN HEARD the vicious question as she stepped into the front hall. "Luke!"

Matt stalked past her to the front door and flung it open. He glared at Luke. "Get out. Now. You might be welcome in Dad's house. Don't bother coming back to mine."

Kristin put out a hand. "Matt—"

But Luke only laughed. "Fat chance, brother. We drew up a custody agreement, remember? Lawyers and everything. I get to see my daughters."

"I don't give a damn about agreements. Get out."

Luke glanced at Kristin. "Sorry. I didn't come to start another fight. Take care of yourself and the girls." He walked out without a glance at his brother.

Matt slammed the door at his back.

"Mommy?" Erin stood in the door at the other end of the hall, with Jenny just behind her. "Who banged the door?"

With a warning glance at Matt, Kristin went to her daughters. "It was the wind, sweetie. Only the wind."

SARAH HAD JUST split the tape sealing the box from *Events* magazine when the phone rang.

"I need your help." Kristin's voice was low and shaky.

"What's wrong?"

"Luke—"

Sarah's heart stopped. "Is he all right?"

"I think so. But you have to find him."

With a thud, her pulse resumed. "Why? Is it his dad?"

"In a way. They're both okay, physically. The Colonel talked to Luke today and the things he said brought Luke over to see Matt."

"They fought again?"

"Only with words. But he looked so...so wounded, Sarah. I know he cares about you very much. And Luke deserves somebody who puts him first, who cares about him more than anyone or anything. He's never been given that in his whole life."

Sarah closed her eyes against tears.

"I don't know whether you love him that way, that much. But he needs you now." Kristin described the brothers' argument. "He's got to talk to somebody who can give him his balance back."

"I'm not sure I'm the right person." Sarah could hardly force her voice past a whisper.

"I think you're the *only* person. Please try."

Any lingering resentment of Kristin had died somewhere amidst all the heartache and conflict. And Sarah had no defenses at all against Luke in trouble. "Okay. I'll try."

BOTH THE TRUCK and the Harley sat in Luke's driveway when Sarah got there. The house looked lifeless. She took a guess and went through the gate into the backyard.

He knelt beside a tomato plant, gently placing brilliant fruit into a basket on the ground. Sarah's sandals brushed the grass as she came closer and he looked up, then sat back on his heels. "Hi."

She saw immediately what Kristin meant by wounded. His face was calm, yet ravaged. "Hi, Luke."

Luke glanced at the basket. "Want a tomato?"

"Can I have a sandwich?"

He hesitated, still watching her. And then said, "Sure. Come on in."

They made their sandwiches in silence, and began to eat. Sarah waited until Luke had finished all of his before she spoke.

"Kristin called me."

His gaze stayed on the slices of bread he'd taken out of the wrapper for a second sandwich. "That must have been a surprise."

She could feel his resistance like a wave of heat between them. "I'm really sorry about your sister. And that your mother—"

"Losing a child has to practically kill you."

"You were a child, too. A baby."

He shrugged.

"Luke."

He poured more tea into their glasses, still without meeting her eyes. "What's there to say? Nothing's going to change. So we just go on. Matt tells me that's the adult thing to do."

"Matt's got a lot at stake. And he was off balance, just as you were."

"He recovers fast."

"He pretends he does."

Luke shrugged again, then began to make his sandwich.

"Okay, then what are *you* going to do?"

He spread mayonnaise carefully from one crust to the other. "I'm leaving town."

She drew a deep breath against the hollow under her ribs. "Running away?"

"You can call it that." He speared a tomato slice.

"What do you call it?"

"Getting out whole."

"You're not whole."

He flashed her a glance of anger and pain. "You made damn sure of that, didn't you?"

At last, she'd gotten some real feeling out of him. "You're running away from me, too?"

"From where I stood, it sounded like I was asked to leave."

"No, you were asked to wait." As if she'd suddenly taken off a blindfold, Sarah recognized the pattern she hadn't seen before. "But from where *I* stand, it looks like you want everything your own way. And if you don't get it, your solution is just to drop out."

He jerked his head up to meet her gaze, letting the half-finished sandwich fall to his plate. "Did you come here to see me bleed? I've gotta tell you, you're good with a knife."

She ignored his question. "That's the way you deal with your family, isn't it? You decided early on that you couldn't compete on Matt's level. So you went as far in the other direction as you could."

In the fading light, Luke's cheeks flushed a dull red. She waited for his comeback, but instead he got up from the table and went to stare out the window.

She spoke to his back. "When your brother returned from Africa, you decided you couldn't compete this time, either. I wonder if you even gave Kristin a chance to discover for herself which of you she wanted. Or did you just forfeit the game, leaving the field to Matt? And now, instead of staying to deal with the girls, the family situation, or with me, you're leaving. Again."

He braced his arms on the counter edge. "Call me the Cowardly Lion."

"Call you a man who hates to fail, so he just doesn't try."

The muscles in his arms and back tightened. "I've tried with all of them. I tried with you."

"What did you try with me?" Sarah stood up. "Did you risk your feelings? Did you put your pride, your heart, anything at all on the line?"

"I asked you—"

"To go away with you. Why? Because we're friends? Because we're good together in bed? Because I like Harleys? Why Luke? *Why?*"

Luke knew what she wanted. He should just say it— *I love you, Sarah Rose. Marry me, live with me for the rest of my life.*

But he wouldn't. Because she was right—when it came to relationships, he was a coward and a fool. He should never have let himself go this far. Safer for them both to have kept the commitment under control.

To keep his feelings, wants and needs to himself.

"Because," he said finally, "I thought we had a connection that was good for both of us. I thought we wanted the same things. I guessed wrong on that one."

When he turned around, he found her staring at him, her eyes too bright, her face pale with doubt and shock and grief. As if someone had died. "I suppose you did," she murmured.

"Not the first time." He squared his shoulders. "So we'll just say goodbye and let each other go. Send me a postcard some day, from somewhere."

"You're leaving town. Where do I send it?"

Luke tried out a laugh. "You're right. Don't bother." Like someone who'd just been shot, he couldn't actually feel the wound...yet. "I'll be looking for your pictures."

Sarah shook her head. "Don't bother. I doubt there'll be any more." Walking around him, she went to the kitchen door. "Good luck, Luke."

"You, too, Sarah Rose." He didn't turn to see her go. "You, too."

THERE WAS going to be a hurricane, and Erin was going to miss it. She wanted to stay home and watch the weather. Instead, she had to go away with Mommy, Jen, Granddaddy and Grandmom Brennan.

But at least Daddy Matt was staying here. Maybe Mommy would find out she didn't miss him while they were gone. Maybe—

Erin flopped over on her bed and stared out the window at the dark. She had to stop wishing for stuff like that. Nothing was going to change. Mommy would stay married to Daddy Matt.

Which would be…not horrible. He could be okay, sometimes. Of course, he had made her take that stupid book back to the store and give it to the manager and apologize, which had just about killed her.

Then they'd gone to the aquarium—just the two of them. They'd looked at the fish and talked about what kind she would like to have. He worked with her to set up the tank, and helped her pick out three beta fish to live there. Daddy Matt knew a lot about fish. That was pretty neat.

If Daddy Matt stayed, then Daddy wouldn't come back home to live. Liking Daddy Matt seemed unfair to Daddy. But *not* liking Daddy Matt made Mommy unhappy. It made Daddy Matt unhappy, too. He didn't say so. But you could see it in his eyes.

Erin yawned and blinked her own scratchy eyes. Sometimes, even a seven-year-old wasn't old enough to figure out what to do. That's why God created parents, she guessed. So kids would have help with the hard stuff.

And as hard as things had been lately, she was almost glad she had two daddies around—she needed all the help she could get!

CHAPTER FIFTEEN

SARAH SLEPT LATE into Monday morning and did her best not to think when she finally did get up. The present had proved to be an unbearable place, so she retreated into the past.

She finally opened the box Oliver had sent, revealing a collection of letters more than two years old. As Oliver had said, they'd been stuck in a box and forgotten about. Slitting each seal carefully, she drew out thin sheets of paper covered with Felix's spiky handwriting. The notes weren't dated, and the postmarks were often smeared, so she didn't have a sense of when he'd written unless he mentioned her assignment at the time. But the words conveyed his inimitable, irascible tone.

"Tourists driving out the locals. Who do they think will take care of them when we go?" A couple of prints accompanied the note—colorized versions of pelicans against a yellow sky. "Don't like this computer nonsense. Stick w/the darkroom."

A comment on Chuck caught her eye. "Boy never will be any good. He'd be better at selling shoes."

Sarah winced. Maybe she was the one who should be selling shoes.

Prints enclosed with another letter showed her Felix's standard style—a deeply focused realism that turned a mere picture into story, or commentary. One in particular—a shot juxtaposing beer cans and bottles against a roadside tribute to a drunk driving death—caught her attention. She'd seen it before, though she didn't remember where. Not in a gallery, she thought. But she couldn't be sure.

A few letters further, she found another familiar view. By the time she'd reached the bottom of the box, she had twelve pictures she could swear she recognized. Of course, Chuck would say she was simply losing her mind.

Sarah listened to her own thoughts. *Chuck would say...*

Before she could chase down the idea forming in her brain, the doorbell rang. Scrambling up off the floor, she tried not to consider the possibility it might be Luke. Last night's goodbye had been angry, as well as final.

The second-last person she expected to see was Kristin. "Come in. And, please, excuse the mess. I've been sorting some old mail."

Kristin gave her a blank look. "Oh—that's okay." She took a deep breath. "Did you find Luke?"

The one subject she didn't want to discuss. "Yes."

"Did you talk to him?"

"We talked, but I don't think I did him any good. He was still pretty upset when I left."

"But at least you're in touch."

"Actually, we basically said goodbye last night." She moved three days' worth of junk mail out of the armchair and onto the kitchen counter "I'm thinking about leaving Myrtle Beach. My...job here isn't working out."

"Oh. Well..." Kristin gripped her purse a little tighter. "In that case, I have a favor—a really big favor—to ask."

"Sit down and ask." Sarah gestured to the empty chair.

But Kristin stayed on her feet. "The hurricane's

headed straight for Myrtle Beach, and the city is recommending evacuation by tomorrow at noon. Matt and Luke are staying in town to work with emergency services. I'm leaving in the morning with Matt's parents and Erin and Jenny to go up to Fayetteville and wait out the storm. Would you...would you come with us?''

Sarah bit back an automatic refusal. "Why?"

"I—I need some help." Finally, the other woman perched on the edge of the chair. "Mrs. Brennan is tired and worried about the Colonel. She adores the girls—I guess we all know why, now—but they're too much for her these days. I can take care of her and the Colonel. I can take care of the Colonel and the girls. I cannot manage all of them at the same time."

"But—" Sarah couldn't picture herself sharing close quarters with Luke's parents. How could she help? "Your family, friends..."

Kristin shook her head. "My dad and mother are staying to work with the Red Cross. My friends have their own families to look after. I made some calls about nurses to hire, or baby-sitters, someone...but nobody's thinking about a new job with a hurricane on the way. So I have to be there for Matt's parents." Her voice trembled, and she bit her lip. "Erin and Jenny need somebody, too. You're my last resort."

Sarah found herself wavering. At the very least, she would have a place to go during the storm, someone to think about besides herself. Yes, she'd planned to leave town, but a permanent move—packing all her gear, selling or renting the condo—would need more than the twenty-four hours before a hurricane.

More important, Luke had gone out of his way to help her when she'd needed him. Even if she never saw him again, she could return the service by helping his daughters. With them taken care of, he might find a little more peace of mind. With a little more peace of mind, maybe he would realize he should—and could—stay in town. For Erin's and Jenny's sakes. And his own.

"Okay," she told Kristin. "I think I can get my stuff together and the place closed up by tomorrow morning. What time should I meet you?"

They discussed details. And then Kristin gave her a smile, bright, but sad. "I do appreciate this. I don't know what I'll ever be able to do to pay you back."

"No need. I'm the one paying a debt. I'll see you tomorrow at ten."

"Great." She started for the door.

"Kristin?" Sarah gave voice to her second thoughts. "Don't tell Luke I'm going with you."

"But—"

"Please?"

"Okay, if that's what you want." Kristin's expression conveyed doubt and dismay. "See you tomorrow."

"Sure." Sarah closed the door. The deadline had given her a burst of adrenaline. She was compelled to think, to plan, to organize. Clothes, money, cameras and bags would all go with her. She'd need to tape the windows on the condo. Maybe cover the furniture with plastic sheets…

Other details occurred to her, and she realized with surprise that she wasn't falling apart, dithering, or hiding from the situation. She was managing her life, for a change. Maybe there were other decisions she'd be able to make now, other plans she could put into action. But first…

First, she had to go back on her word and see Chuck Sawyer one last time. She had some questions she wanted to ask.

THE ANSWER TO ALL Sarah's questions confronted her as she stepped into the dusty darkness of the photo shop. Three of the prints hanging on the wall were enlargements of proofs in the letters Felix had sent. She could visualize at least two others—including the drunk driving shot—which had been here at some point this summer. Those had no doubt been sold.

Too furious to speak, she put out a shaking hand and let it bounce on the button at the top of the old-fashioned metal bell on the shop counter.

"Coming. Coming!" A puff of air blew the black curtain toward her, and then Chuck appeared. "Can I— Oh." His weak smile disappeared. "To what do I owe this pleasure?"

Sarah knew a moment of fear—was he the mugger? But her anger overwhelmed the thought. This was for Felix. She straightened her shoulders. "Fraud."

"Excuse me?"

"These, Chuck." She swept her arm out to indicate the prints. "You're passing off Felix's shots as your own."

"That's absurd. I've got the negatives in my files to prove I took those pictures."

"And I've got letters from two years ago containing those very same pictures. Letters in Felix's handwriting, with his notes and camera settings."

"So?" He pretended to be cool, but his eyes blinked rapidly. He tapped his elbow with his fingers. "Felix can't use the money. I can."

"As his heir, you could have had the money by selling the pictures under Felix's name! Probably a lot more money, since his work is well-known and collectible. Did you think about that?"

"And share *everything* with you?" His face turned red.

"He gave you half the shop that should have been all mine. I'm his nephew. He gave you the attention that he should have given me. If I sold those prints as Felix's, the will would give you half the profit. Thanks, but no thanks."

Sarah clenched her fists to keep from hitting him. "I want you to stop selling those prints with your name on them. That's not fair to Felix."

"And Felix wasn't fair to me!"

"Maybe not. Maybe he should have left the shop to you alone." Sarah stared at Felix's photographs while she thought things through. Then she faced her so-called partner. "I'm leaving town after the storm, Chuck, and probably not ever coming back. I'll sell you my half of the business."

"Like I have the cash on hand to buy half of this place. The land alone is worth a hundred thousand. Or more."

Sarah sighed. "I don't care about the money. I'll charge you a dollar plus the negatives and whatever prints you've made from them, in return for sole ownership."

He practically bared his teeth at her. "So you can sell the prints and take the money? I don't think so."

"I might exhibit them. I won't sell them. As soon as the hurricane's past, I'll go to a lawyer and get an agreement drawn up that will safeguard your interests and mine."

Chuck gazed at her for a long moment. "Okay, it's a deal."

"Good. You can give me the negatives and prints now."

"Sorry, Sarah, dear." That ugly smile again. "I keep those in a safe deposit box in a bank vault in Charleston. I can't get there until the hurricane's gone by."

"Then I guess we'll have to wait. But remember I've got the proofs, and the letters with camera settings in Felix's handwriting. If you back out, I'm giving all of this to the police."

"That won't be a problem. Anything else?" His face had hardened, every trace of expression erased. Sarah didn't like the change.

"I'm taking these prints with me," she countered, and lifted them off the wall. "I'll call as soon as I get back in town. We can arrange for a contract to be drawn up."

"Whatever." He turned and drew back the black curtain, then looked around again. "You know, if you'd just gone away after you got mugged, we'd both be better off." He disappeared into the back room.

Sarah left the shop by the front door, knowing she would never cross that threshold again. Leaving felt like losing Felix all over again. Where would she go after the hurricane? What would she do? She supposed she'd point the Jeep down one road or the other and drive until she simply couldn't drive any more. It didn't really seem to matter very much where she ended up.

Over the course of the afternoon, the bright blue southern sky had changed to dull, ominous gray. The wind felt hot, heavy. A taste of salt hung in the air, blown in from the ocean just a few blocks away. Traffic was horrendous—bumper to bumper with tourists abandoning their vacations, and locals getting to higher ground.

Sarah headed toward the boardwalk, needing the fresh air to clear her brain. She leaned on the rail, staring at the waves thrashing against the sand and a few surfers who'd ignored police advice to stay out of the water.

Surfers and police…Luke. She should leave him a message to tell him she'd be okay. Otherwise, he would worry, maybe even waste time trying to find her. He was that kind of man.

He was bound to find out later where she'd gone, of course, and with whom. The girls would tell him, if no one else did. She might be forced to see him again, to accept his thanks.

Or maybe not. Maybe he would avoid her as carefully as she was avoiding him. And that would be best for both of them.

LUKE GOT Sarah's message at the end of a long day of emergency organization sessions. "I didn't want you to worry." Her voice on the tape sounded huskier and lower than usual. "I'm leaving town before the hurricane hits—somewhere well inland, safe and dry. I'll take the important stuff with me, so don't worry about the condo, either. Just—just take care of yourself, Luke. Keep safe. Bye."

She seemed to hesitate, and he waited for more. But the message ended with a click.

He rubbed the heels of his hands against his closed eyes. Sarah had said she would go, and she had. A woman of her word, indeed.

And he hadn't used the one word that might have convinced her to stay.

After calling to make sure Matt was out of the house, he stopped by on Tuesday morning to see the girls before they left on their trip.

"We're going on a vacation with Granddad and Grandmom," Erin told him. "We're gonna stay in a hotel with a pool and a playground and everything!"

"Sounds like a good vacation to me."

Jenny climbed into his lap as he sat on Erin's bed. "You come with us, Daddy."

Luke hugged her close. "I would like that. But I need to stay here in Myrtle Beach to help people who get in trouble during the hurricane. Not everybody's leaving, you know."

"Why do we have to?" Erin stuck her lower lip out. "I want to see the hurricane."

"You're going so I won't worry about you and your mom and grandparents. It's hard to work when you're worrying about somebody else. You're really doing me a favor."

Jenny sighed and put her head on his shoulder. Erin went on packing her books, explaining the choices she made. Luke listened with pleasure, and thought again how much he loved these little girls.

"Matt's staying here," Kristin told him as he left. "He's going to board up your parents' house and this one, then volunteer wherever he's needed."

"I'm sure we can use the help."

"Would you—" She bit her lip, then looked up at him. "Would you check on him, when you have a chance? Make sure he's okay?"

Thoughts flew through his head, too fast to get into words. He wanted to laugh, to get mad, to be sarcastic. But the bottom line was that Kristin trusted him, knew she could count on him. And so he would do as she asked.

"Sure. Tell me where you'll be in Fayetteville, and I'll check in as often as I can."

Her smile wavered, but he could see she was relieved. "Thank you, Luke. You're...wonderful."

He reached out and pulled her close for a hug. "You're pretty special, yourself." He dropped a kiss on the top of her head and then stepped back. "Be safe."

"You, too."

Luke drove away with the recognition that the situation with Kristin was…resolved. Somehow, over the summer, he'd allowed their relationship to return to what it had once been—a friendship with the woman his brother loved.

Too bad he'd also chased the woman *he* truly loved completely out of his life.

THE TWO-HOUR TRIP TO Fayetteville seemed endless. Sarah took Erin and Jenny in her Jeep, to keep them from annoying their grandparents.

"Why are you coming?" Erin asked, suspiciously. "My dad said he was staying here."

"Your mom asked me to come to give her some help. She's got a lot to do, taking care of your grandparents and you two."

"But we're the helpers!" Jenny piped up. "She always tells us that."

"I know you are. But she might need some grown-up help, too. And with your dad and…Matt…busy with the storm, I'm going along to be that help."

"You aren't part of our family," Erin muttered.

"No." The rain had started, blowing from the east, a heavy dark curtain around the car. Sarah flipped the defrost fan higher. "But I hope I'm at least a friend."

"Do you tell stories?" Jenny asked.

Sarah smiled. "I haven't had much practice. You're the first children I've known well."

"So tell us one now. Then we'll know." A whisper from Erin drew the little girl's attention. "Yes!" she whispered back, loud enough to be heard. "I want a story." She changed her voice. "Go ahead, Miss Sarah."

"Hmm." Sarah tried to remember fairy tales. "Once upon a time…"

"See," Jenny whispered. "She starts right!"

"It's the end that counts," Erin replied.

Sarah made a mental note—*happily ever after.* "Okay. Once upon a time, there was a great big bear. A very tall bear, with shaggy brown fur and long, long, claws, and huge, sharp teeth."

"Stories are supposed to have people," Erin commented.

"Shh!" her sister ordered.

"This bear lived in a big, dark cave...."

She talked for the better part of the drive, telling the story of Zander Bear, a handsome prince caught under the spell of a fairy until he had saved three lives, and Persis, the lovely young woman who wandered into his forest, and nearly got eaten by the bear.

"He saved her life," Erin announced. "Two more, and he can be a prince again!"

"Who else did he save, Miss Sarah? Who?"

"She'll tell us," Erin assured her sister. "Be quiet."

But they had reached their destination. The turn signal blinked on Kristin's green van just ahead. "We'll find out later," Sarah said. "I think we're getting out."

Erin moaned. "Not now!"

But in the back seat, Jenny wriggled. "I have to go potty."

Sarah laughed. "Then we definitely need to stop!"

EMERGENCY PLANNING sessions and a volunteer job assisting city government preparations for the storm kept Matt busy right up to the time Kristin and her caravan drove away. He breathed a sigh of relief, knowing they'd be well inland in just two hours. Hurricane Daniel would come ashore about midnight, according to the forecasts.

In the meantime, Matt had two houses to get ready for the storm.

The rain started as he worked, soaking through his jacket in a matter of minutes. After a couple of hours the wind rose. The metal ladder got slippery, and he wished for the old wooden model he'd used as a kid.

He remembered the hurricanes he and Luke had witnessed in the early years after moving to the beach. They'd always hoped for something exciting, some adventure they could enjoy. Luke had studied weather and tides—he'd tracked the hurricanes and made pretty good predictions. As the eye of the storm passed over, they would go outside, despite their mom's protests, to watch the sky and survey the damage. Broken limbs and toppled trees didn't matter much to adolescent boys.

What had happened to that friendship? What had come between them?

Still thinking about the past, Matt put his tools and the ladder in the back of his truck and finally got out of the rain for the drive to the house he and Kristin shared. Branches had started to snap by the time he got there, so he pulled the truck into the garage to spare the paint as much damage as possible, closing the door to keep water out.

The rain worsened as he worked. Darkness would come early under the black skies. He tracked water into the house to turn on the floodlights, wishing the place had fewer windows.

The ladder swayed under him as he climbed, less from his weight than the push of the wind. Lightning cracked in every direction, and thunder shook the windowpanes. The air felt warm, but Matt was chilled by the rain. If only his hands would continue to function.

He saved the western windows for last, figuring they'd

be the most protected from the wind, the easiest to handle when he was just about exhausted. At the bottom of the ladder, he wasn't sure about that plan anymore. His feet ached from the hours standing on metal rungs. His hands were blistered under the wet gloves he wore. Maybe he could leave this side open—the wind would come from the east, right?

But the west windows looked into Jenny's room and the bathroom she shared with Erin. If he could do anything to keep the girls from being hurt, even if that meant just keeping their stuffed animals dry, then he would. Three more windows. Just three more.

Matt hoisted the plywood sheet and started up the ladder. He lost his footing twice, and the last time came down hard, banging his kneecap on the rung. Hissing with every step, he inched up to the window, fought the plywood into position, put a few nails between his teeth, and pulled his hammer out of his belt.

With one edge of the sheet left to nail, the wind pushed him sideways. Matt grabbed with both hands at the top rung. His heart pounded to a stop as his grip slipped, then caught. He hung there for a while, trying to get his breath back.

And then he realized he'd dropped the hammer.

He cursed all the way down the ladder, using words he'd learned in the Army but rarely used. He couldn't see with the rain in his eyes, and got down on his hands and knees under the ladder to feel around for the missing tool. If he could just get his hands on the damn hammer...

"Yes!" he crowed, as his fingertips touched the claw. He crawled closer, grabbed the whole hammer, and reared back. Kneeling underneath the ladder, aching in every bone and sinew of his body, he struggled to catch his breath.

In front of him at the corner of the house, lightning ripped down a tall pine tree, which exploded into light and flame with a gut-wrenching *boom*. Matt watched in awe as the trunk split into two straight pieces. Flaming pine needles floated through the air, followed by limbs lit like torches. The halves of the trunk held upright for an eternity. And then, pushed by the wind, they started to fall.

Matt scrambled to his feet, slipping in wet pine straw and grass and mud. He heard the pine tree crack at the base as the two pieces broke off. He ran in the only direction he could—toward the backyard gate.

Near the back corner—three feet from safety—he stepped into the center of a coil of garden hose, unseen in the darkness. The loops caught at him like snakes and he tripped, then fell. Swearing even harder, he pushed himself out of the mud onto his hands and his knees.

Driven sideways and down by the force of the falling tree, the ladder hit him across the hips. Stubs of broken branches sliced into the ground beside him. The tree itself slammed onto his head, and Matt went down without another word.

CHAPTER SIXTEEN

LUKE SPENT the night of Hurricane Daniel running emergency calls until the phone lines went down. After that, he patrolled the streets in a cruiser, noting damage sites and looking for victims. The areas closest to the beach had been completely evacuated, down to the gentle old woman and the cats she wouldn't leave behind. Farther inland, more people had stayed. As the winds screamed higher, some of them panicked and tried to leave.

A van tipped on its side in a shallow ditch filled with water turned out to be a mother and her family heading for a shelter at the last second. Luke pulled five kids from the back, three of them still in car seats, the others in seat belts, thank God. The shaky mom sat in the back of the cruiser and cried.

"My husband's with the power company." She took the tissue Luke offered. "I thought I could stay home without him, but it's so *loud*. I was afraid for the babies, if the trees came down."

"We'll get you to a shelter, and you'll all be fine. And I'll leave a message for your husband about where to find you."

She smiled gratefully. "He worries."

Luke turned around and put the car in gear. "Don't we all?" he said, under his breath.

Daniel's eye passed through at 4:00 a.m, with a silence that seemed worse, somehow, than all the noise that had come before. The clouds drew back, and stars were visible. Luke found a homeless man rolled up in the corner of a parking garage and took him to safety. There were so many downed trees and power lines, so many houses with limbs and whole trunks crashed through the roof, that he narrowed his list of reports to only the most critical situations—arcing electricity and dangling branches about to fall.

Then the wind returned, and the rain. The streets filled with sea water and sand—Highway 17 in downtown looked like a quick-flowing creek. On a detour to reach the station, Luke drove past a completely demolished home—four trees had fallen from three different directions. But what first caught his attention was the dog standing on its hindquarters inside the fence.

He stepped out of the cruiser into calf-deep water and approached the house, shining his flashlight through the wrecked windows. "Hello! Anybody home?"

No one answered, and there were no cars in the drive. Easing his way across the splintered porch, he found the front door locked. Luke circled the house, looking through windows, searching for signs of a human being. He finally decided whoever lived in the house had evacuated.

And left their dog tied to the fence.

Just a puppy, he saw as he approached. A puppy that would become a big dog, judging by the size of his feet.

"Hey, there, buster." The dog licked the hand Luke held out and wiggled his whole body, despite the shakes that consumed him. "You look like a Buster. Bet you're cold out here in the rain. Let's get you loose." The knot around the chain link of the fence was wet and tight—Luke gave up right away, wrapped the rope around his hand, and cut through with his knife. The dog yelped and lunged for freedom.

"Whoa, whoa." His arm felt jerked out of the socket. "Not that way, boy. Head for the car."

Buster jumped eagerly into the back seat of the cruiser, behind the grill. Luke gave a thought to the upholstery and shrugged. The department would have to deal with it.

After taking Buster to the animal shelter and telling the folks there that he would be back for him later, Luke rode by Kristin's house. He could see from the curb that Matt had been there—the windows and doors were boarded, everything locked up nice and tight. They'd lost a big tree at the corner—a lightning strike had split the old pine in two. Fortunately one half had fallen out into the empty yard, and the other lay beside the house wall. No damage that a little chain saw work couldn't handle.

The radio blared, describing accelerating winds, already up around ninety-five miles an hour, ordering any units out in the open to take shelter. Luke got himself back to the precinct to wait out the rest of the storm.

By 9:00 a.m. Hurricane Daniel had finished with Myrtle Beach. The clouds rolled off to the west, leaving a sunny, muggy day. People appeared in the streets, examining fallen trees and power lines and wrecked cars, flooded highways and shattered windows. Luke had his hands full keeping the crowds a safe distance away from live electrical wires.

He came off duty at noon. As he dropped into the chair at his desk, the phone rang.

"Brennan."

"Luke, it's your father."

He sat up straighter. "Everything okay? Y'all got there safely? The girls are all right?"

"We're all fine. There was wind and rain, but we didn't even lose power." The Colonel hesitated. "Have you talked with Matt?"

Damn. "No. Have you?"

"No. He told Kristin he would check in, but…"

"If he's been as busy as I have, he hasn't had a chance. The storm's only been gone a little while."

In the background he could hear his mother's voice. The words weren't clear, but the tone said enough.

The Colonel cleared his throat. "Would you locate him for us? We're pretty concerned—Kristin really did expect to hear something before this."

"I'll call the station he was working with right now and get back to you as soon as I can. It may be an hour or so, depending on who's on duty and who knows what. Don't panic."

"We'll stay calm." The line went dead.

Luke stared at the receiver. "Yeah, I'm fine, Dad. Thanks for asking." He dropped the phone on the desk, suddenly exhausted beyond belief.

After a refill on his coffee, he dialed the fire station Kristin had told him Matt would work out of. He got the captain on the line, first try. "I'm trying to locate Lt. Colonel Matt Brennan. He was volunteering with your team during the storm."

"Yeah, we coulda used him." The captain sounded even worse than Luke felt. "We've had some serious injuries, coupla fires, and there's no electricity for five square miles."

The coffee settled like molten lead in Luke's stomach. "You *could have* used him? What does that mean?"

"It means I haven't seen him since the last plannin' session, day before yesterday. However Brennan decided

to weather that hurricane, it sure as hell wasn't working
with my crew!''

"LUKE HASN'T SEEN Matt, but he'll find him.'' Colonel
Brennan's report failed to reassure anyone. Kristin lost
what little color was left in her face.

With a glance into the next room where the girls
watched television, Sarah pulled the adjoining door
mostly closed. "Is Luke okay?"

"He hasn't checked on Matt at all?"

Sarah's question clashed with Mrs. Brennan's and got
lost.

"He's had his hands full.'' Colonel Brennan sat in the
room's only armchair and propped his slippered feet on
the bed. "He said he would get right back to us as soon
as he found Matt.''

"Is Luke okay?"

The repeated question received a puzzled stare from
the Colonel. "I was thinking about Matt…I didn't ask.
But he sounds fine. He would have said something otherwise.''

Sarah glanced at Kristin, who met her gaze, then
looked at her father-in-law. "Would he?"

"I think you're overreacting, Kristin.'' Mrs. Brennan
went to the sink for a glass of water. "If Luke had been
hurt at all, he would have said so. William, it's time for
your medicine.''

Sarah spoke without a second thought. "Are you
sure?"

Mrs. Brennan didn't answer while her husband swallowed his pills. When he leaned back with his eyes
closed, she took the glass to the sink, then looked at
Sarah.

"I may have been…overly harsh recently, as far as

Luke is concerned. But I do care about his safety. I believe he would have told his father if something serious had happened to him. Since Matt is the one missing, I think he's the one we should be worried about." Mrs. Brennan's blue gaze was both stern and confident—she didn't expect any argument.

Kristin drew a deep breath. "We'll let you both get some rest," she said.

Sarah followed her through to the other room, but paused on the threshold. "Please tell us when Luke calls back." Before the Brennan parents could answer, she closed the door. Completely.

Kristin sank onto the bed they shared, her lower lip caught between her teeth, her hands clutched tightly together.

Sarah made a quick decision. "Erin, Jenny, do you want to hear more about Zander Bear?"

"Oh, yes!"

"Then let's turn off the TV and go outside for a while. The playground is shady and we can sit on the swings to tell the story." She glanced at the girls' mother and got a grateful, though shaky, smile in return. "We'll be back in a little while," she promised. Picking up her camera bag on the way out, she herded Luke's little girls down to the playground.

Inside the gated park, under the tall pine trees, Erin took the middle swing of the set while Sarah pushed Jenny gently on another. "Tell more, tell more," the four-year-old pleaded.

Sarah continued the story of Persis and Zander with the rescue of a jaguar cub clinging to the edge of a high cliff.

"That's another life," Erin crowed. "He's saved two lives now!"

"He has, indeed." Sarah stepped back from the swings and eased her camera out of its case. "Do you guys mind if I take some pictures? I bet your dad would like to see what you did while you were here."

Erin and Jenny both got a little silly, trying to outdo each other in posing for the camera. But in between the silliness, when they were distracted by the sheer fun of being little girls, Sarah caught some great shots. She would send them to Luke, as... As a message she couldn't quite put into words.

MATT AND KRISTIN'S house was far enough inland to have escaped the storm surge which had sent an ocean of water crashing into buildings along the beachfront. There didn't seem to be much more damage than he'd seen last night.

Luke picked his way through fallen branches to the red front door. No one answered his ring, or his knock. Matt's truck wasn't parked out front—he might have pulled into the garage for safety. But there were no windows and Luke didn't know the code to open the doors. Besides, even if his truck was in the garage, Matt wouldn't be holed up inside, taking care of himself. He just wasn't the type.

So where was he?

The swing set in the backyard had been toppled, but seemed to be intact. The metal awning from another house had been tossed onto the deck, but Matt had boarded the windows there, too, and nothing looked broken.

That big pine tree struck by lightning had crashed the fence on the side of the house. The thick green needles blended with chips and shards of cedar fencing. Luke stepped over for a closer look at the damage...and saw the rungs of an aluminum ladder woven into the downed branches.

Please, God. No.

"Matt?" He cleared his throat to make the word audible. "Matt, are you in there?" There was no answer. But Luke thought he saw a branch shiver. "Matt?"

Still no reply, and he couldn't get close enough from this side to see anything underneath the trunk. He sprinted through wet grass across the backyard and around the front of the house until he came to the felled pine. "Matt?"

This time, he heard a groan. And he definitely saw a sheaf of pine needles quiver. "Hang in there, bro. I'm gonna see what I can do."

But that wasn't a hell of a lot. He tried shifting the tree trunk by himself, but got nowhere. The ladder was wedged too tight to use as a lever. He wasn't going to be able to do this by himself.

"Matt, I'm gonna get help. If the cell phone works, I'll call. If not, I'm going to have to leave. But I'll be back. Just...just hang on. I *will* be back and we'll get you out of there."

Luke thought he heard another groan in response.

Of course the cell phone wasn't working—the wind would have taken down all transmitters for miles. He made slow progress around fallen trees and flooded streets toward the nearest fire station, but the best help he could get was to put Matt at the top of their priority list. Rescue could still be hours away—other people around town were facing equally tough situations.

Back by the tree, Luke tried feeling through the needles for any part of Matt he could reach. "Are you there, Matt? Can you talk to me?" He inched forward, into the thickest tangle of branches. "I'd really appreciate hearing from you."

"This," a breathless, strained voice said, "is not a good time to talk."

Luke went dizzy with relief. He blinked back the sting of tears. "I don't know—it's not often I have you at my mercy. Maybe I could win a point or two for a change."

"Not…likely."

"Can you give me a status report?"

"I'm flat on my face in the grass with a tree on my back."

Luke gave that comment a bigger laugh than it deserved. "More specifics, please. Pain?"

"Hell, yes."

"Blood?"

"I can't exactly turn to see, but I don't think any major blood."

"Can you move fingers, toes?"

The moment of silence following that question stopped his pulse.

"Yeah," Matt said finally. "Hurts like hell to move my left hand—I'm thinking there's a break somewhere."

"If that's the worst, we're doing okay." Luke probed the greenery, surrounded by the sharp scent of pine, his hands covered in sticky sap and jabbed with aptly-named needles.

Matt cleared his throat. "What…brought you here?"

"A phone call from the Colonel, of course. You didn't check in, and they sent me to find out why." Finally, he saw khaki slacks underneath the green.

"Good thing."

Luke eased several broken branches out of the way, working up toward Matt's head. "Could have been a long wait, otherwise."

"Already has been."

"What time did this happen?"

"Before full dark."

"Damn. But you always did like sleeping outside."

"Not…in a hurricane. Under a pine tree."

"No, I guess not." The plaid of Matt's shirt appeared, and his left arm, twisted at an impossible angle. One more big limb slid to the side…revealing the back of his brother's head. Luke let out the breath he'd been holding. "There you are. Can you open your eyes?"

With a groan, Matt turned his head and Luke saw one blue eye open. "I can't…stay like this too long. The twist hurts."

"Okay, just relax. I don't need to stare at your ugly face, anyway. I've got a thermos in the truck. Do you want a drink?"

Matt turned back. "I've had plenty…of water, thanks."

The situation, as far as Luke could see, was not going to be solved without a crane, or at least a chain saw. Matt had been saved by the falling ladder and the fence, which kept the majority of the tree's weight off him. But some of the thickest limbs of the pine tree remained unbroken. He didn't dare try to saw those off without help.

He placed two fingers at the angle of Matt's jaw, found the pulse strong, steady, a little fast. "The rescue squad will get here as soon as they can. You're at the top of the list."

"Can't be as long as it has been."

"Your house looks okay. Not much damage. Kristin will be pleased." He settled as comfortably as possible into the nest of needles.

"Good."

"They all got to Fayetteville safely, by the way. Dad sounded fairly strong."

"Good."

"Are you cold? Can I get into the house for a blanket?"

"Not without...keys...underneath me. I'm okay."

Luke was quiet for a minute, listening, praying for the sound of a fire truck arriving. When his hopes died, he said the first thing that came to mind. "I'm going to relocate."

"Where?"

"Not sure. Somewhere fairly close, to begin with. Once the girls are...settled...I can get farther away."

"Don't do me any favors."

"Not you. Kristin. Erin and Jenny. I...held on too tight."

Matt didn't say anything for a long time. Luke stirred uneasily. "You there?"

His brother ignored the question. "Leaving is...a... bad idea." He paused. "This is your home."

Luke winced at the strain in Matt's voice. "We can talk about it tomorrow."

"Now. Whatever we...screwed up can...be fixed. I can't talk for...Mom—" Matt drew a breath Luke could hear "—but...we're family. Need to act...that way."

Luke didn't know what to say. "Sure, bro. You're the boss."

He heard Matt chuckle. "Don't...forget it."

They talked sporadically for the next two hours, as the sun peaked and then started toward the west. Luke even dozed occasionally, but his head kept dropping and waking him up. "Matt?"

"You...snore."

"Like you didn't, all through high school."

At four, Luke decided he'd have to go for help again if something hadn't changed in an hour. Lucky for the fire captain, his truck arrived with ten minutes to spare.

The firefighter's first comment was rude, but to the point. "This is gonna be a hell of a job."

Luke had used up his store of patience. "So let's get started."

SETTING THE TACKLE properly took forever. Until the tree was supported and certain not to drop back onto Matt, no lifting could take place.

The firefighters were stretched thin, and Luke pitched in to help. He struggled with the heavy chains, carefully sliding them under the trunk, sometimes digging down into the earth to get enough space.

"Sorry about the gouges in the yard," he said. "Y'all might need to resod."

"I'll...worry...about that...later." The weariness, the faintness of Matt's voice worried Luke. He'd been lying in the wet grass for almost twenty-four hours. Even a strong man like Matt couldn't hold up indefinitely.

"Okay." The team leader surveyed their work. "If we winch it up a ways, we oughta be able to cut some of those branches off. Then we can pull the trunk up far enough to get him out."

Luke knelt by Matt. "Prepare to be rescued. We're gonna hoist this sucker off your back."

Matt blew out a long, shuddering breath. "I'm ready and waiting."

"Hang in there."

Luke retreated to a safe distance. The winch engine ground into operation. With a clatter of gears, the giant pulley began to turn. Chains rattled, then tightened, biting into the trunk. Groaning, the pine lifted. Daylight showed between the tree and the ground.

The urge to run back and drag Matt out from under the horror was overwhelming. Pulse pounding, Luke stayed where he was. A plan was in place. He'd only foul things up if he tried to change anything.

But God, he wanted his brother out of there.

Though the winch engine droned on, the chains stopped moving. The three firefighters stood on either side of the tree, considering. Luke came close in time to hear the bad news.

"That big limb's already cracked. We can't use the saw that close. We lift the tree too far, the limb's gonna break off and land on his head."

He could see what they meant. One of the thickest and longest branches had fallen under the trunk, cracking away in the process. Luke could see the fiber of the tree at the break shredding under the limb's weight. If they didn't hurry, it would collapse anyway.

"You need a brace," he said. "Something to prop that branch while you lift the trunk."

"Any regular brace'll fall off, we get the tree high enough."

"Then you need one that will adjust."

"What kind is that?"

Luke drew a deep breath. "Me."

CHAPTER SEVENTEEN

THE TRICKY PART was crawling underneath the trunk.

Luke took one more extra breath, then lay down on his back in the sodden grass. The firefighters had sawed off as many branches as possible. They couldn't clear a way in, so the rest was up to him.

He felt the trunk sway as he went underneath. Somewhere a branch cracked—he could only pray it wasn't the one he was heading for. Digging in with his elbows and heels, he inched his way through the pine tree. His hair caught on twigs and on sap. Pinecones and needles scraped his face. The pungent smell of evergreen made him dizzy. The air seemed to close down.

He came up alongside Matt's legs. "It's me," he said, feeling for broken bones.

"Kristin…won't be…happy…if that tree falls on…both of us."

"Not gonna happen, bro. We'll have you out in a flash."

With the words, he slid into place under the broken limb. It rested on his chest as he inched further in. He set his elbows on the ground, wrapped his hands around the sticky bark, and lifted slightly, feeling the looseness in the cracked joint. This branch would not last long.

"Okay," he called. "I'm here. Let's do it."

"Right."

The winch motor revved up. Above him, the tree trunk

shuddered, swayed. For a moment, the branch in his hands got heavier.

Gradually, the pine needles lifted off his face. Luke sucked in a great gulp of fresh air, then extended his arms as the branch he held lifted, too. Higher still, and his elbows straightened, hyperextended, his shoulders taking all the strain. The trunk inched up yet again.

With a sound like a shotgun blast, the big branch broke away, its entire weight coming down on Luke's two arms.

He cried out as his arms took the load. Shoulders forced into the ground, teeth gritted, he panted for breath and prayed for strength.

"Luke?" Matt's voice came from very close by. "You okay?"

He couldn't answer, couldn't release his jaw to form words.

All around him needles rustled. "Let's get you clear, Matt," a voice said. "You just relax. I'm gonna hold up this ladder, and the other guys'll pull you out. Don't you try to help."

With his eyes closed, Luke heard heels drag through the grass, and Matt's sharp intake of breath.

"Poor guy," a firefighter said. "Finally passed out. The rest'll be easier that way."

"Now what about you?" the same voice asked a little while later. "Ready to let go of that monkey bar you're holding?"

All Luke could manage was a hiss.

The firefighters wrapped the branch with tackle and raised it farther, using the winch. Releasing the weight hurt. Luke's arms collapsed across his chest, afire at both shoulders. Tears came to his eyes, and he bit his lip. Now was not the time to give in.

"You okay, son?"

When he looked up, he saw the team leader and, behind him, a star-spattered sky. "Getting there," Luke conceded. His voice didn't sound much better than Matt's had. "But you'll need to help me up."

Once on his feet, he went to find his brother. Matt lay on a stretcher at the door of the ambulance. Stiff, tired, hurting, Luke limped over and looked down into his brother's bruised face.

"Next time take on a dogwood tree," he advised. "They're smaller and easier to move."

The blue eyes opened. Matt looked at him for a second, then raised his right hand. "Thanks, Luke," he said. "I'm grateful."

Despite the pain, Luke closed his palm to Matt's. "Anytime." He wanted to say more, but couldn't. "I'll be right behind you in the truck. Meet you at the hospital."

"Not exactly," the EMT said. "We got a gurney for you, too."

Luke shook his head. "I'm okay. I need to—"

"No arguments. Lie down."

Now that he thought about it, he was a little dizzy. But he had to reach Kristin. "Look, I'll get checked out later. I have to make a phone call."

"If you don't lie down on your own, I'm..."

The voice started out strong. But the roaring in Luke's ears got louder and louder, drowning out what the EMT said. As the night turned white around him, he braced a hip against the stretcher. "You know, I think I will sit—"

Those were the last words he spoke for quite a long time.

THE PHONE WOKE them all at 7:00 a.m. "Kristin?"

"No, it's Sarah." She sat up straight in bed. "Matt?"

"Yeah." He sounded incredibly weary. The door between the two rooms opened—the Colonel stood there, a question in his eyes. Sarah passed the phone to Kristin, kneeling on the bed, her brown eyes wide and bright with moisture.

"Matt?" The one word wavered and broke. As she heard his voice, Kristin's eyes closed, pressing tears onto her cheeks. "Are you okay? Is Luke okay?" She looked at Sarah with a giant grin and nodded. "They're fine," she mouthed. "He'll be here by noon."

Choking back tears of her own, Sarah herded Erin and Jenny into their clothes and out to the nearest pancake house for breakfast, leaving Kristin the privacy to celebrate her husband's safety.

Right at noon, a knock sounded on the door of Colonel and Mrs. Brennan's room. Mrs. Brennan squeaked. And then she started to cry.

Scrambling off the bed, Sarah joined Kristin at the door between the two rooms. When she looked around the corner, Matt's big frame filled the outside doorway. He had one arm in a cast and the other around his mother as she sobbed on his chest. "I didn't mean to worry you," he was saying. "I ran into some...uh...delays."

Beside Sarah, Kristin swayed, and started to sink. Sarah caught her—and then Matt was there. "Kris, sweetheart, it's okay. I know you were worried—but I told you I wouldn't get lost again...." Murmuring into her hair, half carrying her, he took his wife into the other room.

At the same time, the little girls slipped past Sarah in a rush. "Daddy, Daddy!"

She was almost afraid to look. But Erin was right—
Luke stepped in through the open door.

"Hey, Erin Bear. Jenny Penny." He knelt with a wince
and put an arm loosely around each daughter. "Having
fun in Fayetteville?"

Then Luke looked up from the girls' bright faces...and
saw Sarah. His eyes widened, dark with emotions she
was afraid to believe. He dropped his chin to his chest,
and blew out a long breath. When he looked at her again,
his face had lost the strain he'd come in with.

"I didn't know you meant you'd be *here,* Sarah
Rose."

"Kristin...asked for some help."

He nodded, carefully. "Thanks."

She shook her head. She didn't want gratitude.

"I would like to be told exactly why we've been waiting here in agony for twenty-four hours." His mother's
soft accent was thick with displeasure.

Luke got to his feet, walked to the nearest bed and sat
down with a daughter on each knee. "Matt was under a
tree that had fallen. It took until after dark last night to
get him out."

"And you couldn't call then?"

"Calm down, Mom." Matt stood behind Sarah in the
doorway to the other room, with Kristin still held tight
in the circle of his good arm. Sarah stepped aside to let
them through. "We both spent the night in the hospital
with concussions. Neither of us was in much shape to be
making phone calls."

Sarah watched him drop a kiss on Kristin's upturned
face, and couldn't help a glance toward Luke. His expression didn't change—was he simply too weary to react
to the couple's intimacy?

The Colonel spoke for the first time. "You didn't say you'd been hurt yesterday, Luke."

"No, sir. I'm not. Just a little stiff from dragging branches off Matt."

"Your father stayed awake all night, which is terrible for someone as ill as he's been." Elena Brennan stepped behind her husband and put her hands on his shoulders. "I would think—"

"Enough." Matt stepped forward, a tone of military command in his voice that sounded very like his father's. "You're out of line, Mom. Again. Open your eyes and really see what's going on—for the first time in almost thirty years."

"I don't know what you mean, Matthew. Your brother—"

"Your *son*, Mom. Your other son, who wasn't the girl you wanted, but who doesn't deserve to be...dismissed...because of it."

Mrs. Brennan gasped, and her eyes went round with shock. She looked at her husband. "You *told* him?"

The Colonel nodded. "A heart attack makes a man think, Elena. You and I have both made some serious mistakes with our boys. I'm hoping we can still repair the damage." He looked at Matt. "Go on. Tell us what happened."

"It's not that big a deal—" Luke began.

Matt overrode his comment. "My brother spent hours yesterday on his back under a tree, holding it up so I could get out. He all but dislocated both shoulders when the weight came down on him, and kept arguing with the EMTs about making a phone call until he passed out from pain and exhaustion. If he hadn't been there, I wouldn't be alive. I'd say that qualifies as considering just about everyone but himself."

Mrs. Brennan stared at Luke as if she'd never seen him before. "But—"

"Thank you, son." The Colonel held out a hand to Luke. "I'm glad you both got out safe enough."

Luke took his father's hand and smiled. "You're welcome, sir."

"On top of all that," Matt continued, "he gave me a dog."

The girls spoke in unison. "A dog?"

Kristin looked over at Luke. "A dog?"

He started to shrug, caught his breath, and stopped. "Somebody left the poor little guy tied to a fence in the middle of the storm. I took him to a shelter but he looked so miserable when I left I told the folks there I'd be back to get him. Buster's his name."

Matt walked over and squatted in front of the girls, who had settled back on Luke's lap. "And I said that I'd talked with you two about getting a dog. Buster sounds like just what we need. You think?"

"Oh, wow." Erin flung her arms around Matt's neck. "Cool!" Then she drew back and turned to Luke. "Do you mind, Daddy? He's your dog. Finders keepers."

Luke shook his head. "I think it's a great idea. I'd love to see you and Jen take care of Buster."

"Why," Kristin asked the world at large, "do I think that's not quite the way all this will turn out?"

Both brothers turned to look at her, their faces alike and yet…different. As he gazed at his wife, Matt's eyes glowed with love and relief. "I can't imagine," he told Kristin with a grin.

"Me, neither." Luke smiled, too. Now Sarah could see that, despite the fatigue, his eyes were calm, unshadowed. He no longer looked like a man haunted by despair. Her heart pounded twice, then seemed to stop still in her chest.

"So," Matt continued, "we need to make some plans. The highways near the beach are still flooded—you won't be able to reach your house, Dad. You're welcome to come stay with us. We stopped by this morning and checked—no major damage."

"That sounds good." The Colonel stood. "I'm ready to get out of this place."

"Me, too. Me, too!" Jenny clapped her hands.

Erin summed up their concerted opinion. "Let's go home and get Buster!"

MATT AND KRISTIN DROVE back to the beach in Luke's truck. Elena Brennan drove the Colonel in Kristin's van. And Luke made sure he rode back to the beach in Sarah's Jeep, with the girls along as chaperons. He would have to take the next steps slow and careful.

"So, what did you do while you were here?" He shifted painfully in the seat to look at Erin. "Did you get all your books read?"

"Every one. And we went to the pool—"

"And played on the swings," Jenny added.

"Miss Sarah took pictures."

He glanced at the woman driving, but she'd avoided his eyes since the trip started.

"I'll look forward to seeing them."

"And we played golf. I won!"

Luke laughed. "You always win, Erin Bear."

"An' Miss Sarah told us 'bout Zander an' Persis."

"Zander and Persis?"

Between them, Jenny and Erin told him about Zander the Bear and Persis, the young woman whose life he saves. Luke heard about the jaguar cub Zander rescued from falling down the cliff into the river. And he listened to the end of the story.

"One day this prince comes through the forest, see, hunting, and Zander sees him and he's been eating mostly berries and he's pretty hungry 'cause it's winter. So he thinks maybe this prince will keep him fed while he hibernates." Erin caught her breath. Jenny was raptly quiet, listening. "Bears do that, you know."

"I know. What then?"

"Zander charges the prince. But at the last second Persis appears. 'No, Zander. Stop!'" The childish voice conveyed high drama. "Hungry as he is, Zander stops. The prince has a bow and arrow, an' he starts to shoot Zander, but Persis stops that, too. Right then the spell breaks and Zander turns back into a prince, himself."

"An' he and Persis get married and live happy ever after," Jenny concluded.

"That's a really great story." Luke kept his gaze on the girls. "But the way I heard it told, the end was a little different."

Sarah's eyes swerved his way.

Jenny bounced under her seat belt. "How, Daddy? How did it end?"

"Well, the way I heard it, once Zander turned back into a prince, then Persis had a choice to make. The prince she'd saved—Prince, uh, Kerin—fell in love with her for her courage in saving him from the wild bear."

"But Zander loved Persis, too!"

Luke nodded. "I know. So Persis had to decide which prince to marry. And while she really cared about Zander, she'd loved Prince Kerin for a long, long time. Even though she'd only seen him from afar."

"Afar?"

Erin supplied the definition. "Way off."

"So Persis married Kerin, and they lived happily ever after."

"What about Zander?"

"That's the really great part of my ending." Luke cleared his throat. "He went back to his kingdom, and there he met a girl who was brave and kind and good. He loved her so much that he promised to give away his crown and all his fortune if she would marry him."

Jenny stared at him with huge eyes. "What was her name, Daddy?"

He thought a second. "Solara. Because she brought sunshine into everyone's life."

"What happened to Zander and Solara?"

"What do you think happened?"

"A dragon flies in," Erin said, "and kidnaps Solara back to his lair deep in the mountains. And Prince Zander has to pass all sorts of tests to rescue her. But when he gets there—"

"That's not what happened!" Jenny bounced again. "I want Zander and Sol-Solara to get married, without any stupid dragons. I like that ending 'cause then everybody gets to be happy."

"So do I, Jenny Penny." Luke turned back to face the windshield and slid down in the seat a little, easing his shoulders. "That's the way all good stories should end."

ERIN OPENED her eyes when the truck stopped moving and realized she'd gone to sleep during the trip back to Myrtle Beach.

They weren't all the way home yet—just waiting for a traffic light to change. Jenny was still asleep in her car seat. The whole truck was very quiet. Sarah and Daddy weren't talking. Nobody had turned on the radio for music. As Erin watched, Sarah looked over at Daddy. He didn't move or say anything—he must have fallen asleep, too.

Erin recognized the feelings on Sarah's face as she watched Daddy sleep. She'd seen them on Mommy's face when she saw Daddy Matt. And when Grandmom Brennan looked at Granddaddy. Erin hadn't seen Mommy and Grandmom cry. But as Sarah turned back to driving, she wiped tears off her cheeks with her fingertips.

Erin closed her eyes to think. Sarah loved Daddy—that's what the feelings were about. Did Daddy love Sarah? Erin wasn't sure—daddies didn't show their feelings the way mommies and ladies would.

But she made him smile—Erin knew that was one reason she hadn't liked Sarah at the beginning. Used to be only Erin and Jenny could make their dad smile and laugh. Now there was somebody else.

If Sarah made Daddy happy, then Sarah should stay. She told pretty good stories. And she liked to swing really high. And maybe she could teach Erin to use the camera. Then they could go to Africa on a safari and take pictures of the animals.... Erin fell into another dream, about lions that talked and monkeys that sang. She didn't wake up again until they got home.

AT MATT AND KRISTIN'S house, Sarah carried the girls' bags inside and helped them unpack. Kristin settled the Colonel in their guest room. To Luke's surprise, his mother had nothing to say about any of the arrangements. She seemed to be totally at a loss.

He found her standing alone in Kristin's living room, staring at one of the pictures Sarah had taken of the girls. She glanced up as he stopped in the doorway, then looked away again, hastily wiping her cheeks.

"Hey, Mom. Everything all right? Can I do anything?"

She didn't speak, and he thought she was going to ignore him completely. But as he turned away, she stirred. "Please come in, Luke. And shut the doors."

Heart pounding, he did as he was told, pulling the glass-paned double doors closed behind him as he stepped into the room.

After another long silence, his mother sighed. "I... think you should know. It wasn't just that you weren't...a little girl."

"We don't have to do this, Mom. It's okay."

She put up a hand. "No. Things have never really been right. Not since the...baby...died. I missed her every minute of every day. I still miss her. And the young woman she would have been."

"I can understand that."

"You see, I grew up with two brothers. My mother died when I was five. All I dreamed of, as soon as I got old enough, was having a daughter of my own, so I could give her the lovely mother-daughter experiences I'd missed."

Luke shook his head. He'd known her family history, of course. He'd never thought about what the situation might have meant to Elena Calhoun as a young girl.

His mother turned toward him, her eyes fixed on her hands, clasped tightly in front of her. "I was glad to be pregnant again. And, yes, I was sure the baby would be a girl." She raised her face and held his gaze. "I admit I was disappointed to discover I'd had another boy. It was a...a difficult birth. They gave me general anesthesia and performed surgery—I could never have another child. My only children would be sons."

"I'm sorry."

She nodded. "But what happened then wasn't so simple. I have always done my duty—carried out my responsibilities. I wanted to be a good mother to you."

"I made that tough, I know."

His mother almost smiled. "You did. Even so...I wanted to try." Her hands loosened, crept up to clasp her elbows. Suddenly, she looked smaller, and tired, and somehow much older than before. "Every time you went to sleep, I worried. I spent hours standing by your crib, watching you breathe. I was so terrified that you would...leave me, too."

Her voice had thickened with tears. "I couldn't bear the worry. The agony of fear. I didn't eat and didn't sleep. I couldn't seem to do anything."

"Mom..." Luke closed his eyes.

"Eventually, I decided I only had one choice. If I didn't care, then losing you wouldn't hurt. A simple solution. I could manage the rest of my life quite well, as long as I didn't let myself...love...you."

Neither of them said anything for a long time.

Finally, Elena took a deep breath. "I can't change the past. I can't even transform the present all at once. But I am grateful that you were there for Matt yesterday. And—and I will work to change my attitude. I would like us to be...friends."

Luke chuckled inwardly. Elena Brennan would never beg for forgiveness. But at least she'd told the truth. The truth was always a good starting place.

"I'd like that, too, Mom." He crossed the room and put his hands lightly on her shoulders. "Thanks for telling me—I know it wasn't easy. But we'll do better from now on, right?"

"I think so, Lu—son." She grasped his shoulders and pulled him close enough to kiss his cheek.

Then she stepped back, and her usual crisp attitude resurfaced. "I think I'd better go see about your father. It's time for his medicine."

"Sure, Mom." Luke put his hands in his pockets and watched her cross to the doors.

With one panel open, she paused and looked back. "I expect we'll be having Sunday lunch here this week. Will we see you?"

He grinned. "I'll be here, Mom. Thanks."

LUKE WAS STANDING by the fallen pine tree when Kristin came up beside him. "This is just horrible," she said with a shudder. "I can't imagine spending a night—even without a hurricane—lying here, helpless."

"Matt wouldn't give up. He was coming back to you—right through hell and high water."

She was smiling as she looked up at him. "You're really okay, aren't you?"

Hope burned inside him like a torch. He couldn't deny its existence. "I think so."

"I'm glad."

He chucked her chin with his knuckle. "And I'm glad for you, Mrs. Brennan. I really am."

Matt and Sarah came around the front corner of the house. "I wanted to say goodbye—" she began. She looked at the fallen tree and winced. "That's awful."

"But it's over." Kristin enveloped her in a hug. "Thanks so much." She sniffed back tears. "I couldn't have made it without you." Then she drew back. "Call me, okay? Maybe we can get together...have lunch...see a movie?"

Sarah's shy smile was a pleasure to see. "That sounds great. I will." She turned to Matt. "Take care of yourself."

"Sure thing. And thank you for taking care of my family." He bent and gave her a kiss on the cheek.

When she glanced toward Luke, her gaze didn't quite connect with his. "You, too, Luke. Be careful." She started for the street.

"I'll walk you to the Jeep. Or..." he muttered as she strode quickly away from him, "I can just follow you there."

Once in the car, Sarah tried to get away before Luke felt obligated to say something...meaningful. "I'm glad things turned out okay." She watched the keys dance as she flicked them with her finger. "Your family is getting stronger again. Maybe if you stay in town after all—"

"Sarah Rose?"

"Yes?" She still didn't look at him.

"We need to talk." He put his hand over hers on the door frame.

"I...no, we...I mean..."

"We need to talk," he repeated. "Now?"

"No!" He wouldn't let her fingers slip away from his. Her cheeks heated. Finally, she looked up into his intent gray gaze. "I need some time, Luke. So much has happened—my life is such a wreck.... I have some things to figure out, decisions to make." Her eyes filled with tears. "I'll call you, okay?"

Luke started to say something, but stopped. "I'll be waiting." He backed away from the Jeep.

"Thank you." She forced a smile and turned to start the car. Could she just drive away and leave him? What if he changed his mind?

"Sarah?" He raised his voice. When she turned, his face was calm and confident and strong.

And his voice rang with conviction as he made her a promise. "Remember, Sarah Rose Randolph. I *will* be waiting!"

CHAPTER EIGHTEEN

THANKS TO STATE and federal agencies, the repair of Hurricane Daniel's damage progressed rapidly. Water receded from the roads, the sand was shoveled off. Beachfront businesses reopened and the tourists returned. Homeowners on the beach started getting back to their houses—some of them to find they had no house left at all. His parents were among the luckier ones. They lost the deck and the pool, but the rest of their house still stood.

Two weeks passed, and Sarah didn't call. Luke didn't try to reach her by telephone—she might find a way to evade him. He wanted to talk face-to-face, to see her eyes as he asked her to stay...to make a life with him.

And so he waited.

In the meantime, he got a different wish fulfilled. The undercover operation to net the serial mugger finally worked. A woman police officer leaving a late movie was assaulted in the parking lot. Luke was on duty when the call came in, and close enough to be at the scene as the guy struggled against the hold of two cops.

He was disappointed, as he came close enough to really see the mugger, to see that this man was definitely *not* Chuck Sawyer.

"They're killers," he cried, as the cops dragged him toward a cruiser. "All of them are killers! We must stop them!"

Luke glanced at Sergeant Baylor. "What was that about?"

Baylor lit a cigarette. "We just ran a background check. The guy's family—wife and three kids—was killed in a DUI accident about six months ago, by a woman driving an olive-green Jeep. I guess he figured if he took away their keys, nobody else would get hurt."

All of Luke's rage against Sarah's attacker drained away. He had come close to losing everything himself. The man's pain must be unbearable. "I hope they can get him some help."

Baylor nodded, his gaze somber as they watched the cruiser pull out. "Me, too."

AT THE BEGINNING of his next four-day break, Luke drove past the photo shop around midafternoon. With a sharp word, he pulled the truck to a stop across the street, rested his arms on the steering wheel, and stared.

Where once a building had stood, bulldozers now crept over the site, shoveling debris. Half the lot had already been cleared. The job would be done by the end of the week and Sawyer's Photo Shop would become a place of the past.

Driving back through town toward the north end of the beach, Luke began to fear the very worst. Had she left without calling? Could she not face him even to say goodbye?

Sarah's Jeep wasn't parked in the condo lot. Despair swamped him; he sat for a minute with his head resting on his hands wrapped around the wheel, all rational thought erased by worry and doubt. What next?

For a cop, he took way too long to think of the logical next step—a check with the complex manager. If Sarah had left permanently, her place would surely be for sale or rent.

Fifteen minutes and some police leverage later, he got the good news that she hadn't notified the management of any changes. As far as they knew, Sarah Randolph still lived in 2-B.

But as far as Luke knew, she still didn't plan to see *him* any time soon.

Leaving the truck where it sat, he hiked the quarter mile to the beach. The crowds had gone inside for dinner and the tide was out, revealing a wide stretch of empty sand. Luke headed south, away from the huge entertainment and fishing pier, seeking as much natural quiet as he could find. As he walked, the big hotels on the right faded from his consciousness. He was alone with the sea and his unanswered questions.

When he realized there was water in front of him, as well as on his left, he stopped and gave some attention to exactly where he'd ended up. After a few seconds, he recognized the small inlet running beside the Sandspur Country Club. The very place he'd met Sarah Rose Randolph for the first time.

Just his dumb luck.

"Luke?"

He heard his name without recognizing it. And then again, closer, louder. "Luke!"

Turning his head, he saw Sarah crossing the sand, slim and graceful in her copper swimsuit, some kind of filmy skirt and a wide-brimmed hat. Just watching her hurt. He dropped his gaze to the shell-crusted sand around his feet.

Her first question was the last one he expected. "You got my message?"

Luke looked up again. "What message?" She'd changed in the days since he'd seen her—the hollows in her face were rounded out, the shadows in her eyes replaced with light.

She nodded. "I left a message this afternoon on your machine. Telling you I'd be waiting here. I thought…" Her golden eyes widened. "That's not why you came?"

That torch inside him started to burn again, using up his oxygen. "I haven't been home since around noon."

"I called about one."

"I missed it, then."

Sarah gazed out over the ocean. Luke stared inland, at a loss for words. Finally, the right ones occurred to him. "What did you want?"

"Why did you come?" Sarah said, at exactly the same moment.

He couldn't help grinning, and her face relaxed into a smile.

"You first," he said.

She started to protest, then pressed her lips together and swallowed hard. "I thought I knew where to start, but now that you're here… Have you been by the shop?"

"Yeah—or what used to be the shop. What happened?"

"It's complicated. I discovered that Chuck's pictures—the ones he was selling—weren't his. Felix shot them all." She explained the letters and the prints. "I offered to sell him my half of the business for a dollar and all the negatives."

"Did he bite?"

"He said he would, but he kept the negatives in a bank in Charleston and couldn't get them right away. Then the storm came and he left the shop without taking any precautions at all. The building was a total loss."

"Why the hell would he do that, if the whole business would have been his?"

"Good question. I finally went down to Georgetown to ask his mother, Felix's sister. According to her, Chuck planned to take the negatives and disappear."

"So he could still try to publish the pictures as his."

She sighed. "I filled out a police report, and I've been in touch with some art theft experts. We'll get the word out to the photographic community and museums that the prints have been stolen. But that's not going to help some individual who sees a pretty shot he likes in a photo shop somewhere and buys it as Chuck's."

"You never know—Chuck may trip himself up one day. Crooks often do." He shoved his hands in his pockets to keep from touching her. "Speaking of which, we caught the guy who attacked you."

"Really? How?"

He gave her the details, and the man's story.

"I'm so sorry," she said. "Will he go to jail?"

"The hospital, more likely. I hope they can help him rebuild his life."

"Yes." She stared out at the ocean, her eyes sad. And then she seemed to shake off that sadness. Her smile returned, with a pleasure that caught like pain in his chest. "As far as rebuilding goes, I'm planning some of my own in the near future."

"Oh, yeah?" A stray curl blew across her cheek. Luke fought the urge to tuck it back.

"The contract for joint ownership of the shop gave Chuck power of attorney for me, and vice versa. Since he's gone, I can make decisions. And I decided to sell the site."

"That'll make you a rich woman."

"I'll be rich for about ten minutes. As soon as that deal closes, I go to sign the papers for a shop in one of the malls near the Hard Rock Café. Prime Myrtle Beach retail space.''

His throat tightened. "A space for…?"

"Let me show you." She turned to walk away.

Paralyzed by a kind of Christmas-morning feeling, as if something he wanted very badly sat just around the corner, Luke didn't immediately follow.

Sarah came back, grabbed his wrist and pulled his hand out of his pocket. "Come."

Her fingers on his skin brought him back to life. He trailed her up to the high point on the beach, where she'd set a blanket, an umbrella, and two low chairs. She gestured to the chairs. "Have a seat. Would you like some juice?"

"No, thanks." Luke dropped into the chair, then slipped off his sandals. The sand's heat came through the blanket with an almost solid warmth.

Sarah reached behind her chair for a canvas satchel and set it in front of her as she took her own seat. She pulled a slim folder out of the bag. "Tell me what you think."

Luke opened the folder on a photograph of Jenny, perched in her childish crouch, inspecting a caterpillar. The silver-gold of her hair, the blush in her cheeks, the intense concentration of a young, innocent girl, put him right there beside her. "Fantastic," he murmured. "Can I have a copy?"

"These are all yours."

He glanced at Sarah, then picked up the next print— Erin, stretched out in a swing, for all the world as if she could fly. Her eagerness and joy in life soared out of the picture. Luke couldn't think of a word to describe what he felt.

The child in the next print was a stranger. But he

shared the universal spirit of boys everywhere as he balanced on his boogie board, seeking to catch a big wave. "What a guy."

All of the prints in the folder featured kids, and all of them created priceless images of childhood. He would frame them to hang where he could see them each day.

He looked at the woman beside him, perched on the edge of her chair, elbows on her knees and chin on her fists. "What can I say? They're great, every one of them."

Sarah nodded, her eyes brimming with excitement. "It's back."

"It..." He floundered for a second. "You mean your instinct for the perfect shot?"

"I found it with Erin and Jenny. I can use it with other kids—with pictures of joy and fun and love."

Luke closed the folder, because the pictures shook with the pounding of his pulse. "So you're opening a studio to do children's photography?"

"Well, mostly. Adults, too. I'll sell and develop film, instant cameras, the usual stuff. But I'm taking pictures again. And loving it." Her face was as bright as he'd ever seen it, her cheeks flushed, her smile wide with joy.

He lost what little breath he had left. "You're staying in town, then."

"I am."

They might have been the only people in the whole world. For as far as Luke could see, the beach around them was deserted. Only the pleas of seagulls broke the silence.

After a minute, Sarah said, "Are you...staying in town?"

The moment of truth. "I guess that depends."

"On...?"

"On you."

Sarah heard the words she'd longed for with a flash of something that felt like pure terror. Or else a terrible, wonderful excitement.

Luke leaned over and slid the folder back into the bag. In the process, his bare arm brushed her leg. As he drew back, she caught his hand and held it between both her palms. His gray gaze lifted. She answered the question she saw there with one of her own.

"What about Kristin?"

His brow creased and his eyes closed, but then he looked at her again. There was no trace of regret in his beautiful face, or in his voice as he explained.

"We share a little girl, so we'll be connected in that way. But—"

At the tug of his hand, she slipped out of her chair and knelt on the blanket between his knees. "But?"

A flick of his fingers tipped off her hat. "What Kristin and I had was good. She needed help, and I was there. But she was never in love with me. And…"

His hands closed on her upper arms, drawing her even closer. "I was never in love with her. In love with being needed, maybe, and being part of a family that worked. But not in love with the woman Kristin is." He curved his palm along her jaw. "I'd never loved like that, Sarah Rose, until I knew you."

"Oh, Luke." She leaned forward and he was there, his lips warm and demanding, his arms tight, his body hard against hers. "I love you. So much."

When at last she recovered a little piece of reality, Sarah found herself cradled in Luke's lap, with his arms around her and his mouth pressed against her hair. As she stirred, his hand slipped to her breast, a warm weight through the thin fabric of her swimsuit. At the sweet pressure, at the caress of his fingers along the edge of the suit's low neckline, she shuddered in longing. ''We're going to get arrested,'' she whispered.

''S'okay,'' he murmured at the corner of her mouth. ''I know a cop who can fix things.'' But after one last, lingering kiss, he let her slip away, bracing her as she got to her feet.

They closed the chairs in silence, lowered the umbrella and folded the blanket. Packed up and ready to go, Sarah turned to look at the ocean. ''I always hate to leave at this time of day. It's so beautiful here.''

Luke circled his arms around her slim shoulders from behind, ''You can come back every day for the rest of your life. I'll come with you.''

He felt her stiffen in his hold. ''That's...that's a long-term arrangement.''

''Marriage is supposed to be.''

''Oh, Luke.'' Now she trembled. ''I didn't think you'd want marriage.''

''I love you, so I want everything. With you.''

After a shaken moment, she whispered, ''Even babies?''

''Definitely babies.'' She was silent so long, he thought he'd said something wrong. Turning her around, he found her face wet with tears. ''Sarah, if you don't—''

Her fingers touched his lips. ''Shh. I just...thought I'd never have...babies. Of my own.''

Luke kissed her fingertips. ''And mine.''

She closed her eyes and smiled dreamily. ''Only yours.'' But then she opened them again. ''What will Erin and Jenny say? And your parents?''

He drew Sarah close against him. ''Jen and Erin will adjust, because we'll help them. My dad and mom—well, we still have some work to do there. But we've talked, recently, and things went okay. When I mentioned you, my mom said you seem like a presentable young woman.'' He chuckled. ''So there's hope. At least Matt and Kristin will come to the wedding.''

''Your brother, your ex-wife, and your daughters, who are also his. A truly unique bridal party.'' Sarah shook her head, still smiling.

''With a wedding picture,'' Luke agreed with a wide grin, ''we'll need a lot more than a thousand words to explain!''

EPILOGUE

AT LEAST the dress Erin had to wear at Daddy's wedding didn't scratch. Sarah had let her help pick the color—green, like the moss on a tree trunk, in a soft cloth that sort of floated when she twirled around. Jen's dress was yellow and she wore a straw hat. Erin didn't like the hat, and Sarah said she didn't have to wear it. Grandmom Brennan had frowned a little about that.

Daddy and Sarah were married underneath an arch of flowers in a big garden with statues everywhere. Erin liked the one of the man reading the newspaper best. Jenny liked the big bear. Sarah took a picture of both of them sitting in its lap.

The after-wedding party was outside in the garden, too. The sun was shining and the cloths on the tables fluttered in the wind. Jenny's hat blew off. Erin walked on the low brick wall between the flower beds and the grass. She'd never known a wedding could be so much fun.

Daddy was having a good time, too. He'd smiled a lot since Sarah said she would marry him, and especially today. He looked very handsome in his suit and tie. Daddy Matt looked nice, too. And Mommy was beautiful in her special dress, a darker green than Erin's but just as soft.

And Sarah…Sarah looked like a princess. Rapunzel, maybe, with her hair long and loose. She wore a veil over her head and a dress that made Erin think of the fairy-tale books she used to read—before she got too old for that kind of stuff.

Now they were all part of a big family, with two of everything—moms, dads, grandmoms and granddads. Sarah had said just to use her name, and Erin was glad, because Mommy Sarah sounded dumb. She was thinking about asking Matt if she could do the same thing with his name. Daddy and Daddy Matt were too confusing when you talked to your friends at school.

"Erin?" She looked toward the voice. "Smile," Sarah said, and took a picture.

"Playing photographer at your own wedding?" Daddy came up and put his arm around Sarah. "That cuts expenses."

Sarah laughed. "And this way I'm sure we get all the right shots. Erin, will you take a picture of your dad and me?"

Erin just stared. "With—with *your* camera?"

"Sure. Let me show you." Sarah knelt in the grass and pointed to a button on the camera. "Look through this window, try to get us in the middle and click!— you've got a picture."

Staring through the window, Erin saw Daddy lift Jenny into his arms, and then high into the air. Holding her breath, she pushed the button. Click!

"Good shot, Erin!" Sarah took the camera back and made a different clicking noise with it. "I'm winding the film. Now we're ready for another one." She ran to stand beside Daddy and Jenny. "Everybody smile!"

Erin held her breath again, put Jenny in the middle of the window and took the picture. "This is so neat."

"And now we need a picture of the four of you." Daddy Matt and Mommy were standing behind her. "I'll take it," Daddy Matt added.

"Be careful," Erin warned as she handed him the camera. "It's very breakable."

He grinned at her. "I'll remember." Daddy Matt smiled more these days, too. Not as much as Daddy. But he was just a more serious person. Everybody was different, right?

As Erin crossed the grass, Sarah took Jenny. Daddy leaned down and Erin let him lift her up. She was a little old for this, but she would be polite.

Matt looked through the camera and did something to the circles on the front. "Looks good. Everybody happy?" He clicked a picture, and then another one.

Daddy looked at Erin. "What do you say, Erin Bear? Are you happy?"

She thought a minute. "Yeah. Except I don't like math in school."

He laughed and Sarah came close. "I didn't like math either, Erin." She jogged Jenny up a little higher. "Are you happy, Princess Jenny?"

But Jenny wasn't too sure about things these days. She put her thumb in her mouth and stared back at Sarah.

"How about you, Mrs. Brennan?" Daddy had put his arm around Sarah. Now the four of them stood in kind of a group hug.

Sarah closed her eyes. "It's the most beautiful, wonderful day of my life." She looked at him again. "What do you think, Mr. Brennan?"

Daddy shrugged. "It's okay."

Sarah's jaw dropped and her eyes went round. Erin punched him on the shoulder. "Daddy! Be polite."

He laughed. "I'm just kidding, Erin." Leaning close to Sarah, he gave Jenny a kiss on the cheek, and another one to Erin. Then he looked at his new wife.

"I've got armfuls of happiness. The best little girls in

the whole wide world—'' Sarah put her hand on his cheek ''—and the friend and love of a lifetime. What else could I want?'' He kissed Sarah's hand, and then her lips.

Erin waited as patiently as she could. But finally she just had to interrupt. ''A piece of cake, Daddy,'' she said as she wriggled down to the ground. ''What you want is a piece of wedding cake. And I want one, too!''

Even though they're married now,
Matt and Kristin still have
a lot to work out.
Watch for their story—

MATT'S FAMILY

—coming from
Harlequin Superromance
in September 2000.

Now turn the page
for an exciting preview.

CHAPTER ONE

MATT WOKE AS Kristin slipped out of bed and left their room. He squinted at the clock. Two-thirty, later than usual. She was often out of bed by midnight or one.

Staring up at the ceiling, he listened to his wife move through the house. Maybe she would just get a drink, then come back.

But minutes passed, then half an hour. The microwave beeped—she'd made herself some tea. A faint glow at the doorway indicated she'd switched on a lamp.

So here they were again, him lying in the dark, waiting, while Kris sat in the kitchen, thinking. About what?

Did she think about the same things he did? Did she wonder how their life could be so good…yet so wrong? How two people could live together and, at the same time, be so far apart?

Matt rolled to his side, facing the door. He'd made love with Kris just a few hours ago. Tonight, as always, she'd given him more pleasure than any man had a right to know. She gave him everything, including her own satisfaction. Her whispers, her sighs, the shudders that ran through her body as he touched and kissed and moved—every reaction conveyed Kristin's delight in what he did.

But she never asked, damn it. Never demanded. Never even abandoned herself to him, selfish—even helpless—in her need for his desire. After nearly a year together, sex seemed almost like a contest to see who could please whom the most. A quid pro quo kind of experience— neither of them relaxed enough to simply take.

Matt knew he never really felt at ease—because he never knew what Kris was thinking anymore. Did she compare what they had to her first marriage, and find something missing? Was she afraid to tell him what she wanted, because she thought he would resent the implication that he'd failed? Or was sex something she did because she saw it as her responsibility in their marriage?

Was the whole marriage simply a matter of responsibility? A debt to be paid?

He closed his eyes at the painful grip of that thought. The idea that Kris had married him because she owed him hurt too much to consider.

In the hallway, her footsteps padded lightly toward their door. She eased back into bed, barely disturbing the mattress or the covers. If he wanted, Matt could pretend he hadn't known she was gone.

That wasn't what he wanted to do. He wanted to take her again—make love to his wife until she was so crazy with passion that she couldn't think, couldn't even respond. Love her until she forgot about loving him back, until she just accepted everything he had to give, until she came apart in his arms and cried out his name. Then he'd know for sure she trusted him, needed him. Wanted him.

But when he finally turned over, he heard her soft, even breaths. She'd fallen asleep. He could wake her, and she would welcome him. Duty, or desire? Matt had no way to know. He wasn't even sure he wanted to find out.

And so he just laid his hand lightly on the blanket covering her hip, and set about making himself go back to sleep.

"THAT'S PRETTY MOMMY!"

"Thanks, Jenny." Kristin patted her daughter's blond head and stepped back from the counter to survey the results of her morning's work—a three-layer chocolate cake, iced with butter-cream frosting and decorated with an American flag. "I think so, too."

The real question was whether her mother-in-law would agree. For the first time, Matt's mother had allowed Kristin to contribute to the family's Memorial Day picnic menu. A bowl of potato salad waited in the refrigerator, as picture perfect as she could make it. Her cake looked professional, if she did say so herself. Surely even Mrs. Brennan would be pleased.

Suddenly weary, Kristin tucked her chin and rolled her head from side to side, trying to loosen the tension in her neck. The picnic started at four. That gave her three hours to get the girls bathed and dressed, the kitchen cleaned up, and herself showered and ready. She smiled ruefully. That might be enough time.

Jenny still sat on the stool by the counter, gazing at the cake. "Hop down, love," Kristin told the five-year-old, turning toward the sink and its collection of dirty dishes. "We're finished."

"Can I have a piece of cake?"

"At the picnic." They'd already covered this ground with the potato salad.

"Why not now?"

"I told you—then it wouldn't be pretty for Grandmom and Granddad to see."

Running footsteps sounded in the family room. "Hey, Jenny, look what I found under my bed!" Sun-streaked hair flying, Erin ran into the kitchen, followed by Buster, the dog. Kristin glanced over to see her older daughter waving a purple stuffed toy.

"That's mine," Jenny said, climbing off the stool "Give me my dragon back."

"I found it, I get to keep it." Erin held the dragon above her head.

Jenny jumped, but couldn't reach. "Mommy, tell he to give me my dragon that Daddy got for me!"

Kristin went back to the counter and picked up the cake to move it before the toy landed on top. "Erin, give Jenny her dragon. You've got one of your own."

As she pivoted toward the other side of the kitchen, a warm furry form wrapped itself between her ankles.

"Buster!" She shuffled her feet, trying to step free The dog gave a loud yelp as her bare heel came down on his paw. Kristin jumped, shifted her weight...and los control of the cake. With a slurp, the plate tilted inward pressing the American flag into the front of her shirt.

Jenny gasped. "Mommy, you hurt Buster!" She broke into tears.

Kristin stood frozen, eyes closed in horror, hands holding the plate against her chest.

Jenny cried louder, working up to a real tantrum. Kristin finally jerked herself into motion and eased the cake back onto the plate. "Hush, Jenny, love. Let's look a Buster's paw, okay?" She set the plate on the counter then knelt in front of the dog, who immediately licked a her shirt. "Which paw did I get, Buster? This one?" He wagged his tail as she checked all four feet. "He's fine Jenny. Don't worry."

Erin stared at her from the end of the counter "Mommy, you've got icing all over you!"

Kristin sighed. "I know." And the top of the cake looked like a bomb crater. "You two go to your room and stay there. I'll come in a few minutes and we'll ge ready for the party."

Once the girls had left, she mopped the flag off her shirt, then stood staring at the ruined dessert. She would have to make more icing, scrape off the top of the cake and the stars piped around the edge, then start all over. Painting that flag had taken her almost two hours. She didn't have time to do it again.

So much for her perfect Memorial Day dessert.

She was whipping icing and wiping tears out of her eyes when Matt came through the door. "Hey, Kris—whoa! Did a hurricane blow through?"

Kristin glanced around the wrecked kitchen, at the ruined cake and her filthy shirt, and blinked back more tears. "Um...I'm sorry it's such a mess. I've gotten a little behind."

"What happened?"

"I had a problem with the cake, that's all."

He frowned. "I thought you were making potato salad."

"I did." She added more sugar to the bowl. "I said I'd bring dessert, too."

"That doesn't leave much for anybody else to cook."

She shook her head at his assumption. "Of course, it does. Sarah and Luke are bringing a green salad and baked beans. Your mother and dad are cooking the hamburgers—"

Matt raised his hands in surrender, laughing. "Okay, okay. I just meant you shouldn't work so hard." He skimmed a dollop of icing out of her hair and sucked it off his finger. "Mmm. Tastes great." He leaned closer and kissed her neck, just under her ear. "You taste wonderful, too." His warm breath sent a sweet shiver down her spine. "Are the girls ready?"

"Not yet. I'll be finished in a few minutes."

"I'll get them dressed." He headed for the stairs. Kristin thought about calling him back—the girls weren't exactly cooperating today. But they liked going to their grandparents' house. Surely they wouldn't put up a fuss. If they did, Matt could handle it. Right?

Thirty minutes later, with a smooth, plain coat of icing on the cake, Kristin hurried down the hallway to the bedrooms. She peeked into Jenny's and found it empty. But the outfit she'd ironed earlier this morning—the one Matt's mother had given them—still lay on the bed. What was Jenny wearing?

Erin's clothes lay crumpled on the floor of her room. She picked them up. "Girls? Matt? What's going on? Where are you?"

"We're in the bathroom, Kris." His voice sounded tired.

She pushed open the door of the big yellow bathroom. Matt, still wearing his uniform and with his brown hair as tousled as hair so short could be, was sitting on the floor with his elbows propped on his bent knees, a spray bottle in one hand, a comb in the other. Facing him stood Erin and Jenny, wrapped in their towels, both with wet, tangled hair.

"What's going on? Why aren't you dressed?"

Matt ran a hand over his head, then simply looked at the girls. Erin stuck out her lower lip. "It hurts when he combs my hair."

Kristin sighed. "Erin, you say it hurts when *I* comb your hair. We're as gentle as we can be. Your hair has to be combed. Did you use the untangler spray?"

Saying nothing, Matt held up the bottle.

She took it from him. "Okay, I'll spray it again. I'll do your hair, Erin, and Matt can do Jenny's. We only have few minutes to get ready."

But Jenny backed up against the vanity. "My hair hurts, too. And he got soap in my eyes."

Jenny always got soap in her eyes when Matt was in charge of bath time. This wasn't a real complaint. This was mutiny, plain and simple.

And the grimness in Matt's face, a despair he was trying his best to hide, testified to the mutiny's effect.

Kristin crossed her arms, fighting down irritation. "Well, we could stay home and let you both sit in your rooms with tangled hair. But that would disappoint Grandmom and Granddad, who are looking forward to seeing you. We're going to be late, as it is. Erin, come here." She held out her hand to Matt for the comb.

He slapped it into her palm and got to his feet. "Sorry," he said in a low voice. "I guess I'll go change." The door closed behind him before she had a chance to reply.

As quickly as she could, Kristin combed and braided the girls' hair and got them into the new shorts sets. That left her exactly ten minutes to get ready. She could arrive looking like she felt—a total mess—or she could take the half hour she needed to look decent for Matt's parents.

So they were late. By the time they got the girls settled in the car and fought beach traffic, they were a long, tense, forty minutes late.

Matt parked the van in his parents' driveway and released the door lock. As if they'd been freed from jail, Erin and Jenny ran through the grass and around the back of the house to the deck on the beach.

When he opened Kristin's door, she took a deep breath and slid carefully to the ground, cradling the covered cake. Then she looked up at him. Her brown eyes were somber and sad. "I'm sorry about the girls."

He set his hand along the angle of her jaw and stroked a thumb across her smooth cheek. "I'll be okay."

She pressed her head into his palm for a second, then stepped away. "I guess we'd better get inside."

Matt followed her toward the kitchen door, carrying the potato salad. Bright sunlight did great things for Kristin's soft tan and shiny gold hair. Her dark blue sleeveless shirt showed off her arms, while white shorts and sandals left a nice length of her great legs in view. The first time he'd seen her, Matt had known she was the prettiest, sexiest girl he would ever meet. More than ten years later, he'd never encountered another woman who could make him change his mind.

His mother looked up in surprise as they came inside. "I wondered what had happened to you. It's after four-thirty."

He bent to kiss her cheek. "Sorry, Mom. Sometimes the girls need more time than we think they will. How are you?"

"Well, thank you." She took the bowl of potato salad out of his hands and placed it precisely on the counter. "Your father is on the deck with Luke and Sarah."

Kristin stepped forward. "Where shall I put the cake?"

Elena Brennan lifted her eyebrows. "Oh, I didn't think you'd have time to make dessert. Let's put yours over here beside mine."

Kristin squeezed her eyes closed as she relinquished the plate. Matt didn't see a problem with the nice, smooth icing…until his mother set Kristin's cake next to her own berry-decorated version. Suddenly, the white cake looked a little drab.

He put a hand on Kristin's shoulder. "Anything else we can do, Mom?"

She appeared to consider, but he doubted she really

had. "No, dear. I believe everything is just about ready. Why don't you start the grill?"

"Sure." He moved Kristin ahead of him. "Don't worry about it," he whispered in her ear as he opened the door onto the deck.

Looking back over her shoulder, she gave him a rigid smile. "Worry about what?"

Matt stared at her as she walked outside. Why wouldn't Kris admit his mother upset her? Was she hiding something so terrible she couldn't share *anything* with him, in case the worst slipped out? What the hell would "the worst" be?

"Well, Matt, it's about time you showed up." Across the deck, his father sat beneath an umbrella, filling his pipe. "You're mother's been wondering."

"Getting two little girls ready for a party doesn't always go smoothly, Dad." He reached out to shake the Colonel's hand.

"Isn't that the truth?"

Matt turned to face his brother. "Yeah—I'm always amazed at how long it takes." They shook hands, then he looked to Luke's right and grinned at his sister-in-law. "Hey, Sarah. How are you?"

"Wonderful." Her clear, sunny smile reminded him of Kristin…back in the old days. "Your wife says you went to work. It's a holiday, remember?"

He sat beside Kris on the glider and put his arm along the back behind her shoulders. "Just paperwork. I get a lot done with nobody else there."

The Colonel snorted as he lit his pipe. "It's about time you gave up this recruiting nonsense, isn't it? Get back to the real Army?"

"I'm still thinking things over, Dad." Matt relaxed his

clenched fist. "It's a big decision, now that I've got a family."

Kristin stirred uneasily inside the circle of his arm. Was she thinking about a time, nine years ago, when he'd made career decisions on his own? And about the dire consequence of those decisions—the five years she believed he was dead?

Like a dog with a juicy bone, his father wouldn't let go of his point. "I'd imagine your commanding officer is wondering what you're waiting for."

"I haven't heard anything so far." Matt tapped Kristin on the shoulder. "Where'd the girls go?"

"They're playing in the sand at the bottom of the steps," she said, without meeting his eyes.

Luke sat forward in his chair. "Do I have time to take them for a walk before we eat?"

Matt pulled in a deep breath against the resistance he couldn't extinguish. "Since I haven't started the grill yet, I'd say you've got about twenty minutes."

"That'll be great." His brother stood up and held out a hand to Sarah. "Will you come?"

"I will." They crossed the deck arm in arm and descended the steps.

"Hey, munchkins." Luke's voice blew back on the wind from the ocean. "Want to walk down by the waves?"

"Sure, Daddy!" Erin loved the ocean.

"Can you carry me, Daddy?" And Jenny loved her father.

The voices faded as the foursome approached the water. Matt sat still, waiting for feeling and function to come back to his brain.

After the bath fiasco this afternoon, he should know what to expect. As far as Erin and Jenny knew, Luke was their father. The hard part for them was understanding what had changed, why their mother had divorced him and married another man.

The hard part for Matt was being that other man.

He put his hands on his knees and pushed himself to his feet. "I'd better get the fire going. Mom's going to be out here with the burgers any minute."

Kristin remained seated on the glider as Matt walked to the grill. His straight back, his square shoulders filling out his knit shirt, were as much a part of him as his military haircut and his natural air of command. But she could read the tension in his body. Luke's relationship with the girls tortured Matt. Erin and Jenny were comfortable around Luke, sure of themselves and him. They spoke the same shorthand language, as people who lived—and loved—together often did. Erin and Jenny and Luke had been a family.

Until Kristin tore them apart.

Suddenly unable to sit still, she got up and walked to the deck railing to stare out toward the ocean. Usually the sound of the waves and the warmth of the sun made life seem simpler, easier to manage.

Not today. Not with Matt closed off from her by a wall of hurt and misunderstanding. Not when she just kept making mistakes, each one more destructive than the last.

Out by the water, Luke and Sarah chased the girls. Jenny squealed as Luke caught her around the waist and lifted her high in the air. They made quite a picture—the handsome black-haired man and his precious silver-blond daughter.

Erin outran Sarah, then kept on running, just for the sheer joy of moving. She loved being outside, like her father. And she moved with the same easy stride, the same long-legged grace Kristin had always adored in

Matt. Erin would be tall one day, with her father's blue
eyes and his serious, considering stare. Luke was tall, too,
but his eyes were a laughing gray and his body more
compact than Matt's.

When would Erin start noticing the differences?

"Is the grill ready, Matt?" Mrs. Brennan stepped out
onto the deck.

"Yes, ma'am. Whenever you are."

"Where are the girls?"

"On the beach with Luke and Sarah."

Even from across the deck, Mrs. Brennan's sigh indicated impatience. "Why does he always take them away
just when we're ready to eat?"

Matt didn't answer. Kristin glanced at his back, which
was all she could see, then turned again to the ocean and
her own thoughts. Almost two years ago, before he'd
even asked her to marry him, she'd made Matt a promise.
One day, as soon as possible, Erin would know the
truth—that she was Matt's daughter, as Jenny was
Luke's.

Every time Kristin thought about explaining, though,
she felt physically sick. The revelations wouldn't stop
with Erin. The grandparents would have to know. How
much would they be hurt by the news? Who else would
hear about it? The country club crowd? Her mother's
church friends—all of them privy to the mistakes Kristin
had made, the poor judgment she'd used? Could she ever
look anyone in the face again?

Out on the beach, Erin stopped her cartwheels and
waved. Kristin waved back, then motioned for them to
come in. Mrs. Brennan would be waiting.

Matt was waiting, too. He never said a word, but Kristin could see the question in his eyes. *When?* he wanted
to know. *When can I tell her she's mine?*

Even worse than facing the disapproval of her parents and his was the knowledge of how much she hurt Matt by hesitating. She wanted to keep her promise. She ached to be open, to stop watching every word she said, to simply acknowledge the facts and move on.

But nothing about what she had to tell Erin felt in the least bit simple. And certainly not easy.

Sooner than she expected, the girls rushed up the steps and across the deck into the house, with Luke and Sarah following more slowly. A gentle hand came to rest on Kristin's shoulder.

"Such a serious face. Is something wrong?"

She looked over at her sister-in-law, who had also become a close friend. "No more than usual." Sarah's dark brows drew together in concern, and she started to say something. But Kristin put up a hand. "No, don't worry about it. Let's not spoil the afternoon. How are you? How's the photography business?"

"Great. And great. The studio has started operating in the black, finally." Sarah took off her hat and let her curly, gold-brown hair ruffle in the wind. "That wedding job you recommended me for has really increased my contacts in the area. Did I remember to say thank you?"

"About a thousand times." Kristin laughed. "I'm glad things worked out. What do you and Luke have planned for the summer?"

"We wanted to talk to you about that. What would you think—"

"Dinner's ready!" Matt brandished a barbecue spatula above his head.

Erin stood at the door to the house. "Come on, Mommy. Let's eat!"

Sarah put an arm around Kristin's waist and squeezed. "We'll talk later, okay?"

"Of course." Kristin joined the rest of the family in
the kitchen, wondering what Luke and Sarah had in mind.
Surely nothing she should dread—and yet she felt uneasy. The air-conditioning raised goose bumps on her
skin. She rubbed her arms, trying to get warm.

"Memorial Day is important." Seated at the kitchen
table with an arm around each granddaughter, Colonel
Brennan started his annual remembrance speech. "Amer-
icans should take time to remember the men who have
died serving their country."

"And women," Sarah said quietly. Kristin would
never have been brave enough to make that comment.

The Colonel cleared his throat. "For five years our
family celebrated this day thinking we had lost someone
we loved in the cause of freedom. Now we celebrate in
thankfulness to have Matt with us again."

Beside Kristin, Matt shifted his weight. She glanced at
his face and saw that his cheeks had reddened. His em-
barrassment was endearing, and she smiled up at him,
linking her elbow through his. He pressed her arm closer
into his side.

"Daddy Matt was gone for five years?" Erin counted
on her fingers. "He left before Jenny was born?"

Tension struck the room like a lightning bolt. Across
the counter, Luke gave a quick smile and a small shrug
which put the answer at Kristin's discretion. "That's true,
Erin," she said. "Even—even before you were born."
Was that the right thing to say?

"Mommy, did you know Daddy Matt before I was
born?"

"Of course, love. I knew…all the Brennans then, and
for a long time before." Matt had gone still as a stone
beside her.

"But—" Erin stopped and seemed to reconsider her question.

"I'm hungry," Jenny announced with a five-year-old's directness.

Mrs. Brennan was the first adult to relax. "Of course, Jennifer, dear. Let your grandfather say grace, and I'll make you a plate."

During the prayer, Matt's stiffness subsided. He didn't draw away from Kristin, but he didn't press her close again, either. Had she disappointed him? Should she have told the whole story right her, right now, to everyone?

What, in God's name, could she say?

After dinner, the adults sat on the deck finishing coffee while the girls splashed in the pool. Matt seemed preoccupied—Kristin could guess with what.

After a pause, Luke sat forward and braced his elbows on his knees. "Sarah and I wanted to run something by you, Kristin." He glanced at his brother. "And Matt. We're spending a couple of weeks in the mountains in June and we'd like the girls to come with us. What do you think?"

Kristin couldn't think at all, for a moment, couldn't decide what her reaction should be.

"We'll be really careful," Sarah added. "We're renting a condo with two bedrooms and a kitchen, so they'll have lots of room."

"Oh, no." Kristin shook her head. "No, I'm sure—I mean, I don't worry about them when they're with you." She caught the skepticism in Luke's gaze, and shrugged. "Okay, not too much."

Her doubt had nothing to do with safety. What effect would so much time with Luke—so much time away from Matt—have on the girls? She looked at him, hoping for help.

His smile was forced. "I think it sounds great. They'll have a good time."

Luke sat back in his chair. Obviously, he hadn't missed the hint of reluctance in Matt's comment. Just as obviously, he'd decided to ignore it. "Okay, then. We'll be away the second and third weeks of the month. I'll wait awhile to tell the girls or they won't sleep between now and then."

"Good idea." Matt stood up and held out his cup. "Anybody else want a refill?" Everyone shook their heads. He looked at Luke's wife. "Sarah, you sure you don't want some coffee?"

She smiled—more brightly than the question called for, Kristin thought. "No, thanks. I'm cutting out caffeine."

There could be several reasons for that decision. Watching Sarah and Luke smile at each other in the soft light of sunset, Kristin had a pretty good idea which one to choose. "Um…do you two have something else you want to mention?"

Luke's grin widened. Sarah looked over. "It's that obvious?"

Kristin smiled back, though her insides felt as if she'd taken the first hill on a roller coaster. "Now that I think about it, yes."

The Colonel drew on his pipe. "What's obvious? What's going on?"

"A minor detail, Dad. We're having a baby."

"Congratulations, son." Colonel Brennan got up to shake Luke's hand and give Sarah a hug. "Maybe we'll get us a boy this time."

"Another little girl would be wonderful," Matt's mother said firmly, still seated in her chair. "When are you due, Sarah?"

"Around the first of December."

Elena Brennan sighed. "A Christmas baby. How lovely."

Babies were lovely at any time of year, Kristin thought. But she couldn't help wondering about Erin and Jenny. What would a new baby do to their precarious balance?

Especially if she rocked their world at the same time with the announcement that Matt was Erin's father?

Matt had stepped over to shake his brother's hand. He bent to give Sarah a kiss on the cheek. "Let's hope, boy or girl, the baby gets your looks, not his." He nodded sideways at Luke.

"Thanks, bro."

"Anytime."

Kristin knew she had to say something. "I'm so happy for you both. You'll love having a baby. Who's your doctor?"

The question led them into a discussion of symptoms and signs and preparations. The men dropped out—Luke went into the pool to play with the girls while Matt and the Colonel talked basketball. Smiling, Kristin listened to Sarah's "discoveries" as if she'd never experienced them, as if she hadn't had two babies herself. Each pregnancy was brand-new. She loved the chance to relive that feeling, even secondhand.

Mrs. Brennan broke into a short silence. "You know, Kristin, you and Matt have been married longer than Sarah and Luke. Don't you think it's about time we heard the same good news from you?"

Kristin gazed at her mother-in-law, scrambling for something to say. It had been months since she and Matt even talked about having a baby. Or anything else important.

"Maybe not just yet, Mom." Matt felt Kristin's stare as she turned in her seat to face him. He kept his eyes on his mother's puzzled expression. "My career is kinda up in the air—if I take a transfer back to Special Forces, we may need to move. Kris might want to go back to school and finish up her degree. Or she might want to get a job away from home. Two little girls is plenty of family for us." He cleared his throat. "For now."

"But surely, Matt—" Brushing back her silver bangs, his mother started to muster her arguments.

"So, you are thinking about going back in. I knew it!" His father pounded the arm of his chair at the same time, drowning her out. "Good man!"

Kristin didn't say a word. Matt felt her gaze leave him, felt her withdrawal like a drop in air temperature. He should have kept his mouth shut. Hadn't he learned long ago to let his mother assume whatever she wanted, just to avoid the hassle of an argument?

But he couldn't imagine a baby in their house, especially after today. Erin and Jenny hadn't come close to accepting him as their dad. How would they feel having about another child—especially *his* child—in the family?

Late in the evening, as he made the drive home from his parents' house with the girls asleep in the back seat and Kristin silent beside him, Matt laughed at himself.

Family—us?

Not by a long shot.

Back by popular demand are

DEBBIE MACOMBER's

Hard Luck, Alaska, is a
town that needs women!
And the O'Halloran brothers
are just the fellows
to fly them in.

Starting in March 2000 this beloved series returns
in special 2-in-1 collector's editions:

MAIL-ORDER MARRIAGES, featuring
Brides for Brothers and *The Marriage Risk*
On sale March 2000

FAMILY MEN, featuring
Daddy's Little Helper and *Because of the Baby*
On sale July 2000

THE LAST TWO BACHELORS, featuring
Falling for Him and *Ending in Marriage*
On sale August 2000

Collect and enjoy each MIDNIGHT SONS story!

Available at your favorite retail outlet.

HARLEQUIN®
Makes any time special ™

If you enjoyed what you just read,
then we've got an offer you can't resist!

Take 2 bestselling
love stories FREE!
Plus get a FREE surprise gift!

Clip this page and mail it to Harlequin Reader Service®

IN U.S.A.	IN CANADA
3010 Walden Ave.	P.O. Box 609
P.O. Box 1867	Fort Erie, Ontario
Buffalo, N.Y. 14240-1867	L2A 5X3

YES! Please send me 2 free Harlequin Superromance® novels and my free surprise gift. Then send me 6 brand-new novels every month, which I will receive before they're available in stores. In the U.S.A., bill me at the bargain price of $3.80 plus 25¢ delivery per book and applicable sales tax, if any*. In Canada, bill me at the bargain price of $4.21 plus 25¢ delivery per book and applicable taxes**. That's the complete price, and a saving of at least 10% off the cover prices—what a great deal! I understand that accepting the 2 free books and gift places me under no obligation ever to buy any books. I can always return a shipment and cancel at any time. Even if I never buy another book from Harlequin, the 2 free books and gift are mine to keep forever. So why not take us up on our invitation. You'll be glad you did!

135 HEN C22S
336 HEN C22T

Name	(PLEASE PRINT)	
Address	Apt.#	
City	State/Prov.	Zip/Postal Code

* Terms and prices subject to change without notice. Sales tax applicable in N.Y.
** Canadian residents will be charged applicable provincial taxes and GST.
  All orders subject to approval. Offer limited to one per household.
  ® is a registered trademark of Harlequin Enterprises Limited.

SUP00   ©1998 Harlequin Enterprises Limited

Return to the charm of the Regency era with

GEORGETTE HEYER,

creator of the modern Regency genre.

Enjoy six romantic collector's editions with forewords
by some of today's bestselling romance authors,

**Nora Roberts, Mary Jo Putney,
Jo Beverley, Mary Balogh,
Theresa Medeiros and Kasey Michaels.**

Frederica
On sale February 2000
The Nonesuch
On sale March 2000
The Convenient Marriage
On sale April 2000
Cousin Kate
On sale May 2000
The Talisman Ring
On sale June 2000
The Corinthian
On sale July 2000

Available at your favorite retail outlet.

HARLEQUIN®
Makes any time special ™

HEART OF THE WEST

Every Man Has His Price!

Lost Springs Ranch was famous for turning young mavericks into good men. So word that the ranch was in financial trouble sent a herd of loyal bachelors stampeding back to Wyoming to put themselves on the auction block!

HARLEQUIN®

Makes any time special ™

Visit us at www.romance.net

PHHOWGEN